MR REDMOND'S MENDING DAY

ALSO BY MICHAEL BARTLETT

SHORT STORY COLLECTIONS
MY VILLAGE IN THE VALLEY
PERSONAL ISLANDS
A DIFFERENT DRUM
RETURN TO MY VILLAGE IN THE VALLEY

NOVELS
DREAMS OF ELEVEN
HUNTING THE HORNETS
MR REDMOND'S MENDING DAY

MICHAEL BARTLETT

MR REDMOND'S MENDING DAY

Crumps Barn Studio

For my sister – Christine Bell
and my brother – Paul Bartlett

Crumps Barn Studio
Syde, Cheltenham GL53 9PN
www.crumpsbarnstudio.co.uk

Cover design by Lorna Gray

Typeset in Adobe Garamond Pro

All our books are printed on responsibly sourced paper from managed woodlands
and recycled material. Printed in the UK by CMP, Poole.

ISBN 978-1-915067-58-6

*This novel is entirely a work of fiction.
It is definitely not the story of our family,
although I have drawn on a number of
personal memories here and there*

"The past cannot be changed.
The future is yet in your power"

Anon

MONDAY/TUESDAY MIDNIGHT

MIDNIGHT. The hour of passing.

In a service flat in central London a man sleeps in a very tidy fashion.

In an apartment in Boston, Massachusetts, a woman is working, her bed not yet occupied.

In an airport hotel near Gatwick a man sleeps restlessly after an exhausting day.

In a suburban house in Melton Mowbray a woman lies in bed dreaming of her garden in spite of the snoring next to her.

In a small flat in Streatham a young woman, at ease with the world, sleeps peacefully.

In a care home in southern England a woman without any memory, sleeps the sleep of absence.

Elsewhere in the care home a man, troubled by pain, lies awake.

The lives of all these people are about to change, though at this moment – midnight, the hour of passing – none of them know it.

Except perhaps the man in pain.

TUESDAY 0:02 AM

HE WAS A MAN WHO HAD NEVER SHIED AWAY FROM DIFFICULT decisions. He never expected to marry the woman he loved – and yet he had. He never expected to rise high in his first company – and yet he had. When he was made redundant he had always assumed he would find another job – and he had. He had always known he was bound to make mistakes in his life – and he had.

But he had never shied away from making difficult decisions and he had no intention of starting now.

The question was, had the time come to make that last difficult decision? He thought it might be.

His eyes strayed to the little felt elephant with the fading coloured patches on its flanks which sat on the chest of drawers. The orange glow from the streetlamp in the car park could just be glimpsed round the edge of the curtain, shining directly onto the elephant's tail which moved gently in the breeze from the half open window.

He heard the church clock strike midnight and he counted the chimes as he always did if he was awake, not noticing or caring that the clock was running slow. The pain that periodically flared up in his belly seemed worse tonight. At his age pain was not surprising but sometimes it was still hard to bear.

To try and distract himself he focused on the elephant. It had been in the family for years but he couldn't remember which of his children it had once belonged to. He thought it was Linda, but it might have been Steven. Either way the little felt fellow was doing pretty well, even for an elephant.

He lay there in the darkness trying to will himself to go to sleep but knowing he wouldn't without a visit to the lavatory. He hated this. Hated the dependence, but there was no choice. His hand reached out for the bell.

It was Ken who came, efficient, jolly and very gentle. The two of them had become good friends, exchanging jokes and banter. The care home staff were meant to use first names to make everyone feel at home but Ken always teased him by calling him 'Mister George'. Now Ken helped him out of bed and across to the lavatory, helped him do what needed to be done, then eased him back into bed. He straightened his pillows and made sure he was comfortable.

"All set now, Mr George?"

"I think so." He winced as another spasm hit him in the belly. He tried to hide it but Ken noticed.

"Pain bad tonight?"

"Bit uncomfortable, yes."

"Is it constant pain?"

"No. Comes and goes. The 'goes' bit is the best."

Ken gave a little laugh. "I like your attitude, man. Wish I could help but I can't give you any more medication just yet."

"No, I know. Don't fret."

Ken smiled faintly. "Anything else? Can I get you a drink, hot milk perhaps?"

"No, thanks, Ken. I'll try and sleep now."

"Okey dokey, Mr George. Sweet dreams." And he went out closing the door gently behind him.

George smiled in the darkness. He liked it when Ken called him 'Mr George', it had become a little joke between them, man to man. All the staff in this home were kind, but he had a real soft spot for Ken. Nothing was ever too much trouble for him.

He settled himself against the pillows and tried to sleep but sleep would not come. He lay there gazing into the darkness. In an unguarded moment the doctor had told him it was only his strength of will that was keeping him going. He liked that idea, the thought that he was still in control. Could choose the moment when he finally let go.

Although he couldn't sleep, he was tired. He thought, wryly, that it was interesting that so many people believed that living into your nineties was an achievement, as if it were something he'd consciously chosen to do. They were the younger ones, of course, who didn't want to contemplate death. He didn't think it was that enviable, especially in his case, having a mind that was still active and functioning but a body that was slowly collapsing. Or so it seemed. He had to struggle to lift himself up in bed these days, couldn't even go to the lavatory on his own, but his mind was as clear as ever. It was knowing what was happening to him that was so hard.

Unlike Dorothy who had taken the other road.

He lived now mostly in his head which even after all these years was still an interesting place to be. It would be easy to give in to despair but he was determined not to do that. He wasn't unhappy. He had a few regrets but not many. As so often when he couldn't sleep he delved back into his memories, searching out the happy ones, the good ones.

He was lucky. So many memories to choose from, his childhood in the little corner shop in Portsmouth, his first job, his marriage, watching his children grow up, family holidays, the unexpected promotion, but at times like this, seeking the happiest of happy memories, he always began with the same one. The summer he first met Dorothy.

GODDESS UNDER THE PALMS

TORQUAY 1949. THE RIVIERA OF THE SOUTH. SUNSHINE. PALM Trees. And Dorothy – name as yet unknown – walking along the sea front. He only catches a glimpse of her on this first occasion

8

but the sight of her makes his heart turn over. Fresh. Smiling. Uplifting.

He is working as a courier for a company that runs local coach trips and someone, somewhere must have taken pity on him. Dorothy is staying in the town with one of her friends and a few days later he finds them on his coach for a trip to Dartmoor with tea at Widecombe. While most of his passengers are wandering through the village, inevitably humming *Old Uncle Tom Cobbleigh And All,* he sits on a wall in the sun. Then suddenly he looks up to see Dorothy and her friend, Marjorie, in front of him.

"Thank you for such a lovely day," says Dorothy.

He's a bit taken aback. He's just doing his job. "I'm just doing my job," he says.

"It must be a lot of fun," says Marjorie, "going to all these different places, meeting all these different people."

"Some are nicer to meet than others," he says daringly and the girls giggle.

"Can we join you?" asks Dorothy. "You've found a nice spot in the sun."

He shifts along the wall a little and the girls sit down.

"What's your name?" asks Marjorie.

"George."

"Well, hallo, George. I'm Marjorie and this is Dorothy."

He turns to look at Dorothy framed against the backdrop of the village, the sun in her hair. She smiles at him and his world is changed for ever.

"Have you had some tea?" he asks.

"We don't really do tea," says Marjorie. "Too much like home."

"We're on holiday," says Dorothy, "we're free, for a week anyway."

"What do you do?"

The girls shrug. "We're typists," says Marjorie.

"Shorthand typists," Dorothy corrects her.

"Does the shorthand bit matter?"

"Oh, yes. More money. We don't just copy type. We take dictation."

He is suitably impressed.

"And where do you do this typing and shorthand?"

"Castleview Insurance. In Salisbury."

"Is that where you live?"

"Nearby, yes. We both get the same bus to work."

"What about you, George?" asks Dorothy. "Do you live in Torquay?"

"Only during the season, while we're running the coach trips here. I've got a room at the back of the town."

"What happens at the end of the season?"

"I'll go back to Bournemouth. That's where our head office is. I've applied for a job there. Don't know if I'll get it."

"What sort of job?"

"Don't know really. The company's not been running that long. I know they want to expand the coach tours business. Might be an opportunity for me there."

"Sounds like fun," says Marjorie casually but Dorothy is more positive.

"I think you'll get that job, George," she says, "and I think you'll be good at it, whatever it is."

He is embarrassed at this unsolicited testimonial but is saved by a toot on the coach horn.

"Come on," he says, "the driver's ready to go."

As they walk side by side towards the coach Dorothy says, "What do you do when you're not working, George?"

"Not a lot," he says, "check on the details for the next day's trip. Go for a walk sometimes. I love it down by the harbour."

"Oh, yes. All those little boats and seagulls perched on their masts."

They reach the coach. He helps the girls up the steps and then takes his seat by the driver for the return trip.

Back on the Torquay sea front he says goodbye to all the passengers but only has eyes for Dorothy as she and Marjorie walk back into the town, waving to him as they go.

Ah, well, he thinks, that's that.

THE CHURCH CLOCK STRUCK ONE. THE LITTLE FELT ELEPHANT drifted in and out of focus. He felt himself getting drowsy now but, as usual, he had saved the best bit of the memory till last. He had an ache down his left side so he eased himself over, trying to find a comfortable way to lay his legs. Then he let his mind go back to that wonderful evening in Torquay, the day after the visit to Widecombe.

DREAMS CAN COME TRUE

THE DAY AFTER WIDECOMBE IS A BAD ONE. THE COACH TRIP THAT day is to Plymouth, theoretically for shopping but in reality to wander round a gloomy, bomb battered town. The rain doesn't help, the passengers are wet and miserable and he's heartily glad to see the back of them when they return to Torquay.

The weather brightens up in the late afternoon and after tea he decides to go for a walk. As usual he heads towards the harbour. He's found that watching the little boats bobbing on the water with the town climbing up the cliff behind is very soothing and today is no exception.

He sits on a bench looking out across the harbour and lets the day drain out of him. He knows it's time to begin thinking seriously about what he's going to do when the summer season comes to an end. There's a night school in Bournemouth where he could do office administration and accountancy but will the firm give him a job in their head office while he studies? If they insist he does the course first, how will he live? He's certainly not going back to the Portsmouth shop. His parents' were killed when their house was bombed and his grandparents took him in, but they are struggling with just two of them. It wouldn't be fair on them, and for him it would be a backward step.

He'd learned early on that the only person he could rely on was himself. In the first few years of the war he had carefully considered his options, come to a decision and volunteered for the RAF in 1942 just before his eighteenth birthday. Growing up in Portsmouth the one thing he knew for certain was that he didn't want to join the navy so, rather than wait for his call-up papers, he made his first positive decision, his 'pre-emptive strike', as he later thought of it.

Then after the war, when he was faced with staying on in the RAF as a clerk or returning to Portsmouth and the dole queue, he broke the pattern again and managed to sweet talk his way into this courier job. He enjoys it but he's not convinced that his future lies in extolling the virtues of tourist destinations to endless groups of new people, even if the coach company would want him again next summer. Looking ahead further, he knows that moving from casual job to casual job is not a long-term solution. He needs a proper challenge and he also needs skills. It's how to get them and survive while doing so, that's the crux of the problem.

Lost in his own thoughts he is hardly aware of the footsteps approaching from behind until a voice says.

"Hallo, George."

He turns to see Dorothy smiling down at him. She is wearing

a flowing dress, tight at the waist with a dome shaped woolly hat on her head that reminds him of his grandmother's tea cosy. With her is Marjorie arm in arm with a young man

He is caught by surprise and his opening conversational gambit betrays that surprise.

"Oh, hallo," he says.

"May we join you?" And without waiting for an answer Dorothy sits herself down on the bench beside him. Marjorie also sits and, after a moment, the young man does the same.

Marjorie nods casually towards him. "This is Albert. Albert, this is George. He took us to Widecombe yesterday."

A brief scowl crosses Albert's face but then suddenly it clears. "Oh, you mean that charabanc trip. You must be the driver."

"Courier actually."

Albert shrugs as if to say what's the difference?

"Albert's an accounts clerk in a big bakery business."

Albert nods. "One of the biggest bakeries up north. Good job, good prospects."

"Up north?"

"That's right. We're based in Leeds. I'm down here for my holiday week."

Suddenly George feels better. Leeds is a long way away.

Albert stands up and looks at Marjorie. "Thought we were going for a walk."

"Yes, of course." Marjorie stands and Dorothy follows her. George doesn't move.

Marjorie says. "Bye, bye, George," and she and Albert begin to walk away. Dorothy looks after them and then down at George still sitting on the bench.

"You going to join us then?" she says.

For a moment the recollection of Albert's disparaging look makes him want to say no but the sight of Dorothy is too much.

He gets to his feet.

"I'd be delighted," he says and they begin to stroll after the others.

They walk in silence for a few moments. There's a light breeze coming off the sea and the sun gleams back from windows along the eastern side of the town. A man carrying a bundle under his arm walks past them and climbs down an iron ladder onto a small vessel. They watch as he takes his bundle down into the tiny cabin. Then he returns on deck, there's a low rumble as he starts the engine, casts off the ropes and turns the little boat's head towards the harbour mouth.

"I wonder where he's going," says Dorothy.

"Off to catch your breakfast probably," says George.

Dorothy laughs. "Not at our guesthouse," she says, "lumpy porridge and weak tea is the best they can do."

"You should try my café," says George. "All I have in my room is a very small gas ring. But there's a great little café on the corner where I can get tea and toast and often a bit of fish if the boats have had a good night. I usually have breakfast there."

"Sounds lovely."

Ahead of them Marjorie and Albert reach the end of the harbour wall and turn off along the seafront.

"Do you want to catch them up?" asks George.

"Not really. He's very boring."

"Oh, okay."

Dorothy turns towards him and gives him her full smile. "We're all right like this, aren't we?" she says.

George, overcome, just nods.

By the time they reach the sea front the others are out of sight and George is wondering whether he's died and gone to heaven. They walk together for about an hour and before long they're chatting as though they've known each other for years.

14

Eventually George walks her back to her guest house and says goodnight.

As he turns to go, Dorothy stops him. "Thank you for a lovely evening, George," she says, "and don't tell me you were just doing your job."

He blushes and shakes his head. There's a pause and then it's Dorothy's turn to blush. He's never seen anything more beautiful.

"I was wondering ... oh, I daresay you're too busy ... but if you did have the time, could we do this again tomorrow? Now Marjorie's met Albert I feel a bit lonely in the evening."

He can hardly trust himself to speak. "Yes, yes, of course. That would be lovely."

"Oh, thank you. Same time, sevenish, down by the harbour?"

He nods and then, feeling rather foolish, puts out his hand. There's a brief hesitation, then Dorothy shakes it and turns to go.

"Till tomorrow then."

The memories are speeding up now. The rest of that week. Meeting Dorothy each evening. The first time she takes his arm as they walk. The conversation that always seems to flow so easily, the laughter, the joy, the enduring of each day until he could see her again.

He remembers the pleasure but there is also the pain of knowing the week is slipping away. Soon she will be gone, back to Salisbury, and he'll be alone again.

On her last evening, sitting on their usual bench beside the harbour, he rather clumsily tries to tell her how much he's enjoyed the last few days. She doesn't respond immediately and he wonders if he's offended her but then suddenly she stands up, turns to face him, strikes a theatrical pose and, to his amazement, starts singing.

When I pretend I'm gay
I never feel that way
I'm only painting the clouds with sunshine

George watches her, dumbfounded, but then she leans forward, takes his hands in hers, pulls him to his feet and makes him dance with her along the side of the harbour.

When I hold back a tear
To make a smile appear
I'm only painting the clouds with sunshine

And suddenly she is in his arms, he is holding her close and she is whispering in his ear. "I've had a lovely week, George, thanks to you."

He doesn't know what to say but she goes on.

"You must apply for that Bournemouth job, George, whatever it is. You'll get it, I know you will. I think you're the kind of man who'll always get what he wants if he puts his mind to it."

"Oh, Dorothy …"

"And Bournemouth's not really very far from Salisbury, you know." She gives him a big smile, frees herself from his arms and goes dancing down the harbour wall.

Painting the blue, beautiful hues,
Coloured with gold and old rose
Playing the clown,
Trying to drown all of my woes
Though things may not look bright
They all turn out alright
If I keep painting the clouds with sunshine.

AND THAT IS HOW IT ALL BEGAN. DOROTHY — THE MOST wonderful thing that ever happened to him.

He shifts in the bed. No position is comfortable for long. With an effort he eases himself over onto his other side, struggling a little to catch his breath.

Dorothy.

Whenever he thinks of the young Dorothy, he pictures her outlined against the sea, the wind pressing her skirt against her legs, her laughter as she tries to control her hair, he laughing at her struggles. The laughter that sets the tone for the next 60 years. They do a lot of laughing, the two of them, as they raise their family.

Dorothy.

Dorothy dressed for a formal dance. Dorothy in her one-piece bathing costume on Swanage beach. Dorothy tending to Steven when he has chicken pox. Dorothy holding the ladder for him as he repairs the garden wall and laughing fit to bust when some cement slips off the board and falls into her cleavage. Dorothy blazing with anger on the telephone telling the coalman he could come back and collect his dust and replace it with proper coal. Dorothy patiently helping Linda with her French homework.

Dorothy.

She has gone from him now though. No more laughing, no more giggling, although her smile is still there as she follows mysterious hidden thoughts of her own.

So many memories and tonight they are working. Imperceptibly he slides into sleep.

TUESDAY 3:00 AM

MIDDLE OF THE NIGHT IN ENGLAND. GEORGE SLEPT UNEASILY IN his Hampshire care home. In the next wing Dorothy was snoring gently, her mind empty of all the memories that George treasured.

Out near Gatwick airport their son, Steven, woke momentarily in his hotel room with indigestion but was asleep again within minutes.

In the Midlands their daughter, Linda, lay in bed with her husband, back to back, she dreaming of her garden, he dreaming of a hole in one.

Across the Atlantic, in Boston, it was mid-evening and their other daughter, Rebecca, was working on a paper she had to give to a scientific conference in San Francisco later in the year.

And in London, in an anonymous flat, their younger son Gary slept, a shallow sleep like a cat, alert to any change around him. He slept as he worked, neatly, flat on his back, arms by his side. Smartphone within reach.

A dispersed family. A family that had not met together in one place for many years. But that was about to change.

TUESDAY 5:55 AM

GEORGE WAS AWAKE AGAIN. ALTHOUGH HE HAD SLEPT HE WAS still tired. He always seemed to be tired these days. This was the worst time of the day, his moment of greatest despair – no chance to sleep again and nothing to look forward to, everything predictable, boring, filling in time. Waiting for … what?

Of course he knew perfectly well what he was waiting for. He was waiting to die. His race was run and after 93 years he didn't resent it. He wasn't entirely sure about this 'strength of will' thing. Was it really possible he could just say "Sod it" turn over and go to sleep permanently? He didn't know, but there was unfinished business that needed to be dealt with first. He'd prepared for this, he'd made plans with Gary some while back and for the last week or so he'd been on the point of ringing him and telling him to go ahead, but at the last moment he had always hesitated. It was, after all, a significant step.

On the other hand it wouldn't do to leave it too late. He knew he would never leave his bed without help again, he couldn't really even dress himself without Ken, and Gary would need time to organise everything so there was no point in delaying. Unlike Dorothy, he could still make his own decisions and now he made this one. Painfully he pulled himself upright in bed, reached for the phone beside him and called Gary's number.

TUESDAY 6:35 AM

IT WAS EARLY BUT HE WAS ALREADY SITTING AT THE COMPUTER IN his home office, his hands floating over the keyboard, caressing the mouse, ready for work and adrift in the only world where he really felt at home.

His personal phone rang, he glanced at the screen, answered it and said: "Hallo, Dad."

He listened for a few moments, nodding to himself.

"I understand, Dad. I'll get everything sorted this end. Leave it all to me."

He rang off and opened the file with the plan of campaign he'd drawn up when George first asked for his help, and ran his eye down the Action List. Rebecca first. She was the most complicated one to sort out. He switched identities on his computer and logged on remotely to the computer in his office. Once the link was established he did a quick search. Yes, there was a flight that would fit the bill, it was operating today and was on time. He worked on the screen for a few minutes, then closed that window and logged off, changing his password as he did so.

Back to his own computer. He briefly reviewed his commitments over the next two days. Routine stuff mostly, so no problem, but there was the Zygon project. That was nearing the critical stage but it would have to go on hold for forty-eight hours. He drafted a short message, encrypted it and then logged on to his office computer again. He sent the encrypted email to the secure server followed by another one saying he had some personal business to attend to. The usual communication channel would remain open but he wouldn't be at his desk for a day or two.

He changed his password again, logged off and immediately

put work out of his mind, concentrating all his thoughts into activating his dad's plan. Gary dealt with facts not speculation. He assumed from his dad's call that his father was dying and so there was no time to waste. He needed to call Rebecca, tell her what he'd arranged. That should be fine, but then he'd have to talk to Steven and Linda and that wasn't going to be so easy. He had promised to re-establish contact with them when George had first outlined what he wanted but it was difficult. Personal relationships were never easy for him and he'd kept putting it off. Now he had no choice. It had to be done. He'd promised his dad he would sort it, so sort it he must.

But first, Rebecca. He checked her phone number in his contacts list and dialled.

TUESDAY 7:17 AM
(2:17 AM IN BOSTON USA)

THE PHONE RANG SEVERAL TIMES BEFORE REBECCA CLAWED HER way to the surface and reached out for it, ignoring the muffled groans of protest beside her.

"Hallo. Who is this?"

"It's Gary."

"Gary? Gary who?"

"Your brother Gary. Who else?"

"Gary? But you only ever email me."

"This is urgent."

Rebecca came suddenly awake.

"Oh, God, Gary. Is it Dad?"

"Yes."

"Is he dead?"

"No, but I think it's very near. He didn't sound good on the phone and he wants to see us."

"All of us?"

"Yes, the whole family. It's important to him."

"When?"

"Today."

"Oh, God, Gary, get real."

Her brother's voice was calm and assured. "Don't panic, Becky, it's all fixed. You're booked on the 0750 flight, your time, out of Logan, first class. I've checked you in online and I'm emailing your boarding pass as we speak. There'll be a car waiting at Heathrow and it'll bring you straight down to Greenacres. I'll be waiting there with Dad."

"How on earth ... Look, Gary ... I don't know about this."

"You said you'd come when the time came."

"Yes, but …" She was struggling to take all this in. "What about the others? Do they know?"

"Not yet. I arranged things for you first, as we agreed. You've got the furthest to come. I'm going to call them now."

"That'll give them a shock." She was forcing herself awake, her mind clearing. "Logan, 0750." She glanced at the clock. "Hell's teeth. I'd better get myself sorted then."

"You do that. Now take down this mobile phone number. You'll be able to reach me on this for at least the next 48 hours, Okay?"

"48 hours? Is that all? Can't you afford the bill?"

Gary ignored that comment, just dictated a number which she scribbled down on a bit of paper.

"Okay, Becky, you'd better get going. Oh, one last thing."

"Yes?"

"Bring your laptop. If it looks as if Dad's fading before you can get here then we'll do a videocall. Okay?"

"On the plane?"

"If necessary, yes. See you later."

And the line went dead. Gary was gone.

TUESDAY 8:03 AM

IT WAS A NORMAL HOTEL WAKING MORNING. THE ALARM ON Steven's watch went off, he rolled over, sighed, tried to tell himself that another five minutes wouldn't hurt and failed. He half fell out of bed, felt the ache in his back and legs and promised himself that he'd definitely take some exercise this weekend. He showered, dressed and headed for the hotel breakfast room making the other usual promise.

"Fruit, that's what I'll have. Fruit, cereal, perhaps a bit of toast. That's all I need in the morning. Must cut down on the heavy meals."

The usual decision, the usual failure. He sighed a little as the full English was placed in front of him. Half a sigh for how nice it looked, another half sigh for yet another failure to live up to his good intentions.

A mushroom and a rasher of bacon had already disappeared and a slice of sausage was on its way, when his phone rang. He looked at the display – no caller ID, so it wasn't Hazel. For a moment he was tempted to ignore it but curiosity got the better of him.

"Steven Redmond."

"Good," said a voice he didn't recognise. "You need to come. Now."

"Come? Come where? Who is this."

There was a sigh on the other end of the phone. "This is Gary."

"Gary? Gary who?"

Another sigh. "Gary. Your brother Gary."

For a moment he thought someone was having him on. "Is that you, Roger. Look, this isn't funny. I'm in the middle of my breakfast."

"It's your brother. Gary. You've got to come now. Dad's not good."

This was all a bit much this early in the morning with the egg still seeping onto his fried bread.

"I don't have a brother."

"Of course you have a brother. Just because we've not been in touch for a while doesn't mean I don't exist."

His mind was gradually coming into focus. "Not in touch for a while? For heaven's sake, I thought you were dead."

"Well, I'm not."

"Look, if this is some kind of joke … How do I know you're Gary?"

Another sigh. "Okay, if you insist. Dad is George, Mum is Dorothy. We have two sisters. Linda and Rebecca. You married Sandra in 1975. I was eight years old. I was very excited. I peed my pants in the church and Sandra's aunt took me outside and cleaned me up. She had bushy eyebrows and whiskers. I was very embarrassed."

He didn't sound embarrassed but Steven remembered the incident well. How could he ever forget?

"And then there was the time you sat on my hamster. I never knew whether that was an accident or not."

"Hamster? Oh, God, yes."

"Was it an accident?"

"Probably. I don't remember."

"It never worked properly after you'd sat on it you know …"

"Worked …? Well, no, I don't suppose it did."

"It went all flat. I didn't like it. I liked it the way it was."

"Yeah, sure. Look, this is all a bit of a shock. Gary? For heaven's sake, where have you been all this time? It must be over 20 years."

"Twenty-seven years, three months and two days, if it matters."

"Of course it bloody well matters. Silence for … however long you said … and then suddenly here you are. What on earth have you been doing all this time?"

"Not relevant. Look you need to come now."

Steven took a swig of coffee wishing it was scotch. "Look, can we start again? From the beginning? Okay, you're Gary. I don't understand but let that go for now. Why are you calling me, where do you want me to come and why?"

"I'm not dead, as apparently you'd just assumed, but Dad nearly is. He wants us all to come and be with him before it's too late. I don't think he's got long to go."

"Where are you?"

"About to leave for Greenacres. Dad called me."

"Dad? Called you? Why you?"

"Because he's dying and he wants to see us."

"Look, I'm having trouble getting my head round all this. What's wrong with Dad? He was fine last time I spoke to him."

"That was five weeks and two days ago. You rang him. A short call. It's three months since you last visited."

"What the hell is this? Have you been spying on me?"

"Care home phone and visitors log. Look Steve, forget the past, just get your arse down there as soon as possible. We owe him that."

"Get my arse … Where the hell have you been all this time, In America?"

"That's not a question it would be safe to answer. Just come. I'll be waiting."

The phone went dead and Steven was left staring at his congealing breakfast.

TUESDAY 8:41 AM

LINDA STOOD IN THE DOORWAY, HER DRESSING GOWN WRAPPED tightly around her, waving as Dennis backed the car out of the drive and headed off for his golf. Several of her friends complained about being golf widows but Linda didn't mind. She liked having the house to herself and already had her day planned.

She was heading towards the shower when the phone rang.

"Hallo, Linda Marchant speaking."

"This is Gary. You need to come. Now."

"Gary? I don't know any Gary?"

"Your brother, Gary. You have to come now."

"Look, I don't know who you are or what you want but it's too early for practical jokes so just piss off." And she hit the red button cutting off the call.

She was in the shower when the phone rang again but she let the voicemail take it. She had her day planned and nothing was going to change it.

TUESDAY 8:50 AM

THE ROOM WAS VERY STILL. THE LITTLE FELT ELEPHANT GAZED impassively out of the window while George lay in bed, nearly as still as the elephant. It was only the rise and fall of his chest accompanied by a slight wheeze that showed he was alive. That, and his eyes, as sharp and as penetrating as ever. He felt quite relaxed. He had set the process in train and there was nothing more he could do.

He let his mind drift back into memory and, as always, the most important memory was Dorothy.

ALWAYS HAVE MORE THAN ONE STRING TO YOUR BOW

THE FIRST FEW MONTHS OF MARRIAGE ARE LIKE A DREAM COME true. They find a little house to rent on the edge of Ringwood, convenient for his work in Bournemouth and Dorothy's work in Salisbury. He isn't keen on the idea of Dorothy carrying on working after they're married. He's the man, it's his duty to support his family, but when he tries to express this to Dorothy she laughs.

"Oh, George, don't be so old fashioned," she says, "Time enough for me to give up work when the children come along. Until then I'm not sitting round the house all day. I don't do dusting."

He hasn't thought of children. His only thoughts have been of Dorothy, but now she's raised the subject he realises he quite likes the idea. But that gives him another worry.

"That's all very well," he says, "but sooner or later it's going to be down to me to provide. I wonder if I should be looking for another job."

"Why? You enjoy what you're doing, don't you?"

"Yes, but what are my prospects?"

"I think your prospects are what you make them, George. You really shouldn't underestimate yourself."

"That's not the problem," he thinks, "the problem is what does the firm think of me. I've done well so far, but I need to push on."

He doesn't say this to Dorothy but she sees he is genuinely worried.

"Look, why don't you talk this through with my father? He might have some ideas or at least set your mind at rest."

George nods. "Good idea. I might just do that."

And he does. He likes Dorothy's father who is an independent man with his own business. In the short time he's known him he's come to have a healthy respect for Frank's common sense so a week or so later they meet in a pub. Frank listens as George outlines his fears, well, not fears exactly, but concerns about his future and his ability to support a family once he and Dorothy have children.

"And so I've been wondering if I should look for another job now. Before it gets urgent."

"Doing what?"

George hesitates. "Well I've no idea really."

"Hmm. Are they reliable, this coach company you work for?"

"How do you mean, reliable?"

"Are they solvent? Are they making money? Are they well run?"

George is slightly taken aback. "Well, yes, I think so, yes to all three. We've just invested in three new coaches with luxury seats."

"And what's your current job with them?"

"Well, the job title is Assistant Office Manager. In practice I do some accounts work but I'm also responsible for the drivers' rotas, booking accommodation on the longer trips and so on."

"So basically routine office stuff then?"

"Yes, but across a broad range of activities. It's been suggested I might spend some time exploring new outlets and destinations for our trips."

"Okay, so that's a kind of business development angle as well. Would that come with a rise?"

"Don't know."

"Well, that's the first thing to ask. Express enthusiasm for tackling something new but ask, politely, for some financial recognition for what you'll be doing."

"Do you think they'd give it to me?"

"Quite possibly, so long as you make it clear you're not looking for much, just a bit of recognition for additional responsibilities."

"Well, I suppose I could try," says George doubtfully.

"You do that, but remember, politeness and confidence. Show them you're willing to take on extra responsibilities but you know your own worth."

"You think I should stay put then?"

"Of course I do. You've got your foot in the door there. Anywhere else you'd have to start from scratch."

"Yes, I see."

"However, might be worth thinking about a flanking movement."

"A what?"

"Think sideways. Acquire another skill."

George's face fell. "Not more night school?"

Frank laughed. "Not as such, no. Look what's the main purpose of your company?"

"Well, running coach trips and holidays of course."

"Exactly. And what's the main necessity for a business like that?"

George looked puzzled. "Well, coaches I suppose."

"Yes, yes. But I'm thinking of people. What kind of people?"

"Oh, I see. Well, drivers and couriers then."

"Precisely."

"Only they don't call them couriers now. They call them Tour Managers."

"I don't care what they call them. You've done that job anyway. I'm thinking of drivers."

"What about drivers?"

"Skilled job, driving a coach. You need a specialist licence."

"Yes, I know."

"So get one."

George is dumbfounded. "Me? Drive a coach?"

"Why not? You can drive, can't you?"

"Yes, they taught us in the RAF."

"Well, then, go ahead and get some training. Get yourself a wotsit licence …"

"PSV, Public Service Vehicle licence".

"Yeah, that. Another skill that's relevant to your firm."

"But I don't want to be a driver."

"Of course you don't want to be a driver but you can never have too many strings to your bow."

"What will the firm say?"

"Don't tell them. Do this in your own time. If nothing else it will give you some extra insight. You'll know a bit more about the problems the key people on your staff face day in and day out. And sooner or later it will pay off, see if it doesn't."

AND THAT'S WHAT HE'D DONE. IT HADN'T BEEN AS HARD AS HE'D expected. During the war the RAF had taught him to drive a

Bedford Armadillo armoured fighting vehicle so handling a large coach was not a complete novelty. He obtained his PSV licence without much trouble but said nothing to anyone at the company and carried on with his day to day work.

His throat was dry and in a moment he would have to push the bell and get someone to bring him a drink. He gazed round the room. He would've liked to turn the clock back, be at home with Dorothy again, but that wasn't possible and at least he could afford this level of comfort in his old age. He hadn't been at all certain about that at the beginning.

He had taken all of Frank's advice. He'd expressed interest in helping to develop new business and asked for a rise with it. His boss had been rather amused but recognised what was going on so entered into a bit of good natured bargaining. The result, inevitably, was a compromise. George got his rise, not as much as he wanted, but more than the original offer, and honour was satisfied on both sides.

He turned out to be a natural at finding new business and soon the accounting and book-keeping duties slid away. He was good with people and concentrated on planning the work schedules of the tour managers and drivers, making sure their lives were as comfortable as possible, always conscious they had to spend a lot of their time on the road and away from home. He was also successful in finding new places for their tours to go, hotels that balanced comfort against economy, interesting places for day trips. He conceived the idea of different trips for different age groups and made a significant contribution to finding customers for this new idea.

His responsibilities in the firm continued to grow and the money slowly crept up as well, so that by the time their second child, Linda, was born he was more confident about the future even though things were still tight. And then, out of the blue, came his big chance.

THE SECOND STRING COMES IN HANDY

IT'S A THURSDAY IN MID-SEPTEMBER. AS USUAL GEORGE IS IN THE office by 8:30, checking the rotas and making sure everything is ready for the various new trips starting at the weekend.

Suddenly his boss, Eric Gurney, erupts out of his office in a flat spin.

"George, we've got a crisis."

"What's happened?"

"That 6-day tour to the Yorkshire Dales …"

"What about them? They're in York today, staying overnight, coming back tomorrow."

"Oh, no, they're not. The driver's got appendicitis."

"What. Donald Cousins?"

"Yes. He's been taken to hospital. They're stranded there and we need that coach for the Welsh trip at the weekend."

George thinks quickly. "Who's the courier on that trip …?"

"Tour Manager."

"Yes, yes, all right, Tour Manager. Oh, I know, Tony Matthews. Well, he's a level headed sort of guy."

"Yes, but he can't drive the coach. And I gather the passengers are stuck in the hotel and getting a bit restless. What the hell are we going to do? Oh, this is a disaster."

George makes a snap decision. "We need to go and get them."

"How can we? All the drivers are out on jobs."

"I'll go. If I get a move on I can catch a train to London, get across to Kings Cross and be in York by this evening."

"And what you going to do when you get there? You can't drive the bloody coach."

"Yes, I can. I've got a PSV licence."

There is silence as Eric looks at George in disbelief. "You've got a PSV licence? Since when?"

"Since some time ago. Look, don't worry about that now. I need to get going."

Eric is still in shock. "Even so they're not going to be happy. They're meant to be doing Fountains Abbey today."

"Good point." He thinks for a moment. "Look, how about this. Ring Tony, tell him to organise some walking trips round York, city walls, cathedral and so on. Get the hotel to lay on lunch – on us. I'll get up there tonight then I'll suggest to them that we can do Fountains Abbey tomorrow, perhaps chuck in Rievaulx as well. Be a longer day but they'll get what they paid for and they'll still be home tomorrow night. That should do it."

"You're going to be knackered."

"Yes, I will, oh, and I suggest we throw in all tomorrow's meals as well – little extra treat. Going to cost a bit but it's better than having a bunch of angry customers bad-mouthing us to everybody."

"Yes, yes, of course." Eric pauses. "Have you really got a PSV licence?"

"Yes, I have. Had it quite a while."

Eric shook his head. "Okay. Well, we'd better get moving then."

It is a long day. The mad rush to Kings Cross, the journey north, meeting Tony at the hotel and then the following morning facing the passengers who are not happy.

He begins with a statement. "Good morning, ladies and gentlemen. My name is George Redmond. I represent the company and I'm here to take you home."

"About bloody time," someone mutters at the back.

George fixes him with a stare. "I'm sure you'll all be pleased to know that Donald, your driver, is now safely in hospital and

I've just been informed that there's a good chance they've caught it in time so they don't think he's going to die."

Silence amongst the passengers. In fact George has no idea how Donald is doing but has rightly calculated that the possibility that a man they've spent the last six days with might die has defused the protests.

"Now I know you were meant to go to Fountains Abbey yesterday but obviously that wasn't possible. However, we can go there today, and we can also visit Rievaulx Abbey which wasn't in your itinerary but is also very interesting. It does mean we'll be back in Bournemouth a bit later than planned."

There is a little murmur from the group but George ploughs straight on. "Of course, if anyone would rather go straight back then I'm authorised to pay your rail fare to Bournemouth via London and we can drop you at the station on our way. The choice is yours."

"What time will we get back?" someone asks.

"Difficult to say exactly. Depends on traffic but the company is willing to pay for any of you to phone home from here if you want to let anyone know what's happening. All today's meals will be on us as well."

There are a few murmurs but no one takes up the train offer. As the luggage is being loaded Tony sidles up to George. "I didn't know you could drive a coach."

George grins. "Nor did Eric. I don't think he's quite over the shock yet."

"Crafty bugger, aren't you?" says Tony.

"Always worth having more than one string to your bow," says George.

It's late evening by the time they get back to Bournemouth and George is absolutely exhausted. He has never driven a coach for such a long distance before and on top of that he and Tony had to find places which could feed thirty people out of the blue. Eric has waited at the depot for their return and claps George on the back.

"Brilliant, George. You're a star. I've got a maintenance team standing by to turn the coach round for the Welsh trip and a taxi waiting to take you home to bed. Don't bother coming in tomorrow. I'll see you on Monday."

George is too tired to argue. He falls into the taxi, falls into the house and, helped by Dorothy, falls into bed.

The following week they receive half a dozen letters from passengers from the Yorkshire Dales trip complimenting the company on the way they handled the situation. There is also one letter of complaint about the delayed return but there is always one and overall Eric is very pleased that a crisis was averted.

A few weeks later George is called into the office. Eric is there with Ron Hutchinson, chairman of the board.

"We just wanted a word about that Yorkshire Dales business," says Eric.

"You did the firm a real favour that day," says Ron, "but what we don't understand is how you came to have a PSV licence and none of us knew."

George shrugs. "Wasn't relevant to my work here."

"So how come you have it at all?"

"It was interesting and I just thought it might prove useful sometime or other."

"Well, it certainly did," says Eric. "Want to do any more driving for us?"

A shiver runs through George. This is what he feared. "Not really, he says, "I enjoy what I'm doing now."

To his surprise Eric and Ron burst out laughing.

"You shouldn't tease him, Eric," says Ron. "Don't worry, lad, you're not going to become a full time driver."

"No," says Eric, "but you are going to become our new Operations Manager, assuming that's okay with you."

Okay with him? Of course it's okay. It's wonderful. Frank's advice has delivered.

LOOKING BACK NOW FROM HIS BED IN THE CARE HOME HE thought nostalgically of those days. He'd loved that job and he'd been good at it. At the time he thought he was set up for life but of course that's not the way the world works. But now more pressing matters came to the fore. Wearily he leaned sideways and pressed the bell.

TUESDAY 9:07 AM

PACKING HIS BAG IN THE HOTEL ON THE EDGE OF CRAWLEY, Steven was trying to decide what to do – should he obey this unexpected summons to go to see his father or not? He'd been away for three days, he was tired and all he really wanted to do was to go home. His work had stopped giving him any pleasure many years ago, the spark had long gone and these days it was all very mechanical, just going through the motions.

"This is the very last time," he told himself, ignoring the fact that he'd said that after the last four courses. There was nothing to stop him retiring but the idea frightened him. Running consultancy training sessions might bore him to death but at least it gave him something to do. If he didn't have that, he didn't know how he would fill the hours.

He thought of his Norfolk home, his study with a view over the garden, the desk where he would open his laptop and complete the paperwork for the last few days. He thought of Hazel, who had changed his life. She would welcome him home, there would be a meal on the table and for a day or two at least he would manage to relax.

It was those thoughts that had kept him going for the last twenty-four hours, through the final session of the course, the final dinner, drinks at the bar with a bunch of people he hoped to God he would never meet again. He had told Hazel he'd be home by lunchtime. Now this call from Gary – where the hell had Gary come from after all these years – had made him stop and think. If Gary was right about Dad, and if Steven wanted to see him again, then he was a lot closer to Fareham while he was in Crawley than he would be in Downham Market.

In the end he did the obvious thing, he rang the care home.

The duty manager at Greenacres was non-committal. George Redmond wasn't any worse as such but he seemed resigned and sometimes with the very elderly that wasn't a good sign. The duty manager wouldn't go as far to say George wouldn't last long, but did say if Steven wanted to see his father again then maybe it was a good idea to come sooner rather than later.

That settled it. He rang Hazel and told her what was happening.

"Of course you must go, darling," she said, "give him my love."

"It may turn out to be a false alarm in which case I could still be home tonight."

He could almost hear her smiling down the phone. "I don't think you will be, Steven. Stay as long as you need."

He hesitated. Should he tell her about Gary? He'd never actually mentioned that he had a much younger brother and this didn't seem the moment to open that can of worms. Anyway, he still couldn't get his head round the Gary angle himself. So he left it.

"Thanks, love," he said, "I'll let you know what's happening when I know more myself."

Twenty minutes later he was in the car heading for the A23.

TUESDAY 10:16 AM

GARY SAT BESIDE HIS FATHER'S BED. THE OLD MAN'S EYES OPENED and he smiled when he saw Gary. He raised his eyebrows.

"Hallo, son. Didn't know you were coming today."

Gary frowned. "But you rang me, Dad. Said it was time to put the plan into action."

"Well, yes, I did. But can't you do that from your place?"

"Yes, of course. I've done it. Everyone's on their way."

George looked puzzled.

"On their way? Now? Today?"

"Yes, that's what you wanted, wasn't it?"

"Well, yes, but I thought it would take a few days to sort it all out. Today? Well, I don't know … And what about Becky. She's in America. She's the one I specially want to see but she can't be here today surely?"

"Yes, she can. It won't be until this evening but she'll be here. Nothing to worry about."

"All the way from America?"

"Yes."

"But how …?"

"Don't worry about it, Dad. It's all fixed."

There was a pause then George said. "And Steven and Linda?"

"I've spoken to them too, Dad. They'll be here soon."

At least I hope they will be, Gary thought. He'd been a little taken aback by Steve's attitude on the phone. Why would he have thought he was dead? Okay, they hadn't been in touch for some years but he'd always known where Steve was. It had never occurred to him that the reverse wasn't true. And as for Linda hanging up on him like that. He just hoped she got the voicemail message he'd left.

George nodded slowly, trying to take it all in. "Today. Well, what do you know."

Gary looked confused. "But we planned all this, Dad. When you said you wanted them to come I thought you meant now."

George nodded. "Well, yes, why not. But I don't understand how you managed it all so quickly."

"It's what we agreed, Dad. We made a plan." Gary was genuinely puzzled. When George had first told him what he wanted, Gary had worked out what would need to be done and agreed it with George. All Gary had done now was to put the first stage into action. It seemed perfectly logical to him.

George was smiling. So we'll all be together again."

"Yes, we will."

"And … and … Dorothy?"

"She's just along the corridor, Dad. I'll fetch her in here when the others arrive."

He'd already arranged with the care home staff that his mother could join them later. It was over six years now since increasing dementia had meant she could no longer recognise any of her family. She certainly didn't know her husband of 64 years, but George knew Dorothy and if his time really had come he would be able to say goodbye

Gary was the youngest of the four children. Steven was already fourteen when he was born. Rebecca, the youngest until then, had been eight. Many of the memories of childhood that Gary cherished were actually second hand memories of things that had happened before he was born. And yet those memories, shared round the supper table, remembered at family gatherings, seemed as real to him as though he'd participated in them himself.

Family firework parties with friends and neighbours, cricket on the beach in summer, decorating the Christmas tree, visits by train to the grandparents, birthday parties, days out in London.

These remembered tales, like an audio photo album, were the closest Gary came to a personal life and he treasured them all.

He sat by his father's bedside, holding the old man's hand, thin and brittle with age, and wondered what it would have been like to have had a proper family of his own. It was never a possibility. The life he had chosen, or the life that had chosen him, was not designed for happy families. Perhaps that was why he clung so fiercely to his own childhood memories or, at least the received memories from his brother and sisters. That was family life for him and he was determined to keep the spirit of it alive.

And then there was Kate. He suddenly jerked in his chair. How could he have forgotten Kate? He had to let her know as well. He knew nothing about Steve and Linda's children but they weren't his problem. Kate was different though. She had a right to see her grandfather before he died. He took out his personal mobile and as her phone began to ring, Gary allowed himself a half-grin. If Linda and Steve thought he had come back from the dead, what would their reaction be when they met Kate?

TUESDAY 10:17 AM

WHEN SHE CAME OUT OF THE SHOWER AND WAS DRESSED LINDA spent some time wandering round the garden. She loved her garden and had great plans to develop it, plans which were constantly changing. Dennis always said she preferred the planning to the action.

It was nearly an hour later when she noticed the flashing light on the answerphone and remembered the call that had come in while she was in the shower. She pushed the playback button.

"Linda, this is Gary, your brother Gary. I don't know why it's so difficult to understand that. If you need convincing, then remember the time I took a new pair of stockings out of your drawer and used them to hang some of my toy soldiers which I'd just court-martialled. Yes, that Gary. Look, I don't think Dad is going to last much longer and he wants us all to be there with him. Don't get mad, just come. Right?"

Linda stared at the phone, not believing what she heard. Gary? She hadn't thought of Gary in years. When he'd come out of prison that time she was quite nervous about meeting him again. What would she say? How did she feel? In the event it wasn't a problem. He had just vanished into the blue and she hadn't seen him since. Now here he was on the phone, years later, saying Dad was dying and asking ... no telling ... her to come. What the hell was all this about? She dialled 1471 but the number was withheld. She was damned if she would call Steven so that only left one option. She, in turn, rang the care home.

A quarter of an hour later she was rushing round the bedroom shoving things into a bag. The duty manager at Greenacres had told her the same as he had told Steven. He been cautious but had suggested that if she wanted to be sure to see her father again then maybe it was a good idea to come now.

She tried to reach Dennis on his mobile but he was probably engaged in digging up tufts of grass while trying to hit a ball and she got his voicemail. She left a brief message saying she'd heard from the care home that her Dad was sinking. She was off there now taking an overnight bag. Didn't know how long she'd be but she'd stay in touch and there were sausages in the fridge for supper. She didn't mention the call from Gary. That situation was too complicated for a voicemail message.

Part of her haste, she acknowledged to herself, was a pang of conscience that she hadn't visited her father more often. There were good reasons, of course, there are always good reasons. The distance was over one hundred and fifty miles each way, it could be done in a day but it wasn't easy. She could always stay over but she was never comfortable leaving Dennis alone. He wasn't a practical man and if she was going to be away overnight she usually provided something he could warm up in the oven. She wasn't sure how he'd cope with sausages on his own, let alone vegetables.

Dear Dennis. Mumbling, bumbling, no self-confidence, always with a worried look on his face but behind all that he was brimming over with love for her and their children. If she was the high flyer of their marriage, then Dennis was the safety cushion to catch her when she fell.

HIDDEN HARMONY IS BETTER THAN THE OBVIOUS

THE FIRST TIME SHE BRINGS DENNIS HOME AND INTRODUCES HIM to her parents they are polite and friendly but she senses their doubts. Many years later she learns that her mother's comment to her father after Dennis had gone was, "Well, if she marries that one she won't have to get pregnant to have a child."

Linda has always had what Dorothy calls 'a strong mothering instinct' and what George refers to as 'a compulsion to help lame dogs'. Linda, rather like her father, holds firm opinions but also trusts her instincts and her instinct about Dennis is that he is an honest and true man in spite of his apparent lack of drive. She has never changed that view.

Before long she is sure that Dennis is the man she wants to marry and she thinks he feels the same but when he still hasn't said anything, after they've been going out for several months she realises it's down to her. She picks her moment carefully. They have a meal in a riverside pub and afterwards go for a walk along the towpath. They're sitting on a bench watching the sun go down when she turns to him and says, "Dennis, will you marry me?"

The look of incredulous joy on his face stays with her all her life.

It's a good marriage. Most of the plans and decisions over the years are made by Linda, though they always discuss things together. Invariably though it ends with Dennis saying something like, "Good idea. Let's do it." And so they do.

At the time of their wedding Dennis is working as an accounts clerk in a department store but Linda encourages him to go to night school and gain a better accounting qualification. By the time he retires he has risen to be deputy manager of a small independent building society. After retiring he spends a lot of time on the golf course. He's not very good at the game, and he knows it, but it gives him great pleasure and, as Linda puts it, "At least he is getting some exercise, unlike a lot of men his age."

Linda suspects that some of their friends wonder how she, who is such an active person, copes with Dennis's passivity, but that has never bothered her. She knows what she has and values it. When trouble strikes she knows she is not alone.

She remembers the time when their daughter, Amanda, aged twelve, is knocked down by a speeding car whose driver fails to stop. When the police arrive with the news Linda goes to pieces but Dennis is calmness itself. He drives them to the hospital but the staff there are reticent about the extent of Amanda's injuries and her prognosis so, while Linda sits holding her unconscious daughter's hand, Dennis goes roaming round the hospital, gently badgering people until he finds someone who will give him straight answers.

Fortunately the car only struck her a glancing blow. Amanda has a broken arm and bruising all over her body, but the real problem is that she hit her head on the kerb while falling and is still unconscious. They do a scan and everything appears normal but it is not until Amanda comes round twenty-four hours later that Linda can relax and then she simply collapses.

Dennis is wonderful. He takes Linda home, puts her to bed with a hot water bottle and brings her endless cups of tea. Making tea is his one, but much appreciated, culinary achievement. He liaises with the hospital, the police and Amanda's school, while Linda lies shivering, imagining what might have been.

Later when Amanda comes home and Linda, to her shame, is still not coping, Dennis does the shopping and makes sure there's always a meal on the table. Later, when it's all over and Amanda is fully recovered, Linda discovers that Dennis had consulted Dorothy about what to buy and one of their neighbours had actually cooked the meals. No matter. Dennis managed the situation and took care of her when she needed it.

For her, he is, and always has been, a man worth loving.

NOW SHE HAS ABANDONED HIM WITHOUT ANY WARNING BUT SHE knew he would understand. She slung her bag in the back of the car and headed for the M1. It would take her the best part of three hours to reach Fareham and it didn't sound as if there was any time to waste.

TUESDAY 10:33 AM

IT WAS A STRANGE DAY AND IT WAS A GOOD DAY. HE FELT MORE relaxed than he'd done for a long time. His back still hurt, there were still occasional pains in his belly which seemed to be getting more frequent but his mind was at peace. He was still more than a little surprised that all this was happening today but if Gary said things were under control he knew they were. Steven and Linda would be here soon, though he was still worried about Rebecca. She was the one he was most desperate to see but she was in America and in spite of Gary's assurances, he couldn't see how she could get here quickly.

But now it was out of his hands. For the moment he could lie here in peace with Gary holding his hand. Gary. What a tortured path that had been but with a wonderful outcome. The prison sentence had hit him hard. He hadn't known how he would respond to Gary when he came out of prison but in the event George never found out. Gary had simply vanished.

Then two years later there was the Rebecca business when they'd had a bitter quarrel and he'd said he never wanted to see her again. That had been bad and he'd regretted it soon afterwards but couldn't find a way back.

Perhaps it was hubris, George thought. We were such a happy family when the kids were little, perhaps a bit smug. We thought we'd got family life sorted but then came those terrible years. Steven got divorced, Gary went to prison, I lost Rebecca through my own narrow minded stupidity. Then after that came the business with Linda's son and the sour feud that erupted between her and Steven. Not much 'happy families' about that lot.

And the final straw was Dorothy beginning to drift away on her own vacant tide never, as it seemed to him, even looking back

48

and waving.

WHERE IS MY WANDERING GIRL TONIGHT?

IT BEGINS SO CASUALLY HE DOESN'T EVEN KNOW THAT IT'S beginning. He comes in from the garden one day and as he enters the house he hears Dorothy call from the kitchen.

"Is that you, Dad?"

He is puzzled. He has known families where the father is referred to as 'Dad' even by his wife, but that's not something they've ever done. He takes off his wellies and walks through to the kitchen where Dorothy is rolling out some pastry.

"What did you call me just now when I came in?" he asks.

Dorothy looks at him. "What do you mean?"

"Just now, you called out."

"Did I?"

"Yes. You said *'Is that you, Dad?'*"

Dorothy makes a tut tut noise. "Don't be so silly, George. Why would I say that? Now if you want to be useful go and get out of those dirty clothes and lay the table. Supper will be ready around seven."

He changes out of his gardening clothes, lays the table but he is unsettled. He knows what he heard but decides it was probably just a slip of the tongue.

Over the next few months there are a number of similar incidents but he soon learns that if he mentions them, Dorothy gets upset. Then a few weeks later he can't find Dorothy anywhere and eventually tracks her down in the garage. To his amazement she has emptied their chest freezer all over the garage floor and is arranging everything in little piles.

"Dorothy, what are you doing?"

"Trying to get this lot sorted out. They're all different sizes which is very irritating."

"But what does it matter?"

"Oh, leave me alone, George. They need to be in order, that's all."

He reaches down and feels one of the packets. It's completely unfrozen and he realises all this stuff will have to be thrown away.

With some grumbling Dorothy is persuaded back into the house where he makes her a bowl of soup and then tucks her up in bed. The next day she apparently has no memory of this at all.

He says nothing to anyone and for several weeks her behaviour is perfectly normal. Then something more serious happens. Dorothy has been spending a few days with Linda and Dennis in Melton Mowbray. George had decided not to go. He likes Dennis well enough but his only topic of conversation seems to be golf and George has absolutely no interest in golf.

It's a Wednesday lunchtime and Dorothy rings to say she's just leaving. The journey normally takes around three and a half hours so she should be home by six. As chance would have it Steven is staying the night with them, breaking the journey on his way home to Norfolk after running a course in Truro. It will be a good chance to catch up with family news.

Six o'clock comes, seven o'clock, but no Dorothy. George is starting to get worried but Steven, wise in the ways of motorways, says it is almost certainly traffic problems. Dorothy has never mastered mobile phones so there is no way of contacting her. At eight o'clock George finally rings Linda who is very alarmed.

"But she left here around two, Dad, just after she'd rung you."

Now both George and Steven are concerned. Their first thought is that she's had an accident but just as they're trying to think what to do next the phone rings. George leaps on it.

"Dorothy, is that you?"

But it isn't. It's a policeman calling from Maesteg in South

Wales. He has found Dorothy sitting in her car outside the town hall there but she seems very confused. The policeman has found their address in her handbag and has rung them.

They can't understand what Dorothy is doing in Maesteg but say they will come and collect her.

"I think that's best, sir," says the policeman, "she doesn't seem to be ill but she isn't quite right, if you know what I mean."

"Thank you. My son and I will come right away but we're in Hampshire so it's going to take us what, oh, I don't know, a good three hours."

"Not to worry, sir," says the policeman, "I'll take her back to the station and probably get a doctor to take a quick look at her. She's quite safe now, that's the main thing."

Steven and George arrive in Maesteg just after midnight to find that Dorothy has been taken to the local hospital.

"Doctor thought it best," says the policeman. "They can have a little look at her and you can talk to them in the morning. I've fixed a bed there for you and your son as well. I'll show you the way."

The next morning the doctor is slightly less reassuring. "She's all right now, Mr Redmond, though she doesn't seem to know how she got here." He pauses. "Can I ask, have there been any similar incidents recently?"

George relates the episode of the freezer and the doctor nods. "Well, I don't wish to be alarmist," he says, "but I think you should get your own GP to give her the once over when you get home."

Steven, direct as always, says. "You think this could be the start of Alzheimer's don't you?"

"I wouldn't be that specific but, yes, these could ... and I mean 'could' ... be early signs of some sort of dementia."

And that is the beginning.

IT'S ALL FOR THE BEST, DAD

THEY NEVER DID DISCOVER HOW DOROTHY HAD ENDED UP IN Maesteg. The only explanation they could think of was that she'd confused the motorway junctions and had ended up on the M4 rather than the M3.

George tried to care for her in their own home as she gradually slipped away from him, but in the end it proved too much and he realised she needed full time professional care. For her sake he knew it had to be done but he missed her desperately. He missed the comfort of her presence, he missed their discussions about every aspect of their lives, he missed the sound of her voice singing as she went about her tasks, but above all he missed the laughter.

For a year after she had gone into a home he battled on by himself but then, as his physical health deteriorated, he had to accept he could no longer cope. He hung on as long as he could but after his second fall when he broke his arm he realised he too needed full time care.

He remembered the day Steven and Linda first brought him here. In spite of their quarrel they had clearly come together briefly for his sake, determined to make the transition as easy for him as possible. However, he could still sense the tension between them even while they were being very kind, very solicitous to him.

They help him out of the car and along the corridor to his room, one either side of him.

Rather like escorting a prisoner, he thinks, and is immediately ashamed of himself. They go into his room. His armchair is there, his favourite family photos are set out on the chest of drawers, but everything else has been disposed of. His whole life is now contained in three suitcases.

"It's a nice room, Dad," Linda says, "and the view across the garden is lovely."

Steven is all businesslike. "I've spoken to the manager and everything is organised. The direct debit is set up and we've left some money with her for odds and ends, underclothes, toothpaste and stuff."

"Will I be able to go and visit your mother?" he asks.

"That's not easy, Dad," Linda says gently. "Steven or I will try and take you from time to time but her home is quite a long way off and it won't be easy."

"Why couldn't I go to the same home?"

"It's a home for people living with dementia, Dad, and you don't have dementia."

"Then couldn't she be moved here?"

"We did ask. But there's no room in the dementia wing of this home. Perhaps later on, eh?"

"I don't like being away from her."

"I know, Dad, but let's face it, she doesn't know who you are any more."

No, but I know who she is, he thinks. *We've been married over 60 years and I miss her, especially the laughter.*

OH, DAD, GROAN, GROAN

MEALTIMES WHEN THE CHILDREN ARE YOUNG ARE OFTEN A RIOT of laughter, sometimes switching to groans as George brings out yet again another bad joke. He is known for his 'groan' jokes but they are never rude.

"What's the difference between an engine driver, a schoolteacher and a glue pot?"

"Go on, Dad. What's the difference?"

"An engine driver minds the train and a schoolteacher trains the mind."

He pauses, then one of the kids asks. "What about the gluepot?"

"Ah, that's where you're stuck."

More groans, then laughter but always a sense of fun.

When the old jokes are repeated, which they often are, Dorothy smiles indulgently but she always enjoys a new one, usually reacting to the punch line a few seconds after everyone else. Once she's got it, she giggles, that long musical giggle that always makes him want to take her in his arms.

An endless flow of family jokes and puns but Linda is often, unintentionally, the star of the show. She sits at the supper table and announces.

"I heard a joke at school today," and immediately everyone starts laughing. Linda looks annoyed. "I haven't told you the joke yet."

George calms everyone down. "Come on, come on, give the girl a chance."

Linda looks round at the family. "What sits at the bottom of the sea and twitches?"

"No idea," says George.

"A grape in a lift," says Linda triumphantly.

Silence, then Steven says, "I don't get it."

"Oh, come on," says Linda impatiently, "A grape in a ... oh." She suddenly realises. "Oh, no, that's the other joke. The bottom of the sea one is a nervous wreck."

"What about the grape?" asks Dorothy.

Linda thinks for a moment. "I know. What's green and hairy and goes up and down."

Howls of laughter, not for the jokes, but for the way Linda tells them.

Laughter, always laughter, in one form or another.

The time when the fence between their garden and the garden next door starts to fall down. George's fence, his job to fix it, but the neighbour, Mr Ramsden, offers to help so one winter's day they gather their tools and start work. It takes longer than expected and they quickly get very cold. At one stage Steven, aged seven or eight, comes to watch and Mr Ramsden gets quite jolly with him.

"Come to watch your dad working, eh?" he says.

Steven just nods.

"Are you going to give us a hand then," Mr Ramsden persists.

Steven shakes his head and Mr Ramsden gives up.

They work on for a few minutes then Mr Ramsden says, "Blooming nippy out here, isn't it?"

"Yes," says George, "I know where I'd rather be."

"Yes," pipes up Steven, "you'd rather be in bed with mum."

There's a silence, neither man knows what to say, then George grasps the nettle.

"He's right you know," he says and both men dissolve into laughter.

TUESDAY 10:46 AM

BATTING ALONG THE A607 TOWARDS THE MOTORWAY THERE WAS a mental traffic pile up in Linda's mind. So many things jostling for attention. Was her dad really about to die? If so, would she get there in time? If she had to stay, then where was she going to sleep tonight? Did Steven know? What about Becky somewhere in America? Did she even know her parents were in a care home? How would Dennis, not renowned for his culinary expertise, manage tonight?

But pushing all those thoughts out the way, like a police car nudging along the hard shoulder, was the thought of Gary. So many years without a word and now this. It was the overriding thing in her head as she grappled with the idea that she was going to see Gary again.

FLASHING BLUE LIGHTS AT THE FRONT DOOR

SHE REMEMBERS THE SUNDAY AFTERNOON ALL THOSE YEARS AGO when the police come to arrest him. She and Dennis have had lunch with her parents but fortunately Dennis has taken Kathryn and Graham off to the swings before the knock comes on the door. She remembers only too clearly the look of shock on her mother's face and the sudden hardening of her father's jaw when the police say why they have come.

Gary is twenty-three but outside the world of computers he is a very young twenty-three. He stands there looking slightly puzzled and when he's told he is being arrested he holds out his wrists for handcuffs as though he's taking part in a television play. Even the police are slightly embarrassed by this. They shake their heads, gently take him by the shoulder and guide him out to the waiting car, before coming back to seize every piece of computer equipment in Gary's room.

When he's been taken away Dorothy slumps down in a chair with an air of complete defeat. George responds in his usual way, with an outburst of anger, against Gary, against the police, against the world. As usual this anger soon burns itself out and then he turns to Dorothy and they cling to each other. They don't appreciate how serious the situation is. Back then none of them really understand the concept or the meaning of computer hacking.

The arrest of Gary, the subsequent trial and the sentence of twelve months in prison hits her parents hard. Gary is the last of their children living at home. Linda and Steven are both long since married and Rebecca is working in Berlin.

Dorothy and George had managed to weather Gary's first caution two years earlier. Then, although they didn't understand the reason, they had accepted his probation order a year ago, but prison was another matter entirely.

"But what's he done?" Dorothy keeps asking. "He just sits up there all day long playing with that computer thing."

Gradually the facts emerge. First, Gary has managed to bypass his parents' phone line so he could use his dial-up modem without incurring any costs. That is described as theft. Then, as one of the early 'virtual back-packers' through cyberspace, he has discovered how easy it is to access other people's computer systems. If he'd been content to simply look and move on, all might still have been well, but Gary couldn't resist the chance to fiddle about in other people's computers. He breaks into the payroll system of a major bank and reverses the salaries so the senior managers are paid as clerks and the clerks receive huge pay hikes. He changes the duty rosters in a nuclear power plant and downloads a lot of sensitive information from a pharmaceutical company.

None of these events go unnoticed and from that moment Gary is doomed. Not that he profits personally in any way from these transactions, a fact which the judge takes into account when sentencing him. For Gary it's all a game. He is simply having fun and exploring the limits of his computer system. When he sits at a keyboard he seems somehow to merge with the computer and, to him, what he's doing is simple and straightforward. He does it because he can and because the systems allow him to, and so Gary, like many similar people around the world, helps set the computer security industry on its first faltering path.

Linda visits him once in prison. Her mother wants to go but doesn't want to go alone. George refuses to go, so Linda and Dorothy make the long, tense drive up to the prison in Cheshire, spend an uncomfortable hour with Gary and then have the long drive home. She finds the visit difficult and does not go again. Dorothy is very upset by the visit but Gary, the object of the exercise, seems totally relaxed.

Gary is a model prisoner and is released after nine months. George and Dorothy receive a card giving his release date but no mention of whether he is coming home. The date comes and goes but no Gary appears. They know he has been released but then he simply vanishes and, as far as Linda knows, no one has heard of him since.

Until now.

LINDA REACHED THE M1, SWUNG INTO THE FAST LANE AS SOON AS possible and put her foot down. She wanted to see her father but she also wanted to solve the mystery of Gary once and for all.

TUESDAY 10:51 AM

IT WAS TIME FOR GEORGE'S MEDICATION. FELICITY, ONE OF THE
care assistants, brought him the tablets and Gary helped him
hold the glass while he swallowed them down. George wrinkled
his nose in disgust.

> *Over the teeth, through the gums,*
> *Look out stomach, here it comes.*

"Now, now, George," said Felicity, "they're for your own
good, you know."

"Won't be needing many more of them," said George, "that'll
save the NHS a bob or two."

"Oh, I think we can still cover the cost of your tablets for a
while yet," said Felicity who assumed he was joking.

When she had gone Gary said, "Are you in a lot of pain,
Dad?"

"Yes I am, son, on and off. To be honest I think I'm ready to
call it a day."

"You mean, you want to die?"

"Well, that's a bit blunt but what's the point me going on?"

Gary nodded. "I understand." He paused. "Do you want me
to help you?"

George was taken aback but realised Gary was absolutely
serious.

"Well, I don't know about that. I wasn't planning to do anything specific about it. I'm just ready to stop. I'm not going to
last much longer anyway."

He knew if he'd said that to Felicity, or any other member of
staff, they'd have said something like, "Don't be silly, of course
you will," but a comment like that would never occur to Gary.

Gary had no understanding of metaphor.

"Well, I'm here to help you, Dad. Whatever you want."

"I know, son, and you're doing just fine. Don't know what I'd've done without you these last couple of years. Mind you, it was a bit of a surprise, you popping up again after all that time."

And a surprise it certainly had been.

THE PRODIGAL RETURNS BRINGING HIS OWN FATTED CALF

GEORGE HAS SETTLED INTO GREENACRES QUITE EASILY. THE ROOM is comfortable and he's well cared for. For the first few weeks Steven and Linda visit him regularly – separately of course – but gradually the visits become phone calls and the gaps between visits become longer and longer. He doesn't resent that. They have their own lives to lead and they both live quite a distance away. But he is lonely.

Then one day there's a tentative knock at his door and a man he doesn't recognise comes into the room.

"Yes," George says, "can I help you?"

"Hallo, Dad," the man replies, "It's Gary."

Gary. A flood of emotion runs through him. Gary, after all these years.

He doesn't know whether to be angry, sad or delighted but to his surprise he finds tears forming in his eyes.

"Gary? I can't believe it."

"It's really me, Dad. I'm sorry it's been so long but I've come to look after you."

"Look after me?"

"Yes. I've only just discovered where you were. I went to the house but it's been sold. I visited Mum in her home and they told me you were here."

"Steven and Linda know this address."

He remembers the blank look that descends on Gary's face. "I'm not in touch with them," he says, "And you must not tell them I've been here."

"Why not?"

"It's complicated, but nothing for you to worry about. I'm here now and I'm going to look after you."

"I'm being looked after. The staff are very good here."

"Is there anything you want you haven't got?"

There's a long, long pause, then he says: "Dorothy."

"I thought as much. Why isn't Mum in this home as well? They've got a perfectly good wing for people who are living with dementia and if she was here you could see her sometimes."

The tears really begin to flow then. "They tried, Steven and Linda, but there were no vacancies."

He remembers how Gary's jaw sets very firm and for a moment he sees a flash of his younger self.

"We'll see about that."

AND HE HAD. WITHIN FOUR WEEKS DOROTHY WAS INSTALLED IN A room in the next wing and George was able to go and sit with her, hold her hand and talk about memories that now only he had. It was wonderful.

Gary himself didn't think of it as wonderful. Just something that had to be done. His employers had clearly not kept the promise they had made him many years ago, so Gary had taken matters into his own hands.

DON'T TAKE ANYTHING ON TRUST

GARY ENJOYS HIS WORK. IT IS PRACTICAL, IT IS TECHNICAL AND IT all takes place in an impersonal environment where he feels at home. He is treated well. He is comfortable, even though physical comfort has never meant anything to him, and he has never regretted his decision to cut all family ties.

However, as the years go by any illusions he might have had about his employers vanish like a deleted hard drive. He realises that basically they have no interest in anything outside their sphere of operations. This leads him to start wondering if they're actually honouring their promise to keep an eye on his mum and dad. His doubts grow, so one day he drives down to Hampshire and parks opposite his parents' house. After a while he sees Dorothy come out, get into her car and drive off. A couple of hours later she is back. Then in the late afternoon George arrives home. Part of him is tempted to go across to the house and knock at the door but he still feels bound by his promise not to get in touch with his family again so he simply drives back to London, reassured that everything seems to be fine.

He repeats this exercise every few months until one day, many years later, he arrives to see a *For Sale* board outside the house. The sight of the board disturbs him so, after a moment's thought, he crosses the road and knocks on the door. There is no answer and, peering through the window, he sees there's very little furniture and what little there is, is covered by dust sheets. Clearly his parents have gone and, in spite of the guarantees he was given all those years ago, he has not been informed.

Gary's outlook on life has always been very simple and now he reasons that his employers have broken their side of the bargain so he has every right to do the same. He returns to London and into his natural habitat of cyberspace and within a very short space of time he discovers that Dorothy is in a dementia care home.

He visits her but she doesn't know who he is. He makes sure she has everything she needs and learns from the staff that George is also in a care home some way away. He has a brief hesitation then. George isn't living with dementia so if he visits him then he will truly have broken his promise made all those years ago. However, the idea, if not the reality, of family has always been strong in Gary and so he goes to see George and discovers that his father is pining for Dorothy and no one is doing anything about it.

So he does.

WHEN THEY HEARD ABOUT DOROTHY'S MOVE STEVEN AND LINDA had expressed genuine delight but when they'd asked how it had come about George had kept his promise to Gary and simply said that a room had become free and Dorothy had been given it.

At the beginning he'd asked Gary a lot of questions. Where had he been all this time? Where was he living? What was he doing? Was he married? But to all the questions Gary had merely smiled and shaken his head.

"None of that matters, Dad," he had said. "None of it's relevant. I'm here with you now. That's the important thing."

He had asked the staff if they had an address for Gary but they shook their heads.

"He calls us regularly," said Pauline Belfort, the care home manager, "and we have a mobile phone number to use in an emergency but that's all we know. We've been asked not to give that number to anyone else." She paused for a moment. "He arrives in a very smart car though," she added.

Gary visited regularly and they talked, mostly about family memories. Gary could never hear enough about 'the old days' and all the family activities, especially the ones before he was born when the other three were younger. Gradually George came to be very close to his younger son, closer than any of his other children.

TIME TO SORT STUFF OUT

HE REMEMBERS THE DAY HE ASKS GARY TO TAKE CARE OF everything for him when he dies.

"I'd like you to be my executor, make sure everything is sorted out properly. And make sure Dorothy is always all right."

Gary pauses. "What about the others? What about Steve? He's the eldest."

"Steven's a good lad and Linda is my darling daughter but you're the one I know I can trust to do everything I want."

"And what do you want, Dad?"

"Well, we were always a very happy family, weren't we?"

"Yes, we were."

"I don't know how it all seemed to go wrong but we're not close now, are we?"

"I suppose not."

"Dorothy's adrift somewhere. I drove Rebecca away. Steven and Linda barely speak to each other. You obviously never see them. Have you quarrelled with them?"

"No."

"Well, I don't know why you won't get in touch with them but I'm sure you have your reasons."

"I do."

"But I need to ask – when my time comes, I would like us all to get together one last time. Can your reasons be put aside then, and will you make sure we're all together, Dorothy too?"

He remembers that Gary turns away and looks out of the window. There is a long pause and then, without turning round, he says in a muffled voice, "I promise, Dad, when the time comes I'll bring us all together again. Somehow."

"I'm not planning on dying just yet, you understand but this is important to me.

"I know."

"However there is one other outstanding matter I need your help with now?"

"And that is?"

"Rebecca. That's the other nettle I have to grasp. I want to see her again before I die. I want to tell her how sorry I am."

"Sorry for what?"

"Doesn't matter. I'll tell you sometime. In the meantime, I need you to find her."

"Find her?"

"I don't have an address. I think she's in America but I don't know. Do you think you can find out where she is."

Gary smiles his lop-sided smile. "I reckon I can do that, Dad. Is she still Rebecca Redmond or is she married?"

There's a pause and then George says. "No, it's still Redmond. She never married."

"Okay then, Dad. You write your letter and I'll get you the address."

And that's what Gary did.

TUESDAY 11:03 AM

STEVEN REACHED GREENACRES JUST AFTER ELEVEN, PARKED HIS car and pressed the button on the front door to be let in. He signed the visitors book and then walked along the corridor to his father's room.

He pushed open the door and went in. George was in bed propped up with a couple of pillows and sitting on a chair next to him was a man Steven didn't recognise.

Suddenly the man moved his head and shook his hair out of his eyes and Steven's focus cleared. Yes, this was Gary, a much older Gary but still his brother. He felt a shiver run down his spine as though he had seen a ghost.

The man was rising from the chair. "Steve. Glad you could make it."

"Hallo, Gary. Been a long time, hasn't it?"

He phrased it as a question but Gary simply nodded. "Yes."

Steven turned to his father. "Hiya, Dad. How you doing?"

A half grin passed across George's face. "Still here. Just about."

There was a short silence then Gary said. "I've got a couple of calls to make. I'll leave the two of you together for a bit."

"No wait. I mean, I don't understand why you're here. How you're here. Where have you been? What's going on."

Gary paused. His eyes were blank. "Steve, I didn't choose to have this meeting but it's what Dad wanted. I appreciate there are some gaps to fill in but let's leave it until Linda arrives. I don't want to do it twice."

"Oh, Linda's coming, is she? That should be jolly. Does she know I'm here?"

"Probably. I don't know. Why? Does it matter?"

A voice from the bed surprised them both. "No, it doesn't

66

matter. That's an old quarrel and it's time to end it. There's more important things now."

Gary and Steven looked at George and then back at each other. Gary turned away. "Well, whatever it is, it's not my business. I'll be back in a while. Oh, I'll get something organised for lunch too." And he went out of the room.

Steven went across, sat down on the chair and took his father's hand.

"How have you been, Dad?"

"Declining. I've lived too long."

"Nonsense."

"It's not nonsense. It feels as though another bit of me falls off each day. I can't even have a piss now without help."

"I guess that's just old age."

"It's that all right. And I've had enough of it."

For a moment a chill ran through Steven.

"You're not going to do anything silly, are you, Dad?"

"'Course not, but at my age with everything gradually closing down, I don't have to do anything. Just accept it."

"I suppose ..." Steven was not entirely sure what his father was saying so he tried jollying him along. "You look pretty perky to me. Got a few years in you yet, I reckon."

"I bloody hope not." The vehemence of the reply surprised them both. "Look, son, it's not a problem, at least not for me. I've had a good time, lots of fun over the years with Dorothy and all you kids, but your mum's gone off into a world of her own now. As for you lot, well you've all got your own lives to lead and that's how it should be. All I want now is for the family to be together again, one last time."

Steven was becoming uncomfortable with the way this conversation was going.

"All of us? What about Becky? We don't even know where

she is."

"Yes, we do. She's in Boston. Gary tracked her down and now she's on her way. He's arranged everything."

"Well, that's the bit I don't understand. How did you manage to find Gary?"

"I didn't. He found me. He's been coming here for quite a while now."

"Oh." There was a pause as Steven tried to take this in. "You never said."

"He asked me not to. Don't know why, but that's his business."

"I suppose."

"He's been very good to me, son. It was him who arranged for Dorothy to be moved here."

"Gary did?"

"Yes. It was such a relief. I go and sit with her sometimes. It's sad, but it's lovely at the same time."

"Oh, Dad. You could have asked me if you wanted it that much."

"I did. Right at the beginning."

Steven began to feel very uncomfortable. "Well, yes, I know but there weren't any vacancies then and after that …"

His voice tailed off. He had meant to follow that up, ask the home to let him know if a room became free, but somehow it had slipped his mind.

Suddenly he found the old man was patting his hand. "No matter, son. She's here now. Dorothy and me, we're as much together now as we ever will be again."

"Yes, but Gary …"

"I know, I know. Don't ask. I can't tell you 'cos I don't know. He suddenly appeared one day out of the blue and now he comes to see me, usually once a week."

"Regular as clockwork, eh?"

The old man thought for a moment. "Now you come to mention it, no. Could be any day, any time. Hadn't thought about that before. One day's much like all the rest in here."

TUESDAY 11:32 AM

GARY STOOD IN A FAR CORNER OF THE CAR PARK TO MAKE HIS calls out of sight of anyone. When he had finished the professional ones he tried Linda again. He was beginning to get anxious, wondering if she had got his message. He'd made Dad a promise and he wanted to be sure she was on her way.

All he got was her voicemail again. "Linda, it's Gary. I hope you got my message. I need you to come. Dad really wants to see us all."

There was nothing else he could do so he sat down on the old stone wall and thought about the hours ahead. He didn't like loose ends. He didn't like not being in control and he was already uncertain about the way the day was going to develop. He had no idea if his father was ill, tired or just worn out, but George clearly thought he didn't have long to live and Gary respected that feeling. He had promised George to gather all the family together when asked and that was what he was trying to do, though it wasn't proving as easy as he'd expected.

He would have to be very careful to deal with this family obligation and then extract himself again. That might be tricky, but one thing at a time. The important thing now was that Dad wanted to see all his family. Steve was here, Dorothy was just down the corridor, Becky would be at Boston airport by now and he just hoped that Linda was on her way too. What else? Oh, of course. He needed to organise lunch for everyone. Happy to have something concrete to do he got to his feet.

TUESDAY 12:07 PM

STEVEN STOOD IN HIS FATHER'S ROOM LOOKING OUT OF THE window across the garden.

"It's a very pleasant view from here, isn't it, Dad?" he said.

There was no answer and, glancing back, Steven saw his father was lying there with his eyes closed. For one terrible moment he thought he may have died but then he saw his chest gently moving and realised he had just dozed off. He looked very vulnerable lying there and for a moment Steven felt a nostalgic pang for the past.

When he thought about it, which wasn't often, he realised how lucky they'd been to have had such a good time when they were growing up. As he'd got older, met more people, lived in more places, faced troubles of his own, he'd come to realise that not everyone's childhood had been filled with so much fun and laughter. He was perfectly well aware that it's easier to remember the happy times – there's more incentive to do that – but even so he reckoned their family life had been pretty good.

With three, later four, children in the family, one-to-one time with parents was always precious. As the eldest he had a slight advantage over the others but he was always the one who spearheaded the way. Silly though it now sounded, he'd always been aware of privileges granted to his younger siblings that he'd had to fight for but now, as an adult looking back, he realised he was the one his mum and dad had learned their parenting skills on.

He was the one who had to fight for the right to go out on the main road on his bike, a right that Linda and Rebecca were later given automatically. He was the one who was blamed the day Rebecca fell in the pond in the park because he was the eldest and should have been looking out for her. When they went for a picnic he was the one who walked alone while Dorothy held Linda's hand and George held Rebecca's. All silly little perceived injustices of childhood that he'd never forgotten.

But all such niggles were far outweighed by memories of good times, happy times, such as the visit to Hamleys Toy Shop in London.

TRAINS, PLANES AND MECCANO SETS

HE REMEMBERS IT WELL. IT'S THE SATURDAY BEFORE CHRISTMAS soon after he'd turned eleven. His sisters are going to a neighbour's birthday party that afternoon but it's all little girls so, although he's invited too, he doesn't want to go. He's moping around the house when suddenly Dad says, "Come on, Steven, you and I are going out."

"Where we going?"

"Never mind. Just get your coat."

They walk down to the bus stop together. Steven pesters his father with questions but they're just met with a smile and a "You'll see."

The bus takes them to the station and they catch the train into London. Then there is a short journey on the tube before they arrive at Oxford Circus. The streets are thronged with shoppers, the Christmas lights are on and there's an air of excitement and anticipation everywhere. Although he's now eleven and feels very grown up, Steven hangs onto his father's hand as they push their way through the crowds.

The day is already wonderful. Simply to be here in London with his father, just the two of them, is magic enough, but things are about to get better. They make their way down a little side road, past the London Palladium and come out into Regent Street.

And there it is. Right in front of them. Hamleys Toy Shop, windows filled with every kind of toy imaginable.

"Well," says Dad. "What do you think of that?"

"Oh, wow. Can we go inside?"

"Of course we can. Why do you think we've come?"

And in they go, into a wonderland beyond imagining. There are toys and games, teddy bears and tops, model railways with trains whizzing round, miniature aircraft hung from strings as though flying, boxes of games, puppets, cowboy costumes, construction kits. A veritable treasure trove.

They pass through a section with dolls of all shapes and sizes.

"Cor," says Steven, "Linda would like it here, wouldn't she?"

"I daresay she would," says Dad and then adds, "Mum and I have bought her one like that" – he points to a doll in a box – "for Christmas but don't you dare tell her."

"I won't," says Steven but he can't help wondering, *If they've bought a doll like that for Linda, I wonder what they've got for me.*

He doesn't know it then, but this is the year he's given his treasured Meccano set with its as yet unborn bridges and cranes and ships.

They move from department to department, from floor to floor until finally Dad says. "Well, I think we've seen just about everything now. Shall we find somewhere and have a bit of cake?"

"Yes, but can we just have one last look at the trains, please?"

"Sure," says Dad, laughing, so they stand again and watch as the little locomotives rush round their tracks, through stations, under bridges, through tunnels and back again. Some of the carriages even have tiny lights in them.

"Come on," says Dad at last, "I'm thirsty."

They find a small café and have a cup of tea and a piece of chocolate cake and then make their way back to the station. Steven falls asleep in the train and Dad has to wake him so they can go and stand in the queue for the bus.

It has been a wonderful day.

LOOKING AT HIS FATHER LYING IN HIS CARE HOME BED, STEVEN felt a sudden pang. For a moment he longed to be eleven again, holding his father's hand, knowing that his world was safe and secure. He gave a wry grin at this unusual burst of nostalgia.

You can't stop the clock, he thought, *we grow up, grow away, make our own lives, our own mistakes. I was certainly good at that.*

The old man in the bed looked smaller somehow than the Dad of childhood memory, more wrinkled, more vulnerable. A bit of fluff from one of the blankets had attached itself to his whiskers and Steven leant forward and gently brushed it away.

"Thanks, Dad," he whispered more to himself than to his father. "You did okay, you and Mum."

He thought about his own son. He'd never taken him to Hamleys though he could easily have done so on one of his access days. The thought had never occurred to him or, if it had, it was stillborn. Perhaps deep down he hadn't wanted to mar his own happy memory with an awkward comparison.

Those isolated days with Tom when he was young were difficult enough as it was. As time went on he became better at finding things for them to do. Pantomime at Christmas, zoo in summer or a boat on Regents Park Lake. But those early days were terrible. He longed for them, or told himself he did, but also dreaded them. It wasn't just the problem of finding something to do with a young boy, it was the questions he always asked.

DAD, WHY CAN'T I LIVE WITH YOU?

THEY'RE IN HIS CAR HEADING FOR THE PARK WHEN THE QUESTIONS start. As always he struggles to find answers that will make sense

74

to a six-year-old. He could lie, but there's still enough decency left in him not to want to do that.

"It's difficult to explain, Tom," he says, "but Mummy and I decided we'd be happier if we didn't live in the same house anymore."

"I don't think Mummy is happy," says the practical six-year-old, "she's always crying and it's very boring."

This isn't information Steven wants to hear so he tries to change the subject. "How are you getting on at school?" he asks.

"Oh, all right." School is clearly not a topic that Tom has any interest in discussing. "Dad, my friend, Alex, has a hamster in a cage. It runs round and round in this little wheel. It's very funny, watching it, 'cos it never gets anywhere."

"Perhaps the hamster doesn't know that."

"Then it must be very stupid." A pause. "Can I have a hamster, Dad?"

How can he answer that? "What does your mother say?"

"Oh, she said no," says Tom in a matter-of-fact voice, "so I thought I'd ask you."

"Well, if your mother has said no then I'm afraid the answer has to be no," says Steven.

"I thought you'd say that," says Tom gloomily, "so I've got another plan."

"What's that?" asks Steven cautiously.

"I could come and live with you. You probably don't cry all the time and I bet you like hamsters, don't you, Dad?"

He plays for time. "I don't mind hamsters and I don't cry a lot, that's true."

"There you are then," says Tom with satisfaction.

He has to grasp the nettle. "However, it's not possible for you to come and live with me at the moment."

The child's face falls. "Why not?"

Steven thinks of his tiny one room bedsit in north London, bed in one corner, basin in another, Baby Belling on the shelf, bathroom down the landing.

"Well, there isn't really room, not where I am at present."

"Oh … Well, can I have an ice cream then when we get to the park?"

Relief. Something he can say 'yes' to. "Of course, you can."

They reach the park. Swings. Roundabout. Slide and then across to the ice cream van. They each have a strawberry cornet and sit on a bench looking at the ducks on the pond while they eat them.

Afterwards he takes his handkerchief and gently wipes Tom's mouth. Then makes a not entirely successful attempt to clean bits of strawberry ice cream off his jumper.

"Mummy always spits on her hanky when she cleans my face," Tom says.

Steven has a sudden flash of memory. "Yes, my mother did that too. I hated it."

"So do I," says Tom.

The wind ruffles the surface of the pond and the ducks bob up and down. There is no more talk of hamsters or coming to live with him. It's as though the child has given up on adults. The day grinds slowly to an end via a lunch time pizza and a visit to the shops. He buys Tom another toy car, delivers him back home, accepts the complaints about his ice cream stained jumper without comment and heads back to the semi-sanctuary of his bedsit, full of shame and relief.

STEVEN WAS WOKEN FROM HIS REVERIE BY THE SOUND OF VOICES outside the window. He moved across and looked out. There were two men going past, one pushing a wheelbarrow, the other carrying a spade, presumably care home gardeners. He'd never thought about the gardens before but now he realised that whenever he came here they always looked lovely, clearly well-cared for.

It'd be nice to have time to sit in the garden, relax and admire the flowers, he thought, but even as the idea came to him he knew it was not something he would ever do.

There was a grunt from the bed and when Steven looked across he could see lines in his father's face as though George was bracing himself against pain even while he was asleep. Watching him lie there Steven realised that he felt rather sidelined. He was the eldest child, the eldest son, and yet it was his younger sibling who seemed to have taken over caring for his father, and his mother too. He felt a twinge of remorse. How often had he planned to come and see them both but then put it off for another day? And all this time Gary had been here, checking on them, making sure they were comfortable and now organising this slightly strange family get-together.

At that moment his father stirred and opened his eyes.

"Gary?"

"It's Steven, Dad. I'm here."

"Oh, yes, Steven. Good of you to come."

"Can I get you anything?"

"Drink of water. There's a bottle somewhere."

Steven saw a bottle of water on the bedside table and poured his father a glass. George's hand shook as he took it so Steven held it steady while he drank.

"Thanks." George relinquished the glass and sank back against his pillows. He glanced round the room.

"Are the others here?"

"Gary's around somewhere and I understand Linda's on her way, Rebecca too apparently."

"Good."

There was a pause and then Steven said. "I've been thinking about the past, Dad. Do you remember that Christmas you took me to Hamleys?"

A tired grin passed over George's face. "Of course I do. Fun, wasn't it, but your Mum gave me hell when we got back."

"Mum did? Why?"

"'Cos you'd got chocolate cake all down the front of your new cardigan, that's why."

Chocolate cake, strawberry ice cream, must run in the family. "Oh, I never knew."

"'Course you didn't, son. She didn't want to spoil your day. It was me got the rocket."

"Can't imagine Mum giving you a hard time."

"Oh, she could do that all right. She had very firm ideas, your mum. But when we clashed it was usually only over small things."

"You were always very close, weren't you?"

There was silence for a moment and then George said. "We still are, Steven, even if she doesn't know it anymore."

Steven felt a lump rise in his throat. He said, "I think I'll pop along and see her in a bit."

"No, that's all right," said George, "Gary will bring her along here soon and we can all be together."

Steven turned away as he felt tears pricking the back of his eyes. He gazed out of the window across the garden. The men had disappeared but he could see sheep in the next field and a flock of little coloured birds he couldn't recognise circling round a feeder hanging from a tree. He stood looking at this picture of peace for a moment and then he said. "I wish my marriage could have been like yours, Dad. Don't remember you and Mum ever having a quarrel."

There was no answer and, glancing down, he saw that

George's eyes were shut again.

"Never mind, Dad," he said softly, "probably just as well you didn't hear that anyway."

But George had heard. He lay there, eyes closed, thinking. *You don't know the half of it, son. No, maybe we never had the sort of marital rows that so many people seem to have these days, but we damn nearly never had a marriage at all. If her father hadn't stopped me being so bloody stupid, then you lot wouldn't even be here.*

His mind drifted back to those terrible few days in 1950. He and Dorothy had been walking out – seeing each other, as they said nowadays – for about nine months. He'd met her family and was slightly in awe of them. They weren't posh, they weren't rich, but they were what his parents would have called 'comfortable'.

Dorothy had been to a good school, had passed her matric and was working as a shorthand typist. George had left school at fourteen, got a job as a van boy but then decided that wasn't for him. He managed to scrape the money together to go to evening classes to improve his written English and he'd done okay. Then came the war and his time with the RAF. He found he had the knack of making people like him and want to help him and he'd gone from strength to strength, but he was very conscious of being way below Dorothy in matters of education. He was also conscious of the difference between her comfortable, stable family home and his grandparents' struggling corner shop in Portsmouth where money was always tight. He was currently surviving by the skin of his teeth in a series of none too salubrious bed sits and had nothing to offer except an uncertain future.

Then in the spring of 1950 it all came to a head.

I LOVE YOU ENOUGH TO GIVE YOU UP

HE ENJOYS HIS JOB AS A COURIER BUT IN HIS HEART HE KNOWS IT cannot last. He likes meeting different people but there are only so many times you can extol the beauty of Dartmoor, the delights of Widecombe, the quaintness of Brixham, the virtues of Dartmouth without wanting to scream.

He considers moving to another company, perhaps one that runs tours in Europe, but deep down he knows it will only be the same thing again and soon Paris, the Swiss Alps, the French Riviera will be just as repetitive and dull as Torquay.

He knows he needs to move on but does nothing about it until he meets Dorothy and suddenly there is more urgency to make something of himself. Fired with a new confidence he approaches his boss to see if the company would contribute towards the cost of a night school course in accounting and bookkeeping. Slightly to his surprise they say yes. He is well thought of, despite of a lack of formal education, and they offer him a trial job in their main office in Bournemouth which could become permanent if he does well with his course.

He launches into this new job and the studying with gusto. He and Dorothy write to each other regularly. Sometimes, at weekends, he hitches a lift to Salisbury and they go to the pictures. Sometimes her father drives her down to Bournemouth for the day.

He meets her parents, kind, competent and successful. He likes them, but is a little overwhelmed by a lifestyle so far away from anything he has ever known. Dorothy's grandfather had owned a furniture shop in Bristol and when he died, her father, Frank, inherited the shop, borrowed some money and expanded it. The business is successful and he now owns three shops in Salisbury, Southampton and Basingstoke. They live in a village on the edge of Salisbury, a three-bedroomed semi-detached house with its own garage and an inside lavatory. They even have a small car. They make him welcome but he is very conscious of the difference between them and his grandparents battling to survive in Portsmouth.

Dorothy is all the world to him and he struggles on for several months trying to convince himself that it can work. But the more he studies, the more he realises how much catching up he has to do and the more he sees of her family, the more he realises the huge social gulf that lies between them.

And so, later that spring, he sits down in his tiny room at the top of an old house on the edge of Bournemouth and writes the letter to Dorothy. The letter he can still recite word for word.

45 Montgomery Road
Bournemouth, Hampshire
17th April 1950

My Darling,
To know that you love me so truly is something I shall cherish for the rest of my life but although my heart has let me dream of a future with you, my common sense tells me it's impossible. Judged by the standards of my background my prospects are quite good, but you and I live and move in different worlds and I love you far too deeply to ask you to sacrifice anything. I love you so much I know I have to give you up. They say the right way is ever the hardest and I hope that you will be happier in the end.

I promised to see you next weekend but I think it would be best if I don't. I know it will hurt at first but

I honestly think I am doing the only decent thing and being fair to you. I shall never stop thinking of you and I shall cherish the memory of the most wonderful thing that ever happened to me until I die.

I hope you will be as happy as you deserve.
All my love
George

He posts it on Monday evening and spends the next two days deep in black despair, yet firmly believing he has no choice.

Then, on Wednesday, as he comes out of the office of the coach company, he finds his way blocked by a thickset man and his heart sinks as he realises it's Frank.

He opens his mouth to speak but a hand is waved in front of his face. "Not a word. Pub. Now."

He is almost marched across the road and into the nearest pub, his elbow gripped firmly, a grip that doesn't even lessen as Frank orders two pints. He's then propelled across the room to a corner table where he's released and half falls into a chair wondering what is coming.

There is silence for a moment. Frank takes a long drink then puts his glass back on the table.

"Right," he says, "now this morning I left my daughter in tears and I want to know why."

George lifts his glass but can't face drinking. "She knows why," he mumbles, "I wrote to her."

"I know you wrote to her. She's shown me the letter. What I want to know is what you really mean."

George struggles to respond to this. "Well, she's, well, you know, she knows things. I can't keep up. It's not fair on her."

"Load of old cobblers."

George is rather taken aback. He is not used to direct language like this. He tries to say it's for the best in the long run but Frank cuts across him.

"Look, there's only two questions here. Question one – do you love my daughter? Do you love Dorothy?"

George is stung to a response. "Of course, I bloody well love her. That's why ..."

Again he is interrupted. "Question two – have you got a job?"

"Yes, for the moment. Whether I keep it depends on whether I can get some qualifications."

"You'll get them. You're a bright kid. Bookkeeping and accountancy, isn't it?"

"Well, yes, and a basic office administration course as well."

"Okay, so you love Dorothy and you've got a job and you'll soon have a better one so where's the problem?"

"Well, there's the difference in our backgrounds ..."

"More cobblers. Listen, son, I don't give a toss where you come from. Your dad could be an Irish horse thief for all I care. If you love Dorothy and you're prepared to do an honest day's work, then that's all that matters. Got that?"

"Yes, but ..."

"No buts. Now how far is it to your digs?"

"About twenty minutes on the bus."

"Don't need the bus. I've got the car outside. Right drink up. We'll go back to your place and you can pack a bag. You're staying with us tonight."

"But I can't. I've got work tomorrow."

"Don't worry. I'll deal with that. You and Dorothy need to get this sorted out. All I'm interested in is my daughter's happiness. Oh, and yours, of course," he added as an afterthought.

A year later George and Dorothy were married.

LOST IN HIS MEMORIES GEORGE MUST HAVE NODDED OFF. WHEN he opened his eyes again Steven was still standing by the window.

"Sorry, son, have I been asleep long?"

"No, only a few minutes. You obviously need your rest."

"I'll have plenty of rest soon. Today I want to enjoy my family."

As if answering a summons, the door opened and Gary came in.

"Okay," he said, "I've organised lunch for us all. I'm assuming Linda will be here by then and Mum'll be joining us too."

"You seem to know your way round this place pretty well." There was a curt tone to Steven's voice but Gary just shrugged.

"Oh, well, you know how it is. You get to know people. Chat with them."

"Chat with them. I see. I never really thought of you as the chatty type, Gary."

Gary looked slightly embarrassed. "Well, no, to be honest, I don't do a lot of chatting. I just smile at people and they tell me things."

"So they tell you things but you don't tell them things? Is that it?"

Gary looked uncomfortable. "Well, if you want to put it like that …"

"How else would you put it?"

"Boys, boys." George's voice cut across them. "Stop this. You're both here, that's all that matters. And I'm very pleased you are. I don't want the day spoilt with your quarrelling."

"Sorry, Dad."

"Yes, sorry."

There was a moment's pause and then Gary's face creased into a big grin.

"Hey, do you remember that holiday in Sandown on the Isle

84

of Wight? The year we found the slot machine in the arcade that had gone wonky?"

Steven said. "Oh, the Kit-Kat machine, yes, I remember. You put a penny in and there were three little balls. You twanged them up into a sort of vertical bagatelle and if they landed in a Win slot you got a Kit-Kat. Mostly they went into the Lose slot though and you lost your penny."

"Yes, but then we found this one that gave out a Kit-Kat whatever slot the balls went into. Obviously had a fault but we cleaned it out of Kit-Kats before they found out, didn't we?"

Steven laughed. "I've never eaten so much chocolate in one go. Didn't want my dinner."

"I remember that arcade," said George, "it was a godsend to your mother and me when it rained. We just gave you all a handful of pennies and sent you down there."

"And what about that crane thing," said Steven. "You had to manoeuvre a sort of grab with little handles and try and catch a prize. Never won anything on that."

"And the film star wheel," said George. "I can see it now. All these pictures of Hollywood film stars, Rita Hayworth, I remember and Ava Gardner, Natalie Wood. You stuck your penny in the slot against their name, pushed the button, the arrow spun round and if it ended up pointing at your picture you won your penny back."

"Only your penny?" said Steven, "just that?"

"Just that. You did it for fun, not to win anything."

"Probably why I never played it," said Steven. "But that arcade was great. Oh, and do you remember the smell of the hotdog stall next door?"

George grinned. "Oh yes, I remember the hotdog stall."

"You and Mum would never let us have one. Said it was dirty and they weren't safe to eat."

"That was your Mum's idea," said George, "she was convinced it wasn't hygienic."

"Pity. The smell was wonderful."

"So was the taste," said George, "as you and I well know."

Steven looked at his father. "You mean, you actually bought and ate hotdogs from there?"

"'Course I did, and so did you." He laughed at the expression on Steven's face. "Did you think we didn't know? Come on, Steven, neither of us was born yesterday. Of course we knew."

"Mum too?"

"Yes. One of those occasions where we decided a blind eye was the best policy."

"And did they make you ill?" asked Gary.

"No, of course not. We were fine. Don't you remember …" suddenly Steven broke off. "Just a minute. I remember that holiday very well but I was only about ten. You weren't even born."

"No."

"So how come you remember the Kit-Kat machine?"

Gary looked a little uncomfortable. "I don't. Not as such, but I remember you all talking about it. It's as though I was actually there."

"You're weird."

"I don't remember you eating hotdogs though after Mum told you not to."

"No, well you wouldn't, would you. It's not something I've ever mentioned until now so it's not a memory you can nick."

"I don't nick them, I just remember them."

"How can you remember something you never did?"

"They're family stories. We told them time and time again. They're part of my childhood."

"But they're not, are they. They're my childhood, not yours."

"But they're our memories, we share them."

"You're living in some kind of fantasy world, Gary. Tell me, have you ever actually been to Sandown."

"Well, no."

"So you've never even been into that slot machine arcade?"

"No." There was a pause and then Gary said in a small voice. "I've never actually played a slot machine at all."

"No, too busy breaking into other people's computers."

"Steven, that's quite enough." George's voice was angry and Steven had the grace to blush.

"Sorry," he said, "I'm sorry, Gary, I shouldn't have said that."

"No problem," said Gary, but he was very pale.

"It's good to remember those happy times," said George, "whether you took part in them or were simply told about them."

"I wish I had taken part," muttered Gary and suddenly Steven felt very guilty.

"I really am sorry, Gary," he said, "it's good to remember all this stuff. It's just that sometimes memory gets enlarged in the retelling."

"Do you mean you didn't win all those Kit-Kats?"

"Oh, we won them all right. Me and Linda. But to be honest I can't remember how many or whether we ate them all at once."

"Oh."

"It just makes a better story if you build it up a bit. I daresay I still had plenty of appetite for my dinner if the truth were known."

"Yes, I see." There was a pause and then Gary said, "I think I'll go and call Linda again. I hope she'll be here for lunch."

He turned and went out and Steven gave a big sigh. George looked at him.

"Yes, yes, I know," said Steven, "I wasn't very nice to him, was I?"

"No, you weren't."

"It's just … well … it's all so odd. Where's he been all this time? What's he been doing?"

"No idea. Does it matter?"

"And then there's all this memory stuff, but they're our memories, not his. It's like he's trying to create some kind of fantasy family."

"We were a happy family. There's no fantasy about that."

"No, no, of course not. Well, until … until …"

"Things started falling apart, you mean."

"Well, I didn't actually mean …"

"Yes, you did, Steven. Don't let's beat about the bush. Somewhere along the line it all veered off course but that doesn't cancel out everything that went before."

"No, I know …"

"And if those are the bits Gary wants to remember, even if some of them are second hand bits, then what's wrong with that?"

"Well, nothing but …"

"Good. Now can you get me another drink of water please."

TUESDAY 1:15 PM

GARY SAT ON THE WALL OF THE CAR PARK STARING AT NOTHING. Today wasn't working out as he'd expected. If 'today' was a computer program he would run a virus scan, then turn it off and reboot. That's why computers were so much better than people. You knew where you were with computers.

He couldn't understand Steve's aggression. Steve obviously loved their father and he, Gary, was doing what George wanted so why wasn't everything running smoothly? And where was Linda? What if she hadn't got his message or had chosen to ignore it? He'd promised George he would bring all the family together again, but it wasn't turning out to be as easy as running a search through a database.

At that moment he saw a dark red Toyota come skidding into the car park, taking the narrow entrance too fast and too wide. He stood up to get a better look. Yes, that was Linda. A bit older and plumper than he remembered but still definitely Linda. He felt a sense of relief.

He walked across to greet her as she got out of the car.

"Linda, hi."

She swung round, startled. "Gary? My God, it really is you."

Gary gave his lopsided grin. "Did you think I was dead too?"

"No. Well, not dead. I didn't know. You just vanished."

"Yes."

"Where did you go?"

"I'm sorry, that's not something I can answer."

"Oh. I see. Well, no actually I don't see."

There was a pause then Gary said. "Steve thought I was dead. Gave him a bit of a shock."

"Yes, well, it's given me a bit of a shock too. But what's all this about Dad? They were a bit cagey on the phone."

"They would be. I think he's dying, Linda. More to the point he says he's ready to die, but that's not something the staff here would acknowledge."

"Is he ill?"

"Not in the sense you mean, no. I think he's just worn out."

"And that's why we're here?"

"Yes. He wants us all together one last time."

"All? What about Becky?"

"On her way."

"So you're in touch with her?"

"Yes."

"Where's she coming from?"

"Boston."

"Boston as in Lincolnshire or …"

"No, Boston in America. I rang her first thing."

Linda thought about this for a moment. "Your first thing would have been a long time before her first thing I guess."

Gary nodded. "Yes, I woke her up. It was around two in the morning there."

"And she's already on her way? How the hell did she get a flight that quickly?"

Gary's face became blank. "I fixed it. Pulled a few strings."

"Bloody hell, Gary. How d'you get to pull strings like that?"

He shrugged. "Doesn't matter. Come on, let's go and see Dad."

"Is Steven here?"

"Yes, he's in with Dad now."

"Oh."

Her tone was less than enthusiastic and Gary glanced across at her.

"Something happen between you two?"

"You could say that."

"Well, forget it, Linda, at least for now. This is for Dad, okay?"

"I guess."

"Come on then."

As they walked across the car park towards the main door, it suddenly opened and a man came out pushing another man in a wheelchair. As they reached the top of the sloping ramp the man pushing lost his balance for a moment and the wheelchair careered off down the ramp on its own. It was soon recaptured and they stood aside to let it go pass. As they went into the building, Gary laughed.

"That reminds me of the year we went to visit Great Aunt Annie in that home in Cliftonville. You remember, the wheelchair race in the corridor."

Linda looked at him blankly. "The what?"

"Oh, come on. You remember. We were on holiday in Westgate and one day Dad announced we were getting the bus to Cliftonville to see this old aunt none of us had ever heard of."

FORMULA ONE IN A WHEELCHAIR

THE STORY IS VIVID IN HIS MIND. IT IS SOMETIME IN THE MID-60S and they're staying in a family boarding house in Westgate-on-Sea for their summer holiday. Steven is around nine or ten. They are lucky with the weather, mornings on the beach, walks along the cliffs, ice creams, sandcastles, cricket on the sand. They visit Dreamland in Margate and Dad wins a teddy bear on the rifle range and gives it to Rebecca, the youngest. Then one morning Mum announces they're taking a bus through Margate along to Cliftonville to visit Aunt Annie in her nursing home.

"Who's Aunt Annie?" the children ask.

"Well, she's actually a great aunt," Dad says.

"Not even that really," Mum chips in. "She's your grandfather's sister-in-law."

That stretched-out relationship is beyond their imagining but they enjoy the bus ride along the seafront to a big old house on the clifftop. There they're presented to a very elderly person, with more whiskers than they'd ever seen on a lady, lost in the depths of a large armchair. The grown-ups start their inevitable "Do you remember this? How's old so-and-so?" chat and the children slip away. They go into the room next door where they find several wheelchairs and soon the two girls are in a chair which Steven is pushing up and down the corridor pretending to be a racing car. It is only when Matron appears and Steven runs over her toes that the fun comes to an end.

Later they are admonished by their parents but there is a twinkle in Dad's eye even while he is saying how naughty they are. He promises the Matron they'll be punished and on the way home he buys them each an ice cream cornet, telling them they would have had two each if they had not been naughty so that was their punishment.

Oh, yes, Gary remembers the visit to Great-aunt Annie.

"WELL, I DON'T," SAID LINDA, "AND I DON'T SEE HOW YOU CAN either, Gary. If it was the mid-60s then you weren't even born."

"Well, no, but you all used to talk about it so I do kind of remember it."

"Well, that's more than I do," said Linda and they went on down the corridor in silence.

TUESDAY 1:29 PM

AS LINDA CAME INTO THE ROOM STEVEN STOOD UP. FOR A MOMENT brother and sister regarded each other, then Steven said, "Hallo, Linda. How are you?"

"Fine." A brief pause. "And you?"

"Fine. Dennis well, is he?"

"He's fine. And Hazel."

"Also fine."

There was a long pause which was broken by George.

"If you two have finished being unnaturally polite to each other, how about saying hello to your old Dad?"

"Sorry, Dad." Linda moved rapidly across to the bed, Steven stepping nimbly out of her way. "How are you keeping?"

"Well, I'm not fine, that's for sure."

"Oh, I'm sorry to hear that. What's wrong?"

"I'm old. I'm falling to bits. I've lived too long."

"Now, come on, Dad."

"He said the same to me," said Steven.

"Why not? It's true."

"Oh, Dad, please don't say that." Linda was down on her knees beside the bed, her arm round her father's shoulders.

George smiled. "Don't worry, love. It's not a problem. Just being realistic."

"Yes, but …"

"And now I definitely need a pee. Who's going to help me get over there?"

"I will, Dad." And suddenly Gary was there, gently helping the old man out of bed and across the room to the toilet.

The door closed behind them and Linda and Steven were left looking at each other.

"What is all this?" asked Linda. "Is he ill?"

"Don't think so, not as such. Gary thinks he's just given up."

"And that's why we're here?"

"I guess so."

"And Becky is on her way?"

"So I'm told. From Boston of all places. I don't understand how that's all been arranged."

Linda sighed. "Gary told me he'd pulled some strings."

"What sort of strings?"

She shrugged. "He didn't say."

There was a pause. Behind the closed door they heard the toilet flush.

"And where the hell has Gary come from after all this time?"

Steven shook his head. "Haven't a clue, but Dad says he's been visiting him for quite a while now."

"He has?"

The toilet door opened and Linda fell silent. She and Steven watched as Gary guided George back across the room and started to help him into bed. Suddenly the old man stopped him.

"No, I don't want to go back to bed. I want to sit up here in the chair so we can talk."

"Okay, Dad."

Gary settled his father in the armchair and Linda took a blanket off the bed and tucked it over his knees.

"There. How's that?"

"Top notch." He looked round. "It's good to have you all here. Is Rebecca really coming?"

"Yes, but not till much later, Dad," said Gary. "She's on her way but her flight doesn't get in till early evening."

George nodded. "Well, in that case I'd better make sure I hang on till then."

Steven and Linda exchanged glances. "'Course you'll hang on

94

till then, Dad. You're doing fine."

"Maybe. It's wonderful to see you all but I must make my peace with Rebecca."

There was a silence. Casting round for something to say Linda suddenly spotted the felt elephant on the chest of drawers.

"Good heavens," she said, "you've still got Nellie."

"Who?" said Steven.

"Nellie. My little elephant. I used to take her to bed with me. I thought she'd been lost long ago."

"Well, she turned up," said George. "Couldn't remember if it was yours or Steven's."

"Not mine," said Steven, "I had a lion with a zip down its tummy."

"A lion with a zip?" said Gary.

"Yes. I kept my pyjamas in it. I called him Albert."

George laughed. "Albert Ramsbottom," he said, "I remember reading that to you."

"Was Albert a neighbour?"

"No," said Steven. "It's a poem, Gary, or rather a monologue."

"Oh." His brow furrowed for a moment. "I've never really understood poems."

"Nice to see Nellie again," said Linda. She went across and picked up the little elephant. "She's not in bad shape for her age either."

"Better than me, that's for sure," said George. He glanced up at Gary. "Can you get Dorothy now?"

"Sure, Dad. I'll go and arrange it." Gary turned to Steven. "I'll just go along and get Mum. We could do with a couple more chairs in here. Could you deal with that? You'll find some in the sitting area just down the corridor."

"Well, yes, of course. That's okay, is it? The home doesn't mind."

"Not at all. It's cool."

"What about Mum?"

"I'll bring her across in a wheelchair. She'll be fine in that."

"Right, I'll get that organised then."

TUESDAY 1:37 PM

SHE LIKED SITTING IN THE SUN. SHE LIKED THE WARMTH ON HER face. She closed her eyes and tilted her head upwards. It was peaceful here – wherever 'here' was. She didn't know but it didn't matter.

If she opened her eyes a crack she could see white clouds scudding across the sky. They seemed to form shapes, interesting shapes, always moving, always changing.

She hoped they would bring her a cup of tea soon. There was always a cup of tea. She would quite like one now but it didn't matter. There was the warmth of the sun, the clouds changing shape. Nothing to worry about.

She began to sing gently in a soft voice.

> *I'm dancing with tears in my eyes*
> *'Cause the man in my arms isn't you*
> *Oh, yes, I'm dancing*
> *Dancing with somebody new*

The clouds were beautiful. She felt contented. Perhaps they'd let her have cake with her tea. Fruit cake with thick icing.

She suddenly felt a slight jerk as someone took hold of her wheelchair. She stiffened slightly. She didn't want to be moved. She was enjoying the sun.

"No," she said.

The voice was very gentle. A soft voice. A kind voice.

"It's all right, Mum," the voice said. "I'm just taking you round to see Dad. Steve and Linda are there too and Becky's on her way."

She didn't understand what it meant but the voice was

soothing and kind so she smiled.

Her chair began to move, gently. The warmth of the sun vanished as they moved further back into the room.

"Where are we going?"

"We're going to see Dad and Steve and Linda."

"Oh." The words didn't mean anything but it didn't matter. They'd bring her a cup of tea soon. She liked a cup of tea. And perhaps they'd let her have a cake with her tea – cake with icing. Then later she could look at the clouds. Enjoy their different shapes.

Trying to smile once in a while
But I find it so hard to do
I'm dancing with tears in my eyes
'Cause the man in my arms isn't you

The wheelchair moved softly and gently along the corridor.

TUESDAY 1:38 PM

LINDA LOOKED DOWN AT HER FATHER IN HIS CHAIR. HE SEEMED smaller somehow.

"Dad, I don't understand why you're suddenly gathering everyone together. You're not going to die, are you?"

"We're all going to die, Linda."

"Well, yes, of course, but … oh, you know what I mean."

"Look, love, I'm 93. Half of me doesn't work properly any more. Your mother's gone beyond reach. You kids are all settled and I'm in a lot of pain. What have I got to live for?"

"Oh, Dad, that's so gloomy."

"No, it's realistic. I've got nothing to look forward to these days except Bingo day in the main hall. As for this gathering, well, I just had a hankering to have all my family around me one last time. We were all so close once."

"Yes."

"I don't know how it all blew apart."

"Things happen, Dad. It wasn't your fault."

"Some of it was." George paused and seemed to be gazing into space. "Rebecca was my fault. I drove her away. I was judgemental, Linda, angry. I said some awful things."

Linda was silent and a tear appeared in the corner of George's eye. "It was such a shock, came right out of the blue, and when I realised I was the only one who didn't know, I lost it. I spoke hastily and then couldn't retract it and I've regretted it ever since."

"Oh, Dad."

"I drove her away, Linda." He sniffed and wiped his eyes. "Do you ever see her?"

There was a pause then Linda said. "No. I heard about what happened from Mum. I tried to get in touch but by then she'd gone to America and I didn't know where. I've not heard from her since."

"I know. She just cut us off. All my fault."

"Don't blame yourself completely, Dad. From what I heard at the time I don't think Becky handled things too well, either."

"No, it was my fault. And then there was Gary. I wasn't much use to him either. Do you remember when you and your mum visited him in prison?"

"Of course I do."

"I should have gone. Not left it to you. But I was so angry."

"I know."

"A son of mine in prison. I was angry and I was ashamed, but for me, not for him."

"It was a difficult time."

"Yes. But I made it worse. When we knew he was going to be released I couldn't think what I was going to say to him, but then he came out and vanished so I never had the chance to say anything. I should have met him from prison, brought him home with me, showed him we still loved him in spite of everything."

"Why didn't you?"

"Pride. He was the one who'd done wrong. He should come to me. Bad decision."

"Well, he's here now anyway. Where's he been all this time? What's he been doing?"

"I've no idea."

"No idea at all?"

"No. He won't talk about it. He just visits, chats about the old times and … well … he cares for me. And your Mum."

Linda felt a sense of guilt. Why hadn't she visited more often, made sure her parents were all right. She didn't know what to say but was saved by a thump on the door. She went across and opened it and there was Gary with Dorothy in a wheelchair and behind them Steven with a chair in each hand.

"Hallo, Mum," said Linda.

"Hallo, dear," said Dorothy smiling up at her. "Nice to meet you."

There was a bit of a bustle as Dorothy was wheeled across to sit next to George and the other chairs were set out round the room, then they all sat down and looked at each other.

There was a moment's silence then Gary said, "Lunch will be here in a minute. I've arranged for Mum and Dad's meal to be brought in here and I've organised some sandwiches for the rest of us."

"Is there anything you haven't organised?" asked Steven.

Gary flinched, as he'd so often done in childhood when challenged, then he stiffened.

"I'm just doing what Dad asked me to," he said.

"Yes, that's right," said George. "I asked him to get you all here. I want to see all my family together again before I go."

"Oh, Dad," said Linda, "please don't talk like that."

"Well, okay," said Steven, "I understand that, but I still don't understand about Gary." He turned to his brother. "Where the hell have you been all these years and why suddenly pop up now?"

Gary shook his head and said nothing. George said, "It's not suddenly. He's been visiting me for quite a while."

"A fact you chose not to share with us." Steven turned to Linda. "Did you know Gary had re-joined the family circle?"

She shook her head. "No. Not until this morning."

"Okay, then. So why all the mystery?"

They all looked at Gary who sighed. "I'm sorry. I don't want to be mysterious but where I've been, what I've been doing is simply not relevant. This is a family occasion. Let's just enjoy it?"

Linda said, "Are you in trouble again?"

Gary shook his head. "No, nothing like that. I can assure you

I am completely trouble free. Honest as the day is long."

"A winter's day? Or a summer one?"

Linda glared at Steven then turned back to Gary.

"Are you still involved with computers?"

Gary looked at her for a long moment, then said, "Yes, I think I can say that much."

"Oh, for heaven's sake." Steven was getting impatient but he was interrupted by a knock on the door. Lunch had arrived.

TUESDAY 2:03 PM
(9:03 AM IN BOSTON USA)

WHEN THE AIRCRAFT HAD LEVELLED OFF AT ITS CRUISING altitude Rebecca undid her belt, reclined her seat and tried to relax. Since Gary's phone call in the middle of the night it had been all go. Dressing, packing – difficult as she didn't know how long she'd be away – messages to her office, explanations to Chris who'd come wide awake once she'd started rushing about.

Then the cab to the airport through the dark streets wondering how efficient Gary's preparations had been. She need not have worried. They were expecting her at the airline desk, all the paperwork was in order, she was given priority through security and she even had time for some breakfast in the First Class lounge before boarding the flight.

Now there was nothing more she could do until Heathrow, where she hoped the car Gary had mentioned would be waiting for her.

If her physical body had stopped moving, her mind had not. She was in emotional turmoil at the prospect of seeing her father again after all these years. If Gary was right and he really was dying, this would be the last chance to repair their relationship.

YOU CAN NEVER REALLY ESCAPE FAMILY

WHEN THE LETTER FROM HER FATHER ARRIVES SHE CAN HARDLY believe it but, ironically, her first thought is to wonder how he knew where to find her. The letter is apologetic, an old man reaching out across the years to try and rebuild broken bridges. But it is not a warm letter – there is something rather remote about it.

Later she thinks the 'remoteness' might be in her own mind, that perhaps George was struggling to express his feelings on paper and it's ended up more awkward than a face-to-face conversation would have been.

She talks it over with Chris but she knows in her heart she can't ignore the appeal in her father's letter so she sends a brief note in acknowledgement, saying she'll write later at greater length. But the letter has opened a door in her mind that she'd thought she had closed for ever. Now, not for the first time, she wonders how much she herself is to blame. If she had stayed in England a reconciliation might well have been possible but she had come straight to America, buried herself in her work and shut off all memories of her past life – or so she had thought.

Now those old memories, never dead, only dormant, come flooding back and she finally realises how much she has missed her parents. In his letter her father tells her about her mother's dementia, and she has a moment's pang as she realises the chance of a reconciliation with her mother has gone for ever. And now her father, who from the tone of his letter doesn't think he has long to live, is offering an olive branch.

After their terrible row she had come to America vowing never to have anything to do with her family again, but now she wonders whether that was just stupid pride. She could have stayed in touch with Linda and especially Steven, but had never made the effort. She accepts the fault is hers, they have never known where she is so could hardly make the first move.

Gary is different. She hasn't seen him since he went to prison then, when he came out, he'd performed a disappearing trick of his own, long before she did the same.

She is still thinking about how to follow up her first letter when she has another surprise. She receives an email from Gary.

Hi Rebecca, I guess this will be a bit of a shock after all this time but by now you should have had a letter from Dad. I've been taking care of him for a while now, making sure he has everything he needs and so on. I'm sure you'll be wondering why I disappeared all those years ago and have never been in touch since. I'm afraid I can't tell you about that. I would have preferred to leave it that way but Dad has asked me to make some arrangements for him and I have to contact you to do so. Would you please email me at the address below and tell me if you're okay with that and then I'll tell you what I've promised to do. Gary.

This is just as big a shock as the letter from George but it helps her make a decision. She emails back.

Hi Gary, I can't believe it's you. I have a thousand and one questions but I guess they'll keep. Of course it's okay to contact me. What does Dad want? Becky.

The reply is almost instant.

Hi Becky, thanks for replying. Dad has asked me to be his executor and I've agreed. However, the main thing is that when the time comes he wants me to get all the family together again one last time before he dies. This poses a few problems. I don't know anything about it but I gather you and he had a big bust up of some kind which he now regrets. The thing is, we may not get much warning and if I'm to get you here in time from Boston – assuming you want to come – then some advance planning is essential. Will you come? If so, I'll start sorting it out. Please reply using this email address. Gary.

This message needs a bit more thought. She discusses it with Chris who, level-headed and supportive as ever, gently helps her realise that "No" is not an option. She will have to go. She's missed the chance with her mother, she can't miss the chance with her father.

She's surprised to see that this email from Gary comes from a different address but she replies saying of course she'll come if it is humanly possible. She's tempted to ask about the aura of secrecy that seems to hang over Gary but suspects questions won't be answered, so she doesn't. However, she does ask if he's also in touch with Steven and Linda.

> Hi Becky, not in touch directly with them, no, but I know how to get hold of them when I need to. Dad wants us all with him before he dies so I will contact them then. However, I feel more relaxed with you, maybe because we're closer in age, maybe because you're the only one who bothered to write to me when I was in prison.

She is curiously moved by that last sentence. She'd heard about Gary's prison sentence while she was working in Germany and had tried to find out what was going on but George was angry and Dorothy simply didn't understand what Gary had done. From the little they could tell her Rebecca had put two and two together and in her own mind had a pretty shrewd idea what Gary had been up to but saw no value in trying to explain it to her parents. The fact was her younger brother was in trouble so she wrote to him. She only had one brief postcard in reply but over the nine months he was in prison she wrote five or six times, light, chatty letters telling him about her life in Germany and the interesting scientific work she was doing.

Then came the information that Gary was about to be

released from prison so she wrote, saying she'd be back in the UK shortly and was looking forward to seeing him again. But she never heard another word. Until now.

Over the next few days Gary contacts her several times, bringing her up to date on what has been happening to George and Dorothy. She asks him if she should fly over now but Gary says no, George is very clear that he wants the whole family around him when he feels the end is near and that's not yet. In one way she's quite relieved. It would be difficult for her to leave the work she is currently engaged on unless it is a real emergency so she accepts this decision.

She's pleased to get these messages from Gary but she is puzzled. Every time he emails her he gives her a different address to reply to. She tries hitting the 'Reply' button but when she does that her email just bounces back. Once she tries re-using one of the first email addresses he sent her but that bounces as well. The upshot is that she can never contact Gary unless he contacts her first.

SHE STRETCHED HER LEGS, REVELLING IN THE SPACE A FIRST CLASS seat offered. Her main concern now was that if George really was dying, would she get there in time? She decided she needed an update so she used the cell phone in her armrest and dialled the number Gary had given her.

TUESDAY 2:17 PM

LUNCH WAS FINISHED, PLATES CLEARED AND SANDWICH WRAPPERS in the bin when Gary's phone rang. He glanced at the screen then said, "I'll take this outside. Won't be long."

He walked down the corridor and out into the car park before taking the call. "Hi Becky. How you doing?"

"Fine. Everything went very smoothly. You must know a lot of useful people."

"You could say that. Flight on time?"

"So far. How's Dad?"

"Not too good. Seems to be in a lot of pain. Keeps dozing off then jerking awake again. He perked up when I went and got Mum."

"Who's there with you?"

"All of us, bar you. Dad, Mum, Steve and Linda."

"How's it going?"

"It's a bit chilly. Steve and Linda weren't exactly over the moon to see me. Suppose that's not surprising really. But they're also a bit frigid with each other. Still not sure what that's all about."

"Families, eh?"

"Didn't used to be like that. It used to be wonderful. I've been thinking about all those marvellous Christmases. The tree, all the family together, opening our presents, Nanny coming for the day helping Mum in the kitchen, carol sing-alongs…"

SANTA CLAUSE IS COMING TO TOWN

IN MEMORY CHRISTMAS IS ALWAYS A HAPPY FAMILY TIME. ALL THE usual bits and pieces are removed from the top of the piano and a little silver tray appears with a bottle of sherry, a bottle of port and a bottle of ginger wine.

The week before Christmas they make paper chains, loops of coloured paper stuck end to end and linked together in circles. These are lovingly pinned up in the bedrooms, fixed to the picture rails with drawing pins. Later the real family decorations box is taken down from the loft, expanding paper chains, flat shapes that open out to become coloured bells and lanterns, cotton wool snowmen and yards and yards of tinsel.

Then comes the day when they go out with Dad to buy the tree, not a big one, there isn't much space in the living room, but a real tree. Another box from the loft is opened and the various tree decorations are attached, each of the children taking it in turns to put one up, from the silver fairy sparkling at the top – which Dad always does – to the little plastic Santas and reindeers lower down. And then there are the lights, tiny bulbs that never work the first time so Dad has to work his way through them one by one to find the duff bulb that's breaking the chain.

The excitement of Christmas Eve, the certainty you'll never get to sleep and then suddenly you're awake on Christmas morning and you stumble downstairs in your dressing gown to see the piles of presents on the chair in front of the fire. The thrill as the wrapping is torn off and the contents revealed. Then the smell of turkey or goose pervading the house as Mum – helped or hindered by Nanny – battles with the Christmas dinner, singing all the while.

Reindeer on the roof top,
Santa in the flue,
Mother in the kitchen
With far too much to do.

The neighbours dropping in for a glass of sherry. Christmas

dinner, setting fire to the pudding – an act that's never quite understood – the slow, lazy afternoon, pantomime on the telly around tea time and finally stumbling upstairs to bed, tired but content.

Such happy memories.

"I DON'T REMEMBER ANY CAROL SING-ALONGS," SAID REBECCA, "I remember helping to decorate the tree, of course, but Nanny? Surely she was dead before you were born?"

"Well, yes, I suppose she was, but I can still see her there somehow."

"Perhaps you're remembering the photos. What happened to all the albums? Do you know?"

There was silence for a moment then Gary said, "No, I don't know. I've got a few very old photos. I found them in the lining of Mum's suitcase but I don't know what happened to the family albums."

"Perhaps Linda or Steven took them."

"Maybe." There was a pause then Gary said, "I would really love to have them."

Rebecca was a little surprised. "Would you? But surely most of them date from before you were born."

"Exactly. They're the family memories I don't have myself."

"Oh, I see." But she wasn't really sure she did.

"They're important, Becky. They're a record of our family."

"Well, yes, I suppose." Rebecca turns this idea over in her mind then says. "I don't remember much about family Christmases to be honest, Gary."

"But you must. You used to talk about them, I remember it so clearly."

"Well, maybe. Memory's a funny thing. Oh, they're starting to serve a meal. I'd better go."

"Okay. Talk to you later."

Gary walked back down the corridor, deep in thought, slightly worried that Becky didn't remember the Christmases he remembered. Especially as she'd taken part in them and he hadn't. By the time he'd been old enough to help decorate the tree the others had lost interest and not long after that the real tree had been replaced by a self-assembly plastic one. But he still treasured the memory of the Christmases he had so often heard described. Wonderful times. Family times.

TUESDAY 2:51 PM

GEORGE WAS CONTENT. HE WAS UNCOMFORTABLE, OF COURSE, but that was offset by the way the day was shaping up. He felt certain in his own mind that this was a fitting conclusion to a long life but it was Rebecca he most wanted to see. At one stage he thought he'd never see her again which caused him great distress.

He had always regretted that dreadful day, but had never known how to undo the damage he had done. It was a final act of desperation when he asked Gary to try and find her, never expecting he would succeed. But he had.

Once he knew where she was he wanted to write but didn't know what to say, he was still so ashamed of his behaviour, but when the pains started getting worse and more frequent, he realised that unless he did it now it might be too late. So he had written, struggling to express how he felt, how stupid he had been. After a while she had replied, a slightly formal reply, but at least they were in touch again. But he so, so wanted to see her.

He had explained this desire to Gary and Gary had emailed Rebecca. When he told George that she had agreed to come when the time came he felt a huge sense of relief.

Now, he was certain that time was running out. Each day was more of a struggle than the last and he was tired. But first there were things to do. Gary was keeping his promise, rather faster than he had expected, true, but Steven and Linda were here and Rebecca, his Becky, was on her way. He could hardly wait. This was his final piece of unfinished business.

But now, for the moment, he was alone with Dorothy. Gary was still out in the car park, Linda was trying to organise some tea and Steven had gone to phone home.

He reached out towards Dorothy and took her hand.

"Well, Dottie," he said, "most of the family are here. Nice to be together again, isn't it?"

Dorothy did not appear to notice, just continued to smile, her eyes fixed on something across the room or in her mind.

George felt a moment's pang for what they had lost but firmly put that thought aside in favour of remembering all they had had.

"We were okay, Dottie, weren't we?" he said, not expecting or getting any response. "Lots of good times, good kids. Went a bit pear shaped from time to time, guess that's inevitable, but on the whole I wouldn't change anything, would you?"

Not true of course. He'd like to be able to turn the clock back to change the way he had behaved with both Rebecca and Gary. They were his main regrets. Other stuff, well, nothing ever goes completely smoothly. As one slimy American once said, "Stuff Happens", and when it happens, you deal with it. That was always his approach, or almost always.

"It's been a great life, Dottie," he said, "and although I know you don't understand what I'm saying or ..." he swallowed hard, "... even know me anymore, I want you to know you're the most wonderful thing that ever happened to me and I wouldn't have missed any of it for the world."

He paused. For a moment he thought she had gripped his hand a little tighter but her face was still absent though the smile remained.

It hadn't all been beer and skittles of course. It had often been a struggle to bring up three, later four, children on his income but he had fiercely resisted Dorothy's suggestion that she should go back to work. He was the man, he was the breadwinner. Until suddenly he wasn't.

He had never forgotten those terrible few weeks in the sixties.

A time when he came as close to despair as he had ever been. Three kids and one on the way. The timing could not have been worse.

LOOK ON IT AS AN OPPORTUNITY

FRIDAY LUNCHTIME. HE'S JUST SEEN THE VARIOUS COACHES depart for their weekend destinations and he's already looking forward to a couple of days off. Might take the kids to the park. If the weather holds could even have a picnic.

The summons to the office sets off no alarm bells. He strolls in expecting to see Eric for one of their periodic 'state of the nation' chats. Instead he is faced with a stranger. A stranger in a very natty suit.

"Mr Redmond?"

"Yes."

"I'm Ronald Fitzroy, the new Chief Executive."

"We don't have a Chief Executive. We have a Managing Director, Eric."

"Eric Gurney has retired with immediate effect. I will be replacing him."

"Eric said nothing to me."

"Mr Gurney was told not to say anything to anybody."

"Oh, right. Having a leaving do for him, are we?"

"Mr Gurney has already gone. He chose not to be, shall we say, cooperative so, no, there will be no 'leaving do' as you put it."

George opens his mouth to comment, thinks better of it and waits for what is to come.

"Now let me see, you've been with this company for quite a while."

"Twelve years or so."

"And you're the Operations Manager."

"That's right."

"Just what is it that you manage, Mr Redmond."

George doesn't like the sound of this, and he certainly hasn't warmed to Ronald Fitzroy in their brief acquaintance, but he controls his temper and answers as civilly as he can.

"I manage the fleet of coaches, organise the tours, sort out the drivers' rotas, couriers' rotas, book the hotels and so on. Plus I do a fair bit of new business development."

"Do you mean *marketing*?"

"I don't know. Do I? That's the modern term for finding new business, is it?"

"It's the correct term, but I ask myself why would an Operations Manager be involved in marketing."

"Why not? I know the sort of trips our customers like. I know the places they like to go. Seems obvious."

"Hmm. I would have thought a professional marketing person would be more effective."

By now George is feeling decidedly uneasy.

"I brought in a ton of business last year."

"I don't know what constitutes a 'ton' when applied to new business but the results don't look too impressive to me."

"Okay, I agree demand is falling off a bit. It's these cheap flights and package holidays. Not doing any favours to the coach tour trade."

"Interesting you use the word 'trade'. I would prefer to think of the market as opportunities. In fact, it is clear to me that this company cannot continue doing what it has been doing. A lot of people have a car these days and a few coach trips to stately homes and out of date seaside resorts are not the future."

"Then what is?"

"Chains. Everything in one package. Hotels, coaches, individual trips planned to a personal itinerary, excursions. Perhaps in time even our own airline."

"I see."

"So to prepare for this we need to streamline the whole operation."

George nods grimly. "So Eric's been streamlined, has he?"

"In a manner of speaking. We need a new breed of company manager, preferably people with a degree."

"A degree?"

"It's the future, Mr Redmond."

George is no fool. "And I'm not the future, am I? Rising forty and no degree. I'm for the chop, yeah?"

"Look on it as an opportunity. A chance to expand your horizons. Have a change."

"I don't want a change."

"Well, I'm sorry but you're going to get one. As far as I can see you don't have a formal contract with the company …"

"I've never needed a contract. Eric and I have always got on without any legal stuff."

"But as I've just explained, Eric Gurney is no longer here."

"No, you've made that very clear." He has a sudden thought. "I do have a letter of employment."

"From when you first joined the company, yes, it's in the file. However, it has no legal value."

"So what are you saying?"

"I'm saying that without a formal contract all you are entitled to is one week's notice so that is what I am giving you today."

"A week? That doesn't give me much time to find something else."

"You'll have the week free, Mr Redmond, in fact you'll have more than that. A week's notice means a week's pay but we do not wish to be ungenerous so in view of your length of service we will give you two week's pay."

"Two weeks?"

"Yes, but there's no point you hanging on to work out your notice. This is your last day in this company. Goodbye."

George finds himself outside the door. He returns to his own office to find it locked and the contents of his desk in a cardboard box in the corridor. He puts the box in his car, drives down the road to a public phone box and rings Eric.

"What the hell is going on? You might have warned me."

"I'm sorry, George, but they said I wasn't to talk to anyone. They threatened to take my pension away."

"They can't do that."

"I can't risk it, George. I'm nearly 60. Where the hell would I find another job at my age?"

"And you had no idea this was coming?"

"None. Things haven't been the same since Ron retired from the board. It seems that the new guy sold the company, just didn't bother to tell anyone."

"Bloody hell."

"I'm sorry, George, I really am but I've got to go. Please don't ring again."

George doesn't know what to do. He thinks of challenging the decision but he's been around long enough to know there's no point in flogging a dead horse.

Instead he just goes home.

He doesn't tell Dorothy what has happened, partly through shame, partly because he doesn't want to worry her when there's another baby on the way.

Another baby on the way. Soon it will be four kids. He has to have a job.

On Monday morning he gets up as usual and leaves the house at his usual time. He spends the morning in the library working his way through the Jobs Vacant adverts. Nothing. In

117

the afternoon he calls a couple of other tour companies. Still nothing. He returns home at his usual time, cheery as ever on the outside, slightly desperate on the inside.

Tuesday is much the same as Monday. He gives the library a miss and makes personal calls to other coach companies. Still nothing, a lot of sympathy but most of them are struggling too, though none of them seem to be thinking about owning their own airline.

Wednesday, Thursday, Friday pass in the same way. That weekend he gives Dorothy the usual amount for housekeeping without telling her this is his last but one pay packet.

The next three weeks are grim. He maintains the pretence, leaving the house at the same time each day, returning at the same time each night. In desperation he has moved onto hotels, car hire firms, taxi companies, travel agents. Nothing.

He begins his fourth week of unemployment as close to desperation as he has ever been. His few savings are dwindling. He sits in the park at lunchtime consuming the cheapest sandwich he can find. He has to have a job. He cannot let Dorothy and the kids down.

He thinks back all those years ago to that meeting with Dorothy's father in the pub in Bournemouth. The two questions that changed his life.

"Do you love Dorothy and have you got a job?"

The answer then had been "yes" and "yes" but now he didn't have a job. What would he say to Frank now? Not that he intends to say anything, he's too ashamed. After all the trust shown in him how can he tell him that he's finally failed? George thinks about his father-in-law. Frank was successful. He had taken over a small business and turned it into a much bigger one. George had asked him once how he had done it.

Frank had shrugged. "It's not difficult," he had said, "you

identify a need, fill it, then give good service. A lot of firms think it's a privilege for you to buy from them. That's bollocks. People want to be looked after, people need to have confidence that you can do what you say you can do, and do it well. Simple."

George thinks back over this. Good advice, but how can he apply it to his present situation. He has no idea but then the following day, out of the blue, he is presented with a possible answer.

Neighbours three doors down from George and Dorothy are moving only moving day has come and gone and they're still there. By chance George meets Andrew in the street and asked him what's happening.

"Bloody removal firm", said Andrew, "couldn't organise a piss up in a brewery. I chose a small local firm because I thought they'd give good service. Fat chance. First they come a day early but we can't move out then – got nowhere to go. Then they say they're fully booked the day they should be moving us and finally they say it's going to cost more than they first thought because they hadn't realised how much stuff we had. I told them to get stuffed but now I'm stuffed too."

George, with Frank metaphorically peering over his shoulder, suddenly senses an opportunity.

"Tell you what," he says, "why don't I round up a few mates, hire a van and we'll move you?"

Andrew is taken aback. "Could you do that?"

"Don't see why not. Let's have a look at how much stuff you've got."

George is not the only one who has been kicked out of the coach company so he has no trouble rounding up a few hefty helpers. He hires a large van, thanking Frank yet again for the foresight that got him his PSV licence, and Andrew's move is safely accomplished. Two days later George walks away with a pocket full of cash and Andrew's thanks ringing in his ears.

"That was nice of you, dear," says Dorothy. "It's good you could get the time off work."

For a moment he is tempted to confess but he's had an idea and wants to explore it first. The following morning, he visits the office of Dobson Removals, the firm that let Andrew down. At first the receptionist doesn't want to let him in but George is prepared for that.

"You tell your Mr Dobson that if he gives me ten minutes of his time, not only can I prevent his firm being sued to hell and back but I can also increase this firm's profits."

The sheer cheek of this approach gets him into Mr Dobson's office.

"What's all this about being sued?"

George explains about Andrew, how angry he is, how he works for a major bank and how he is talking of suing for breach of contract."

"What breach of contract? We never had a contract."

"And that's your other problem," says George, "you need to tie these jobs down, not just for your own safety but so the client can't change their mind after you've done a deal."

"What the hell do you know about the removal business?"

"Specifically about removals, not a lot. But I do know a lot about managing a fleet of vehicles, organising driver rotas and teams, interacting with people, providing sensible informed quotes and giving good service so people recommend you, rather than taking you to court."

There's a pause, then Dobson says. "You say you can stop this bloke suing us?"

"Yes, I think I can."

"And what do you want?"

"A job," says George simply.

"A job? What as?"

"Your assistant. Give me three months and I'll help you improve the efficiency of this firm and increase business. What have you got to lose?"

"Three months' salary," said Dobson with a rare flash of humour.

"Worth a gamble, isn't it?"

Dobson eyes George for a moment. "Okay, we'll give it three months and we'll see what happens."

That evening when the kids have gone to bed and he's doing the washing up George says casually to Dorothy. "Oh, by the way, I've got a new job. I start on Monday."

"That's nice, dear," says Dorothy, "you've missed a bit of egg on that plate."

Something about the casual way she says this makes George put down the plate he is washing and turn towards her, soap suds dripping onto the floor.

"You knew all the time, didn't you?" he says.

Dorothy blushes. "Well, actually, yes," she says.

"Why didn't you say anything?"

"I trusted you. I didn't want to worry you. I knew you'd sort it out somehow and I knew you would tell me if things got really desperate."

"Oh, Dorothy, I was so afraid of letting you down."

She comes across to him and puts her arms round him. "You could never let me down, George. But I want you to promise me something."

"What?"

"Never keep a secret like that from me again. This marriage is a partnership and we share everything, the good and the bad. Will you promise me that?"

"Yes, yes I will."

"Thank you. Now I think we should finish the washing up and go to bed."

Within three months Dobson realises that recruiting George – that's the way Dobson remembers it – was the best thing he ever did. Within a year the turnover has doubled, within five years they have six offices in towns all over the south of England, a whole fleet of vans of different sizes for different kinds of jobs and a reputation for service second to none. In the early stages George himself does all the estimating – a novel idea to Dobson – and always follows up with a personal visit to the customer after the move. He has found his niche. As his salary increases he uses his own company to move his family from the house in Ringwood to a bigger one near Eastleigh.

GEORGE WAS STILL HOLDING DOROTHY'S HAND WHEN THE DOOR opened and Linda came in carrying a tray of tea, closely followed by Gary and Steven. Linda smiled when she saw them, she put down the tray came across and took her mother's other hand. "Oh, Mum, isn't it lovely to all be together again?"

Dorothy smiled.

"We're not all here yet," said Gary, "but when Rebecca arrives we will be. Just like old times."

"Not exactly," said Steven, but catching a warning glance from Linda added quickly. "We're all a lot older for one thing."

George grunted. "Yes, and I'm way out in front."

"Well, we're none of us getting any younger," said Linda, then blushed at the trite cliché.

"Of course not," said Gary taking her literally, "that's not possible, but that doesn't stop us remembering the good times, does it?"

Linda caught Steven's eye. "It's not all been good, has it?"

Gary shrugged. "Maybe not, but why remember those bits?"

"Why be selective?" said Steven. "Good bits, bad bits, they all make up the whole."

"Maybe they do," said George, "but I'd quite like today to be about the good bits, if that's okay."

There was a silence and suddenly in that silence there was a knock on the door. Linda moved across the room and opened it. Outside was a young woman in her early twenties holding a bunch of flowers.

"Can I help you, dear?" said Linda.

"Hi, I've come to see Grandpa," said the girl. Her voice was soft but there was an unmistakable north American drawl.

"Well, I don't think your grandpa's here. Are you sure you've got the right room?"

"Sure I have," said the girl. She came into the room and went across to George, kissed him on the cheek and gave him the flowers.

"These are for you, Grandpa George."

"Thank you, Kate. They're lovely."

"I came as soon as Pops called me." She glanced round the room. "I guess you're Aunt Linda and you must be Uncle Steve."

Linda and Steven looked at each other.

"I don't understand," said Steven, "who are you?"

Gary suddenly stepped forward and put his arm round the girl's shoulders. "This is Kate Managan. She's my daughter."

TUESDAY 3:16 PM

STEVEN SAT ON THE WOODEN BENCH AT THE EDGE OF THE Greenacres car park looking out over the gardens. He'd suddenly felt a desperate need to be on his own. Too much was happening too quickly. The sudden urgent summons to visit his father. The baffling re-appearance of Gary after all this time, a Gary nothing like the introverted, naïve young man he remembered but a confident Gary, a Gary who seemed very much in control. Coming face to face with Linda with all the tension that still existed between them, the possibility of seeing Rebecca again after so long. And to cap it all, the sudden realisation that he had a niece he hadn't known existed and that Gary was her father. It was all a bit much to take in.

His hand went instinctively to his pocket, then paused. It was over thirty years since he'd stopped smoking but sometimes the habit of reaching for a cigarette still took over. This was just the kind of moment when he could have done with one but he wasn't going back down that road again. Instead he reached into his other pocket, took out a mint, unwrapped it and began sucking.

He sat back on the bench trying consciously to let his body and mind relax as the counsellor had taught him. He understood the value of such relaxation and he managed the body bit okay, but trying to relax the mind was a different kettle of fish. How do you close down your thoughts, think of nothing?

"Imagine a quiet, peaceful scene, something that gives you pleasure," James had said and he'd done his best. He had tried imagining the sea with waves lapping gently on the sand. He had tried imagining green hills under a summer sun with sheep grazing peacefully in the distance. He had tried imagining sitting on the terrace of a thatched cottage looking down the hillside across farmland to a river sparkling in the evening light. None of them had worked. It wasn't that he couldn't create these pictures in his mind, he could, it was just that he couldn't hold them there and very quickly the other thoughts, the ones he didn't want to think about, came tumbling back.

Many of them came tumbling back now, spurred by the sight of Dad and Mum together again. He still didn't understand the Gary situation but, although he felt irritated by the mystery surrounding his brother, he realised he was pleased to see that Dad and Gary had somehow been reconciled. He knew how much his parents had been hurt by Gary's prison sentence. He'd been angry with Gary at the time for causing his parents so much pain but now, looking back, he acknowledged he didn't have the right to throw the first stone.

"We all hurt them in our own way," he thought. "They hated it when Sandra and I split, then there was the bust-up with Rebecca and then all that trouble with Linda's boy. Between us we made a right balls up of it."

He remembered his own part in that balls up, the day he told his father that he and Sandra were separating. That was a day he would rather forget but was one of the things he could not.

WHAT MAN HASN'T THOUGHT ABOUT IT?

EIGHT YEARS INTO THEIR MARRIAGE STEVEN AND SANDRA AGREE to part, initially for a trial period but it doesn't take Steven long to realise that, for him at least, it is permanent. Six weeks after he moves out, with tears, sadness and recriminations on both sides, it's his son's birthday. Thomas is five and Steven agrees to go back for the day so Thomas can spend it with both parents. It was never going to be an easy visit and then he learns that Sandra has invited his parents to lunch.

"You can't be serious?" he says.

"Why not?" says Sandra, "we always invite them for Thomas's birthday."

"But they don't know we've split."

"Then it's high time they did. Take your Dad down the pub before lunch and tell him then. I don't want Thomas upset more than necessary."

So that is what he does. They find a table in a corner and Steven gets the drinks. They chat about this and that for a while and then George says. "Well, you might as well tell me and get it over with."

"Tell you what?"

"I don't know. Whatever it is you've brought me here to say. I can sense an atmosphere a mile off, son. Have you and Sandra had a row?"

Steven is silent for a moment. "You could say that," he says finally. "Actually we've separated. I moved out a few weeks ago."

"Bloody hell." A brief pause, then. "Does your mother know?"

"No."

Another pause, then George gestures at the empty glasses and when Steven nods, he gathers them up and heads towards the bar.

When he returns he takes a deep swallow then says, "So do you reckon this is permanent or just a spat like, that will pass?"

Steven thinks for a moment and then says, "I reckon it's permanent."

"Right. Well, I think you're a bloody fool but that's not going to make any difference, is it?"

"No." Steven is quite ready to match bluntness with bluntness.

Silence. Then George says, "I have to ask, Steven. Is there someone else?"

This is the question Steven has been dreading but there's no dodging it. "Yes, I think there is."

"Ah," and in that one expression George manages to convey resignation, disapproval and sadness.

Steven hurries on trying to justify himself. "Things haven't been right between Sandra and me for some time. We've had a lot of quarrels, things have been said. I hadn't really thought of leaving, not really but then, well, I met Vanessa. You know how it is, Dad, I mean I ask you, what man hasn't thought about it?"

George raises his eyes and stares straight at Steven. "I never thought about it. Your mother has always been the only one for me. I've never even looked at another woman."

No, thinks Steven, *I don't suppose you ever have.*

George drains his glass and puts it back on the table. "Well, that's that," he says, "it's your life, Steven, we're all entitled to go to hell in our own way. Come on, we'd better be getting back to the birthday lunch."

As they stand up Steven says, "There's just one more thing, Dad …"

"You'd like me to be the one to tell your mother." He sighed. "Yes, I'll do that for you, but not today. Let her enjoy her grandson's birthday first."

IT HAD BEEN A DIFFICULT TIME. HIS MOTHER HAD BEEN VERY upset but more because of Thomas, Steven thought, than for him and Sandra. When the divorce finally came through he made a point of telling his parents at once but they seemed indifferent to the news. Apart, divorced, what was the difference, Thomas was still growing up without his father. Sandra had remained on good terms with both George and Dorothy and from time to time would take Thomas to stay with them, even after she had married again. He was glad about that. A small compensation for having bought his freedom at their expense.

Vanessa hadn't lasted. In fact, from the moment their relationship moved from being an exciting dalliance to a permanent arrangement it had all gone rapidly downhill. Vanessa's flat was quite small and they very soon got on each other's nerves until finally, after only a very few months, he had moved out. He found himself a tiny bedsit and began a lonely life which he hated but knew he had no one to blame but himself.

This was the time when he began to go to pieces, not seeing any way forward and yet knowing that retreat would be disastrous. His work was suffering, he wasn't sleeping and, having disappointed his parents, there was no one he could talk to.

It had been a very bad period in his life.

TIME TO GET YOUR ARSE IN GEAR

HE IS SCREWING UP BIG TIME. HE KNOWS HE'S SCREWING UP BUT doesn't have the energy to do anything about it. At best he is coasting at work and in the world of management consultancy, coasting is not good enough. He wonders how much longer they'll go on tolerating his below par performance but that's still not enough to stop him feeling sorry for himself. He's in a downward spiral and lacks the motivation to do anything about it.

Then one afternoon he receives a phone call in the office. It is Rebecca, bubbling over with excitement. She has just heard that she has been awarded her PhD and wants to celebrate.

"Sorry I've not been touch for ages. It's been a bit full on the last couple of years but now it's done. Mum and Dad can't get up to London, Linda's stuck in the Midlands with two young kids. It's you and me, brother, let's hit the town."

He doesn't want to hit the town. All he wants to do is what

he always does, retreat to his bedsit and sit there in lonely misery. He tries to find excuses but something in his voice must have alerted his sister who suddenly becomes very serious.

"Steven. What's wrong."

He brushes it aside. "Nothing, I'm just tired."

"Pull the other one, it's got bells on. Tell me, Steven."

He snaps, as he does so often these days. "Just leave it, will you, I'm not in the mood for celebrating."

"You've made that very clear, but it won't wash, brother. Stay there. I'm on my way."

He doesn't believe her but half an hour later she walks into the office. She takes one look at him and says, "Get your coat. We're out of here."

He points out it's only four-thirty but she's having none of it. She drags him down the street and into one of the tiny little graveyards that are scattered all over the City of London. It is shadowy there and empty. They sit on a bench and Rebecca takes his hand.

"Okay, Steven, tell me all about it."

He tries to resist, but the warmth in her voice is too much and suddenly he is in tears and it all comes pouring out. How he and Sandra had split, but how nothing has gone right since, he's lonely but Vanessa was a mistake, he can't function, he hates himself, he doesn't know how he can go on, he feels guilty, he feels he has nothing to live for.

Rebecca listens quietly, still holding his hand until finally he runs out of words and sniffs into silence. There's a short pause, then she says. "One key question, Steven. Do you want to get back with Sandra?"

"God, no. Nothing's changed there, and anyway she's got a new bloke now."

"Okay, so it's you we need to sort out, right?"

"Forget it, Becky, it's not your problem and I don't want to spoil your day."

"It'd be spoilt even more if I leave you like this. Come on, you're coming home with me."

"But I can't. What about your flatmates?"

"They won't mind. You'll have to sleep on the sofa but I'm not leaving you alone tonight."

He's shivering now so he takes the line of least resistance and goes with her. Back at her flat they talk some more then Rebecca says, "I think you need professional help."

"Oh, no. No psychiatrists for me."

Rebecca smiles. "Thought you'd say that, but I'm thinking of something rather different."

"What?"

"Counselling. And I may know someone. Let me give them a call."

"I'd rather not. This is my problem. No one else can help."

"Bullshit." Suddenly Rebecca is very angry. "For God's sake, Steven, you're not doing too well on your own, are you? It's time to get your arse in gear, mate, and don't be too proud to accept some help."

He is taken aback at her vehemence and suddenly feels very ungracious.

"Well, okay then. Maybe."

She makes her call and two days later he meets James – he never learns his other name – and to his surprise he finds that he can talk rationally to him. It takes a long time, the best part of two years, but gradually he finds a sense of balance again. There is no magic formula in what James does, but with his gentle guidance Steven manages to rediscover a sense of self-worth. He learns to acknowledge how he feels and James helps him find ways to manage the bad times when they come, as they always will.

He is very grateful to Rebecca but she brushes it aside. "You're family. We help each other."

He remembers that sometimes, with shame. After her row with their parents and her disappearance into America somewhere he should have tried to find her. He is sorry he wasn't there for her when perhaps she needed him. Maybe today will give him a chance to make amends.

LOST IN REVERIE HE HEARD A STEP ON THE GRAVEL BEHIND HIM and he turned round, half expecting, half dreading to see Linda, but instead it was Kate. She gave him a cautious smile and gestured at the bench.

"May I?"

"Sure." He shifted along a little and she sat down. He delved into his pocket again. "Mint?"

"Thanks." She took one, he took another and they sat there, side by side for a moment, sucking and looking straight ahead.

After a moment Kate said through her mint, "I guess you and Aunt Linda didn't know about me."

"No, we didn't. Well, I didn't anyway."

"She didn't either. That was obvious." There was a pause and then she said. "Pops is not exactly forthcoming about stuff."

"No. I gathered."

"Did you know he's been visiting Grandpa for some years now?"

"No, no I didn't. Not until today."

"He's gotten a very strong sense of family. Took me a while to get used to that."

"Am I right in thinking you're from the States?"

"Sure. Ma and I live in Philly, that's Philadelphia, Pennsylvania."

"I know. I've been there."

"Oh, okay." She paused. "But you didn't know we were there?"

"I didn't know you were anywhere. Does Gary live with you in Philly?"

Kate laughed. "No way. He lives in London. Far as I know he's never been to the States."

"Oh, I see. Um ... forgive me, I'm having a rather strange day. I can't quite understand how you and your mother live in the States and Gary lives in London. Did your parents split up?"

Kate shook her head. "No, they never split, they were never together in the first place."

Steven blinked. "Oh, I see, well, I think I see." He paused for a moment. "But they must have been together at some time or ..." his voice tailed off and Kate laughed again.

"Oh, sure, they were together for that. Ma was doing some kind of secondment to London which is where they met. Then she went back to the States and a while later found she was pregnant with me."

"Oh, okay."

"Pops had no idea and Ma never got round to telling him, why rock the boat she said."

"But then she did rock it."

Another laugh. "I love your British sense of humour. Oh, yeah, she rocked it all right. She was sent back to London for three months when I was about eight years old and she took me with her."

"And that's when you met Gary."

"When I first met Pops, yeah, only I didn't know he was my Pops at that time."

"It must have been a bit of a shock."

Kate thought for a moment. "It's odd but I'm not sure it was. It was kinda cute in a way. Most of my friends had parents who were divorced and most of them squabbled. I was different. My parents had never gotten divorced, they'd never even gotten married, but it was clear they liked each other, just chose to live in different places. That's cool. I'm comfortable with that."

Steven was silent, thinking back to his divorce from Sandra. They had never openly quarrelled but their relationship had become very impersonal, an attitude that sadly had extended to his son. Initially he had tried to keep in touch with Tom – or at least so he told himself – but life often got in the way and it never really worked. Sometimes, to comfort himself, he thought it would be better when Tom grew up and he could explain things to him man to man. That amorphous hope was finally destroyed on the day of Dorothy's 70th birthday party.

FORGET IT, DAD, WHAT'S THE POINT?

THE PARTY IS HELD AT GEORGE AND DOROTHY'S HOME AND everyone – apart from Rebecca – is there. Steven comes with Hazel, Sandra brings her husband Nick, together with Tom who's in his final year of an engineering degree at university. It is Dorothy's day so everyone is being studiously polite to each other.

Steven hasn't seen Tom for some time so when he comes across him in the garden towards the end of the afternoon he makes an effort to talk to him.

"How's the course going?"

"It's okay."

"Still enjoying it."

A shrug. "It's okay."

"Any idea what you'll do when you graduate?"

"No."

This is hard work but he perseveres. "Lots of opportunities in engineering these days."

Silence for a moment then Thomas turns to face him. "Look, Dad, let's cut the crap, shall we?"

"Do what?"

"Let's stop pretending that we're father and son having a proper conversation. You don't really care about my future and I'm not interested in yours. You made your decision about me and my mother years ago. Nothing's changed. Let's just call it a day, eh?"

"That's not true, Tom. I've always cared about you."

"Oh, spare me that."

"Look, I know it wasn't easy while you were growing up but I did my best. And we're both adults now. Surely we can have a civilised conversation."

"What about?"

"Well, you know, stuff. What fathers and sons usually talk about."

"Which is what? You have to have a shared existence to have anything to talk about, otherwise you're just making polite, inconsequential conversation. I can't be bothered with that."

In spite of himself Steven is starting to get angry. "Okay, so you don't want to talk to me. Your choice. But you were happy enough to take my money to help you through uni, weren't you?"

Tom shrugs. "Of course. Why not? You owe me that."

For a moment there is silence then Steven says. "So that's it then, is it?"

"I think so, yes. Can't see the point. I'll send you a Christmas card if I remember. Have a good life." And Tom turns and walks off.

Steven doesn't know whether to feel sad or angry, guilty or relieved. In the end he settles for a mixture of all four. But he doesn't seen Tom again.

hand. "Hey, I'm sorry, Uncle Steve. I think I've upset you. Pops told me you're divorced. I didn't think. I'm sorry."

"Don't be. All water under the bridge." A thought struck him. "You say Gary knew about my divorce."

"Sure. As I said, he's real big on family. He's told me all about you kids and all the stuff you used to do together."

"You see, this is what I don't understand. I haven't seen Gary for, oh, it must be getting on for thirty years. I know nothing about where he's been, what he's done since ... um ... since ..."

"Since he came out of jail?" Kate finished the sentence for him.

"Oh, so you know about that."

"Sure. It was one of the first things he told me when we really became buddies. I was in my teens then, on another visit to London with Ma."

"Oh. Right. Well, my point is we haven't seen each other for all those years. I know nothing about him but he, apparently, knows all about me. That's what I don't understand."

Kate shrugged. "Can't help you there. I don't know much about Pops either, apart from the stuff we do together when I'm in London."

"Are you on a visit now?"

"No. I'm in the UK for a couple of years. I'm doing a post-grad course in mathematical analysis at Imperial."

"So you're living in London?"

"A little apartment in Streatham. Pops found it for me."

"And you've visited my father before?"

"Grandpa George? Sure several times." She laughed. "He was a bit surprised the first time I met him too."

"I bet he was."

"He and Pops are pretty close, you know."

"Yes, I'm beginning to realise that."

"I think they're good for each other. Pops looks after Grandpa and Grandpa makes Pops feel he's still part of the family. Pops is very big on family."

"So you keep saying. Not big enough to get in touch with my sisters and me though."

Kate was silent for a moment. "No. I don't understand that. I asked him about it once. He was talking about family days out, what fun they were with all of you together and I asked him why I couldn't meet you and Aunt Linda. He changed the subject."

"We have another sister too. Her name's Rebecca and she lives in …"

"Boston. Yeah, Aunt Becky. Pops has told me about her too. I'm looking forward to meeting her. Maybe I can visit with her next time I'm home."

"According to Gary you'll meet her later today. That's if you're staying, of course."

"Oh, I'm staying. But I do like the idea of one of Pops' sisters living in the States near Ma and me."

"Boston and Philadelphia aren't exactly close."

Kate grinned. "That's so English, Uncle Steve. You probably think Scotland is far away. The States is a big place. Boston's only about five hours' drive from where Ma and I live."

"Well, if you put it like that …" Steven paused to gather his thoughts. "I'm sorry if I seem a bit vague, Kate, but today is turning out to be very weird. I haven't seen or heard from Gary for years and years and then suddenly there he is. There you are too. A real surprise, a pleasant one I might say, but still a surprise. To be honest if I thought about him at all, I probably thought Gary was dead, but now I discover he's not only very much alive, but has actually been in touch with our parents and Rebecca for some time.

Kate scratched her head. "I don't think he's always been in touch with Aunt Becky. I think that's pretty recent. But from the way he talks I do think he feels quite close to her."

"So by inference he doesn't feel close to Linda and me?"

Another pause. "No, I don't think he does," said Kate. "I get the impression you didn't always get on too well together when he was growing up."

"Except in happy family memories apparently."

"Hey, Uncle Steve, I'm sorry, I really don't understand any of these family dynamics."

"Why should you? Not your fault."

They sat in silence for a few minutes. Then Steven said, "Do you think my father's dying?"

There was a pause before Kate answered, then she took a deep breath. "Yeah, maybe not actually dying but I think he's ready to go. I guess that's what today's all about."

"So you don't think Gary's over-reacting?"

"No. He told me a while back he'd made this promise to Grandpa. To get the whole family together one last time to say goodbye. That's what Grandpa wants." She was silent for a moment and then she said, her voice breaking slightly. "That's why I am staying here until … until … Oh, Uncle Steve, Grandpa's such a lovely man. I'm so very honored to be part of all this."

Suddenly Steven realised that he liked this young woman very much. Instinctively he reached out and put an arm round her shoulders in a brief hug. "Of course you're part of it. You're family."

She turned towards him and he saw the hint of tears in her eyes. "Do you mean that? I really am family?"

"Of course you are. You're Gary's daughter and Gary is my brother. Welcome to the Redmonds."

"Oh, wow, thank you." She sniffed. "Perhaps we'd better go back inside. See how they're getting on."

"Yes, perhaps we'd better." Steven stood up. "Come on then."

"And perhaps we can persuade Grandpa to tell us some of his wonderful jokes."

"Wonderful? Are you kidding? His jokes are awful."

"No, they're not, they're very funny. We don't have jokes like his in the States."

"Just as well," muttered Steven but Kate was in full flow.

"D'you remember that one about the funeral director?"

Steven sighed. "Not particularly."

"Oh, it's great, there was this guy, he only had one leg, he was six foot six tall and had bright red hair and, do you know, the funeral director refused to bury him."

Steven could recognise a cue line when he heard one. "Why did he refuse to buy him?"

"Because he wasn't dead." And with Kate's laugh ringing out they went back into the care home.

TUESDAY 3:27 PM

THE CONVERSATION IN GEORGE'S ROOM WAS DYING AWAY. GEORGE himself was clearly sleepy and Gary's small talk was as non-existent as ever. Linda desperately trying to think of something to say, turned to Gary.

"Kate seems a very nice young woman."

"Yes, she is."

"How old is she?"

"Oh ... um ... early twenties, I think."

"You think?" Linda gave a little laugh. "Don't you know when your own daughter was born?"

Gary looked confused. "Well, no, I don't actually. I think she was about eight when I first met her."

Linda's jaw dropped. "You didn't know her until she was eight?"

"No, I didn't even know she existed."

Linda was speechless and Gary realised that something more was required of him.

"Her mother's American, you see. Well, I suppose Kate is too, come to that. She was born over there, of course."

"That's amazing."

Gary was puzzled. He thought 'amazing' was an odd word to use. It all seemed perfectly logical to him. He hadn't known about the pregnancy. How could he have known? He thought back to that summer twenty odd years ago, his recent promotion, the joint meeting between them and the Americans. His first meeting with Rhonda.

THE SPECIAL RELATIONSHIP – PART 1

HE FIRST SEES HER AT THE MORNING BRIEFING MEETING. SHE'S sitting next to Arthur who introduces her as Bonnie. That's her operational name, of course, he doesn't learn her real name until much later. She's an American, from a specialist cryptology unit somewhere in Kentucky, her own speciality is lateral and oblique mathematics and she's here for six months to work with the team trying to unravel the complexities of the Andaman malfunction.

Gary is not someone who ever pays much attention to women, or men come to that, but something about her strikes a chord. For a start she looks happy, not exactly a scientific description but a sufficient contrast between her and most of his colleagues to make her stick in his memory. She is tall and yet doesn't look big. She is wearing a slim line trouser suit which to his eyes just looks smart but which later, much later, he learns has been specially tailored for her. Gary, who never notices what he himself is wearing and has never considered visiting a proper tailor, is seriously impressed.

Occasionally over the next few months their work paths cross but then one evening as he's leaving the building he finds her close behind him. As they emerge onto the pavement they exchange greetings and then somehow fall into step with each other.

As they wait for the traffic lights to change she suddenly says, "You busy tonight?"

Gary is caught on the hop. "Well, no, nothing special."

"D'you fancy grabbing a pizza someplace. I am just so, so sick of eating on my own."

And Gary, who seldom thinks about what he is eating or when he is eating it, finds himself saying, "Sure. Sounds great."

And that's how it all begins.

LINDA SHOOK HER HEAD. "I JUST CAN'T IMAGINE THAT. FANCY not knowing you had a daughter until she was eight years old."

"But they were in America. I didn't even know Rhonda was pregnant."

"You'd have thought she'd have got in touch though, let you know you were about to be a father."

This idea had never occurred to Gary. "But she was fine. She had a good job. She didn't need any help."

"Gary, it's not just about money. You had a right to know."

Gary was still puzzled, not following the line of argument.

"I don't think it's important. Anyway I know now and, as you say, Kate's great."

"Well, yes, but what about Kate herself? Didn't she have the right to know she had a father somewhere? An English father?"

"I don't see what difference it would have made. She's always been well cared for."

"Oh, Gary, can't you see, that's not the point."

"Isn't it?" He could see that Linda was upset by this though he didn't understand why. He searched for something to make it easier for her.

"Kate and I liked each other from the first moment we met. I bought her an ice cream and took her on the London Eye."

"Did she know you were her father?"

"Not at first, no. That's why I bought her the ice cream."

He smiled to himself, remembering the look of joy and surprise in the little girl's eyes when he presented her with a strawberry cornet.

THE SPECIAL RELATIONSHIP – PART 2

THEY MEET ON THE SOUTH BANK OUTSIDE THE NATIONAL Theatre. He assumes Rhonda has chosen this spot for operational reasons but then he sees her coming towards him holding a young girl by the hand. Their greeting is warm, if a little restrained, but that seems quite normal to him after a gap of eight years.

"Kate, this is my friend Gary I told you about."

"Hi, Gary."

"Hallo, Kate."

He offers his hand and the child solemnly shakes it. He glances sideways at Rhonda and raises an eyebrow but Rhonda shakes her head silently.

Then she says, "Kate, why don't you go over to that wall and see how many boats you can see. I just want a quick word with Gary."

"Okay, Ma," and the child obediently trots off.

Left alone Rhonda and Gary look at each other.

"Good to see you, pal, after all this time," says Rhonda.

"Good to see you too." He nods towards the child. "You married now?"

"Nope."

There's a pause as Gary's logical mind works through the options. Then he says, "Is she mine then?"

"She's ours, Gary. Not yours."

"Yes, of course. I only meant, am I her father?"

"You sure are, pal. I had to come over to the UK so I figured I'd bring her with me. Give you a chance to get to know her."

"Thank you. I'm glad." He pauses. "Bit surprised though. Does she know about me?"

"Nope. I figured we could tell her together."

He nods. That seems perfectly logical to him. "Let's do it then."

They walk across to join the little girl at the parapet looking down at the river.

"How many boats have you seen?" asks Gary.

Kate looks up at him. "Well, that kinda depends on what you mean by 'boats'. I've seen seven barges, two small launches, nine of those bathtub shaped things with crowds of people and loudspeakers, and two men in a rowing boat."

"Oh, right."

"I've also seen four black-backed gulls, not sure if they were lesser or greater, seventeen herring gulls, five black headed gulls, a mute swan and two ducks, probably just ordinary mallards but they were a bit far away."

Gary is slightly taken aback at the assurance of this child.

"Do you like birds, then?" he asks.

"Oh, sure. When Ma told me we were coming to England I got a book about British birds and read up about them. You seem a bit short of vultures over here though. We have a lot of turkey vultures back home."

"True. There's not a lot of vultures in London," Gary says. "Not ones that fly anyway."

"Hey, that's cool. You mean you've got some non-flying vultures?"

Gary, who hadn't intended to crack a joke, looks slightly bemused. Behind Kate's back Rhonda is smiling broadly.

"Er ... not exactly," he says, "look why don't we go and get an ice cream. Your mother and I have something to tell you."

"Cool, I like you." And the child takes his hand and skips along the pavement beside him.

They buy ice creams – strawberry cornets all round, not something Kate has seen before.

"Hey, aren't these cute? I love ice cream. Back home it comes in little pots."

They sit on a bench in the sun, licking away.

Conversation with anyone never comes easily to Gary and he has no experience of young children. He searches his mind for something to say.

"When you've finished your ice cream would you like to go on the London Eye?" He makes a vague westward gesture. "It's like a sort of big wheel."

"Cool. That'd be fun. You coming too, Ma?"

"Sure am, honey."

The three of them walk along the embankment, the child between the two adults, all holding hands. Kate is exuberant.

"Hey, this is great. London's real cool." She turns her beaming smile on Gary, "and I like you too, Gary. I wish you were my Pops."

Gary and Rhonda exchange glances. "Well, actually, Kate," says Gary, "as it happens it would seem that I am your … er … Pops."

"Are you? Hey, that's really cool."

She stops and turns to look at them. "I'm not that surprised really," she says seriously, "Ma always said she'd take me to meet my Pops one day and when she said we were coming to London I did wonder."

Rhonda smiles down at the child. "So what d'you reckon on him now you've met him?"

Kate's brow furrows. She stands back and looks Gary up and down. "I kinda like the idea. Do you live in London?"

"Yes, I do."

"Are we gonna live in London now, Ma?"

"No, honey. We're only here for a few weeks and then we'll be going back home."

The child considers this for a moment. "Are you coming back to the States with us when we go, Gary?"

Gary shakes his head. "No, I'm not. Sorry, Kate, but I live here. My work is here."

"Okay. But we can visit with you, right?"

"You certainly can. Whenever you want."

"Cool." She thinks for a moment. "Well, I guess …" She breaks off.

"You guess what, honey?" says Rhonda.

"I guess I'd better call him Pops, not Gary, yeah?"

The two adults laugh. "You can call me whatever you like, Kate," says Gary.

"Pops," says Kate firmly. "And now, Pops, Ma, where's this eye thing we're going on or shall we have another ice cream first?"

TUESDAY 4:06 PM

IT WAS WARM IN GEORGE'S ROOM WITH SIX OF THEM IN THERE. George was nodding drowsily with an occasional grimace of pain. Dorothy was smiling in her abstract world, occasionally her lips would move as though she were singing to herself. A care assistant had come in a while ago, wheeled her out for a pee and then brought her back again. The three siblings sat there, not knowing what to say and therefore feeling slightly awkward. Kate was doing something or other on her phone.

Linda felt somehow that it was incumbent upon her to ease the tension. But how? If she and Steven had been on their own they would have had plenty to talk about but would probably have ended up fighting again. If she was alone with Gary she could try and talk to him to find out where he had been all these years, learn more about his relationship with this Rhonda and what kind of relationship he now had with Kate. She would love to know more about all of that but, based on her experience so far today, doubted whether Gary was going to be very forthcoming.

If she had Kate on her own she could ask her about Gary – she might learn more that way. In any case she would have welcomed the chance to talk more to this surprise niece but she could hardly say, "Come on, dear. Let's go and have a girly chat and you can tell me all about your mysterious dad."

Steven didn't know what to think or what to say. His father didn't look any worse than the last time he'd seen him, a bit more lethargic perhaps and he suspected George had more physical pain than he was letting on. He wasn't sorry that he'd come but he found this enforced family gathering oppressive and, if it hadn't been for Gary's conviction that his father was dying, he'd have been wondering how soon he could reasonably make his excuses and get away. Then he remembered Rebecca somewhere over the Atlantic heading towards Heathrow. In the circumstances he could hardly go before her arrival. He sighed. He would just have to grit his teeth and sit it out.

Gary was also feeling uncomfortable. He liked tasks that were clear cut and precise. The start of today had been easy for him. Way back George had told him what he wanted and Gary had arranged all the practical details. Then this morning, following George's call, he'd put that plan into action. Successfully. Rebecca was in the air, Steven and Linda were here, as was Mum. What he hadn't thought about was what would happen next. The answer seemed to be nothing. He didn't want his father to die but if that was the plan then why didn't he get on with it? He fretted quietly to himself. After so many years of isolation he wasn't comfortable in this family gathering set-up. There was a huge gulf between family memories and family reality and he wasn't at ease with it.

An awkward silence hung over the room, each of them lost in their own memories.

A NIL-NIL DRAW

STEVEN IS STANDING IN THE PARK WITH GEORGE ON A DAMP Saturday afternoon in spring. George is a keen follower of the local youth club football team and often spends Saturday afternoons watching them play. Steven has no interest in football whatsoever, but he does want to talk to his father privately and the opportunities for that back at home are rare.

"Oh, for God's sake, did you see that. Come on, ref, that was a foul."

To Steven it is all meaningless. He plays football at school, he has no choice, but why anyone would choose to spend a precious weekend day running around in the mud if they didn't have to, is completely beyond him. Still he makes the effort.

"Nice bit of passing that, eh, Dad?"

"What? Oh, yeah, not bad. But it's only sideways, doesn't gain any ground."

"Oh, yes, see what you mean."

What Steven wants to talk to his father about is his future. This coming autumn he is due to start his 6th form year at school and study for his A-Levels but he has changed his mind. He's had enough of formal education, he just wants to get a job. Any job, it doesn't matter. He's fed up with school and wants to earn some money.

He knows this decision won't be popular. His mum is very keen for him to get what she calls 'a good education' and to 'make something of himself'. He doesn't want to hurt her but he does feel he has a right to his point of view, if he can find a way of expressing it and find someone who will listen. He reckons his Dad is more likely to be amenable and if so he will help him deal with Mum.

But first he has to find the words and the opportunity which is why he's standing on the touchline in the park on this chilly Saturday afternoon. There's a flurry of activity round a goal mouth. Dad cheers his side on and Steven joins in with as much enthusiasm as he can muster. The ball goes out of play. No goal is scored.

Half time comes. Perhaps this is his chance but another supporter wanders over to talk to his Dad.

"Hiya, George, how's tricks."

"Not so dusty, Bill. You met my lad, Steven?"

"Pleased to meet you Steven. Come to support your Dad's team, eh?"

"Yeah."

"Good lad. Heard you cheering just now. That should have

been a goal, shouldn't it?"

"Suppose."

"Good to see enthusiasm."

"I have to cheer Dad's team or I don't get any tea."

George and Bill burst out laughing and George gives him a gentle cuff round the ear.

"Get on with you, Steven."

He's pleased to have cracked a successful joke but he's no nearer broaching the subject he wants to talk about. The longer he waits, the harder it gets. Perhaps on the walk home he'll get his chance. But when the time comes he can't find the words and the two of them get absorbed back into family life with the conversation stillborn.

He feels resentful. Tries to tell himself that George wouldn't listen but deep down he knows the failure is his. He never does share his thoughts about his future with his parents. He takes the easy path, stays on for the 6th form, does his A-Levels, gets good results, goes on to do a business studies course at a Technical College and never looks back. Probably everything has worked out for the best, but he always has the feeling that somewhere along the line he took a wrong turning and he keeps a vague feeling of unfulfillment all his life. Apart from anything else he never forgets that Saturday afternoon moment of personal failure. His nil-nil draw.

LINDA SAT THERE WATCHING HER PARENTS, TRYING HARD TO remember them as she wanted to remember them. Her mother lively and encouraging, her father fun and supportive. In her mind's eye she smoothed away the wrinkles and the vacuity back to the time she was nineteen and announced she proposed crossing America on a Greyhound bus with a friend.

GREYHOUND TO ADVENTURE

SHE IS NERVOUS ABOUT TELLING THEM, NOT SURE WHAT THEIR reaction will be. The original plan for this trip was for three of them to go but Jane has already dropped out. The legal age of majority may have been lowered to eighteen but Jane's parents were having none of it. They said a flat, "No."

She and Margaret agree to approach their respective parents on the same evening and now that evening is here. She waits till tea is over. Rebecca is upstairs revising for her A-levels and Gary is playing in the garden. The coast is clear.

"Mum, Dad," she says, "can I talk to you for a minute?"

They look mildly surprised but Dorothy says, "Of course, Linda. Is there a problem?"

"No, not a problem as such but there's something I need to tell you, no, ask you, well, yes, I suppose tell …"

George grins. "Doesn't sound like you're pregnant then," he says, a remark which earns him a sharp rebuke from Dorothy.

"George, that's not funny." There's a beat pause and then she says to Linda, "you're not, are you?"

"'Course not, Mum," says Linda, "it's nothing like that."

"Then let's go and sit down and find out what it is like," says George and leads the way through to the sitting room.

She has rehearsed this moment and has decided the best plan is to come straight out with it.

"Margaret and I want to go abroad for three months. We want to travel across America by Greyhound Bus."

There's a short silence then Dorothy says, "Good idea …"

"That'll be a 'tell' then, not an 'ask'," says George.

The relief is huge. "You don't mind? Jane's parents have refused to let her come."

"Well, I'm not sure I'm too keen," says George, "two girls

travelling alone, all that way."

"Oh, come on, George. It'll be a great experience for them."

"I'm sure it will, but what happens if something goes wrong?"

But Dorothy is having none of it. "You can't go through life wondering what would happen if something went wrong or you'd never do anything."

"Yes, okay, but America. On a bus. You hear so many stories."

"Yes, and that's probably what most of them are – stories. She's young, George, this is the time to have adventures. You have to take some chances or life would be deadly dull."

"Maybe dull is safe."

Now Dorothy is getting quietly cross. "Oh, yes, dull is safe but who wants to be safe all the time? If you'd stuck to 'safe' neither of us would be here now, would we?"

"What do you mean?"

"Remember that letter you wrote to me all those years ago. That was you playing safe, wasn't it?"

Linda is looking from one parent to the other in fascination.

"Oh, now come on, Dottie. Play fair."

"I am playing fair. I'm reminding you how my father talked you out of being safe. Never regretted it, have you?"

"For heaven's sake, 'course I haven't. You know that."

"Well, then, what do you think my father would say if he could hear us now?"

There's a moment's pause. Then George sits back in his chair and to Linda's astonishment roars with laughter.

"Okay, Dottie, you win. If Frank was here now he'd take me down the pub and say 'If you don't let that girl go to America, then I'll push your face through that wall'."

Dorothy giggles. "Yes, he probably would."

Linda is completely dumbfounded, not quite sure which way the argument is going.

"So can I go?"

George nods. "Technically," he says, "we can't stop you. You're over eighteen, an adult in the eyes of the law."

"Yes, but …"

"You can go, Linda, and go with our blessing," says Dorothy, "but can we ask some questions?"

"Of course you can."

"What about college? What do they think?"

"They're happy to put my course on hold for a year. They say I'll make a much better health visitor with some wider experience behind me."

"Okay, I can see that," says George. "Now, what about money?"

"I've been saving and I've never touched that money granddad left me."

George laughs. "Frank again. I think he'd be tickled pink to know how you plan to use it."

"Where will you stay?" asks Dorothy.

Linda shrugs. "Apparently there's a lot of cheap motels around but Margaret's got a friend who did this last year and she says they often took overnight buses and slept on those."

"Well, if you're going to spend three months sleeping on a bus," says George, "much better you do it now while you're nineteen rather than forty-nine. I'd rather have my bed these days."

"When do you plan on going?"

"Late summer. When term ends at college. I need to take a year out so when I get back I'll get a job somewhere until the new college year starts, then pick up where I left off."

"Well you seem to have it all planned. Where will you go first?"

"We thought New York. Margaret's friend stayed at the YWCA there and said it was fine. Then we'll probably head down to Washington and carry on south. I'd like to go to New Orleans and after that, well, we'll see."

"Quite an adventure," says Dorothy.

"Yes, but it's something I really want to do."

"Then do it," says George. "Your Mum's right – as she usually is."

"Of course," says Dorothy.

"One proviso," says George.

For a moment Linda is suspicious. "What?"

"I'll give you some message money. Don't spend it on anything else. Just use it to send us an occasional telegram, or whatever they call it over there, to let us know where you are and how you're doing."

"Oh, I see. Right."

"And," continues George, "if you run into money difficulties let us know first. If you need money, I'll get it to you somehow. Don't want you getting into debt in a foreign country."

Linda is overcome. "You're wonderful," she says, "you're both wonderful."

"As your Mum's just reminded me, I've always liked a challenge myself," says George, "but these days I'd draw the line at sleeping on a bus."

LOOKING AT HER FATHER NOW, SHRUNK INTO HIS CHAIR, twitching occasionally with pain, Linda struggled to remember the man who loved her enough to let her go. Suddenly the room felt very oppressive and she could not simply go on sitting there.

"Anyone fancy a walk?" she said, getting to her feet.

To her surprise Steven also got up. "I'll come with you," he said.

She glanced across at Gary but he shook his head. "I'll stay here," he said, "You two go."

TUESDAY 4:36 PM

THEY LEFT THE BUILDING AND HEADED OUT INTO THE GROUNDS of the care home. They walked past the seat where Steven had talked to Kate and took the path around the lawn towards the shrubbery.

For a few moments they walked in silence and then Linda said. "How do you think he's looking – Dad I mean?"

"Not good."

"No."

"When I first got here I thought it was all a bit of a wild goose chase but he's faded noticeably during the day."

"Yes, I thought so too. And he's obviously in quite a lot of pain."

"Yes. A bit weird though, all this, isn't it?"

"You mean, Gary?"

"Gary, Kate, Becky flying in from the States. This whole family gathering thing."

"If it's what Dad wants …"

"Oh, sure. It just feels so … so … planned."

"It has been planned. That's quite clear."

"Yes, I don't really mean … planned. Perhaps contrived is a better word."

"Mmm! But he desperately wants to see Becky."

"Ah yes. The final loose end." Steven was silent for a moment. Then he said. "Do you think he really is about to die?"

Linda thought for a moment then nodded. "Yes, I think I do. I didn't when I first arrived but now I'm not so sure."

"But he can't just decide to die when it suits him, can he?"

"I don't know. All I know is I'm glad I came."

"Me too."

Suddenly Steven stopped and took Linda's arm, forcing her

to stop too.

"Look, Linda, this is as good a time as any to say I'm sorry. Sorry for what I said about Graham back then. And this time I really mean it."

She looked at him, then nodded. "Thank you." A pause. "You hurt me though, Steven, really hurt me."

"I know."

They stood there, together, in the sunny peace of the garden, remembering.

ANOTHER TIME, ANOTHER JAIL – LINDA

SHE REMEMBERS THE CALL VERY CLEARLY. SHE CAN NEVER FORGET it. It's September, a Thursday morning. She's about to put some soup on for lunch when the phone goes.

At first she thinks it's a cold call. One of those "*Madam, you have a problem with your computer but we can help you solve it*" calls. But then she hears Graham's name.

"I'm sorry," she says, "I'm sorry, what did you say?"

He is a lawyer calling from Pattaya in Thailand. His English is good, though heavily accented, but not so accented she cannot understand what he is saying. Graham, her son Graham, has been arrested on drugs charges and is in jail. For a moment it feels as though the world has come to an end but then she takes hold of herself, notes the information he is giving her before ringing off and calling Dennis.

Dennis, as always, is an emotional tower of strength. A practical man he is not, but he is always there in times of crisis, comforting, supporting, encouraging. He has no idea what to do, Linda has to deal with everything but, as always with Dennis beside her, she never feels alone.

She refuses to remember the next few months in detail. The

consultation with lawyers in the UK, the journey to Thailand, talking to lawyers there, being allowed to see Graham briefly. Perhaps that was the worst of all, the way he just shrugs it off.

"It's no big deal, Mums. It's only a bit of coke. Everyone's doing it. It won't come to anything."

But it does come to something. They go back to Thailand for the trial and she has a real struggle to stay calm when Graham is sentenced to five years. They tell her he's lucky. Many drug offences carry longer sentences. Some even face the death penalty.

Occasionally she feels she is drowning in all the complexities but Dennis is always there with a cup of tea or a comforting word. He is very supportive. He never reminds her that he wasn't in favour of Graham's backpacking trip through the Far East. But Linda was determined he should go, remembering the way her parents had supported her trip across the States all those years ago.

They return to the UK, consult more lawyers and eventually a year later they manage to obtain permission for Graham to complete his sentence in an English prison. For the second time in her life she finds herself going through a prison gate at visiting time.

ANOTHER TIME, ANOTHER JAIL – STEVEN

THE FIRST STEVEN KNOWS ABOUT WHAT'S HAPPENED TO GRAHAM is a call from George.

"I thought I should let you know, son," he says, "Linda's boy has been arrested in Thailand. Something to do with drugs."

For a moment Steven is taken aback and then, without really stopping to think, he says, "Is he indeed. Well, I can't say I'm surprised."

This isn't the response George is expecting. "Why not?"

"Well, he's always been an arrogant little plonker, hasn't he? Gives 'stupidity' a bad name."

George is silent for a moment then he says. "I didn't know you felt like that."

"No. Well …"

"I know he hasn't always been the best behaved teenager. To be honest some of the things he's done made me very angry. If any of you had behaved like that I'd've walloped you but you can't do that these days apparently."

"No."

"But when all's said and done he is my grandson and you have to stand by your own. Nobody's perfect."

"No," thought Steven, "nobody's perfect, but not everyone goes out of their way to prove that fact as consistently as Graham does."

"I wish it hadn't been drugs, I can't excuse that, I grant you. But now it's Linda we have to think about."

Steven, perhaps defensive because of the failure with his own son, does not feel inclined towards sympathy.

"I still think the brat deserves all he can get." He pauses. "Do you think I should give Linda a call?"

"Not if you're going to say things like that," says George and uncharacteristically he hangs up.

Steven decides to wait until Linda calls him, which she doesn't until several weeks later and then she makes no mention of Graham so he doesn't either. And that should have been that.

Except it wasn't.

IN THE GARDEN OF THE CARE HOME BROTHER AND SISTER HAD arrived at the same memory. The setting was the community hall in the village where Linda and Dennis lived. The occasion was the party for Linda and Dennis's silver wedding. There were around eighty guests, family, friends, children of friends. A local band was belting out 1970s hits and the pile of vol-au-vents was steadily decreasing. A pay bar in the corner was doing steady business.

Like most crises, especially family crises, this one came out of no-where and exploded like a landmine in a china shop.

WHEN YOU'RE IN A HOLE, STOP DIGGING

SHE IS HAVING A PRETTY GOOD EVENING ON THE WHOLE, although at first she finds it hard to put on a cheerful face. A few days earlier she'd visited Graham in prison for the first time since his transfer from Thailand and it had left her deeply depressed. She is not in a mood for celebrating so she suggests they should cancel the party but Dennis points out that the hall is booked, people invited, band and caterers paid in advance and cancelling won't help Graham in any way at all.

She sees the sense in that and hopes that the party will dull the pain, at least for a while. And to some extent it does. No one mentions Graham, whether out of tact or ignorance she doesn't know, so she is spared endless commiserations and sympathy.

Ten o'clock comes. They cut the cake, there are a few innocuous speeches and she settles down for the last two hours before the midnight curfew on the hall. Then it happens, an unlucky combination of the wrong people coming together at the wrong time.

She is talking to her mother when Steven and Hazel drift into the group.

"How was Graham when you saw him?" Dorothy is asking.

"Not good," says Linda, "the jails here are certainly better than the ones in Thailand but it's still prison and it isn't very nice. He's putting on a bold face but underneath I think he's a bit frightened."

"Serves the little shit right," says Steven.

There is a stunned silence, then Linda says. "What did you say?"

"Steven, come away now." Hazel has hold of his arm and is trying to pull him out of the group but Steven is having none of it.

"I said, serves the little shit right," he says. "He was always going to end up like this."

Dorothy steps in. "That's enough, Steven. I think you've had too much to drink. Come on, Linda, let's leave him to it."

But Linda is blazing. "How dare you talk like that about my son. At least I was there for Graham. I didn't walk out on him like you did with Thomas."

Hazel is hanging on to Steven and Dorothy is trying to edge Linda away but brother and sister are now face to face.

"Being there for Graham didn't do him much good, did it? At least Thomas knows how to behave. He didn't spend his teenage years bullying other kids and getting cautions from the police."

"One caution, just one, and that wasn't his fault."

"Oh, no, of course it wasn't. Try telling that to the old lady he knocked flying when he was nicking those fags."

"He wasn't nicking them. He was on his way to pay for them when she got in his way."

Steven let out a roar of laughter. "The sad thing about that is that you probably actually believe it. The same way you think he was hard done by in Thailand instead of being just another nasty little drug pusher."

"You bastard." And she slaps him hard across his face which catches him by surprise.

"You bitch." He takes a step forward but suddenly George is there, thrusting in between them.

"That's enough. Both of you."

"Did you see what she …"

"I don't care who did what to who …"

"Whom …" mutters Dorothy from long force of habit, an intervention which causes Hazel to give a nervous giggle.

"Steven, you will apologise to your sister," says George.

"Like hell I will." And he turns to walk away.

"Steven …" George's voice is like a whiplash. "Do as you're told."

The ingrained habit of a lifetime kicks in and Steven stops in his tracks.

"And you, Linda," says George, "you will apologise to your brother for hitting him."

"Apologise? To him? After what he said?"

"Yes. Apologise. We do not settle disputes by violence in this family."

There is a long pause. The rest of the hall has fallen silent. A few people, embarrassed, are examining their drinks with close attention. The band, rightly assuming the evening is over, start packing up their instruments.

After a long moment. "I'm waiting …" says George.

Reluctantly Steven turns back to face his sister.

"I am sorry for the things I said," he says coldly.

Another long moment then … "And I'm sorry I hit you," says Linda, her face like stone.

"Good," says George. Then he turns to face the rest of the hall. "Thank you, ladies and gentlemen," he says, "I regret that a family disagreement has brought the evening to an untimely end. However, before we all leave I think we should remember why we came here in the first place. We came here to celebrate the silver wedding of my daughter, Linda …" He reaches out and takes her hand … "and her husband, Dennis. Dennis, where are you?"

An embarrassed Dennis emerges from the crowd and George takes his hand too.

"Now we need to end this evening positively so, although we've already done it once, I am going to ask you to raise your glasses again to Linda and Dennis and then give them three cheers. Are you ready?"

There is total silence in the hall.

"I'll take that as a 'yes' then," says George grimly. "Right ..." He starts to raise his arm, realises he doesn't have a glass, looks round spots one on a nearby table, grabs it and raises it high.

"To Linda and Dennis and their family."

The mesmerised crowd follow suit.

"To Linda and Dennis."

"Now then," says George, "we're going to end on a high. Right? Okay then, three cheers for Linda and Dennis. Hip hip ..."

The first cheer is somewhat muted but then the Dunkirk spirit kicks in and the final two cheers echo round the roof of the hall.

"Thank you," says George, "now I think it's time we went home."

He puts his glass down on the table and makes a face. "I don't know what that drink was but it tasted like a whore's armpit."

"George. That's quite enough of that." And Dorothy drags him away.

Linda and Steven look at each other. Apologies have been made but the only result is an uneasy truce that will last for the next twelve years.

SOMEWHERE IN THE TREES A BLACKBIRD UTTERED A WARNING call. A cloud drifted over the sun and, briefly, the garden seemed

161

dark. Linda glanced over at Steven and in spite of herself, a wry grin crossed her face.

"That was one hell of an evening, wasn't it," she said.

For a moment Steven looked surprised then he grinned back. "Yes, it was rather. Thought the old man was terrific though."

"Put us in our place, didn't he?"

"Yes. Reminded me of the time he dragged me out of bed because I'd forgotten to do one of my chores. Sent me out into the garden in my pyjamas to fill the coal scuttle."

"I don't remember that."

"I do," said Steven with feeling. "And I'll tell you something, I never forgot again."

"They were great, weren't they? Both of them. Mum and Dad."

"Yes. And now he's dying. And Mum's gone off on a journey of her own." There was a pause then Steven said, "What's Graham doing now?"

"Ah, you're not going to believe this but he's an actuary working for an insurance brokers in the City."

"An actuary?"

"Yes, he began studying while in prison and qualified a couple of years ago."

Steve shakes his head. "Talk about from the sublime to the ridiculous."

Linda laughs. "I know what you mean. I'm pleased for him, of course, at least he seems to have settled down. To be honest I don't really know what an actuary does but I do know he can bore for England on the subject."

"And Amanda?"

"Still happily married. As equable as ever. I did wonder whether I should call her and Graham when I realised what was happening today but they couldn't just drop everything and come and anyway, what could they do?"

"True."

Silence for a moment apart from the sound of the wind in the trees, then Linda said, "And what about Tom?"

There was a long, long pause before Steven answered. "Tom. Yes, well I screwed up good and proper there. I haven't seen or spoken to him for nearly twenty years."

"What? Are you serious?"

"Yes."

"But why not."

"His choice. He said it wasn't worth the bother. We didn't have anything to say so why pretend we liked each other just because we were father and son."

"Oh, Steven."

"Trouble is, I can see his point." He paused. "Still makes me sad though."

Linda took his hand. "Of course it does. But Sandra ..."

"Oh, Sandra keeps me in touch with what he's doing and so on but we have no direct contact. He got married a few years ago, apparently. I wrote to him then but it was returned, unopened."

"I'm so sorry."

Steven shrugged. "It is what it is."

"Does Dad know?"

"No idea. Probably. Sandra tells me Tom keeps in touch with him, birthday, Christmas cards and so on. Don't know if they ever meet though."

There was a silence as brother and sister thought about their offspring. Finally Linda said, "Didn't do too well, did we, either of us?"

"No."

"I never condoned what Graham did, you know."

"Of course not."

"But he's my son …" her voice choked slightly. "And you've got to look after your own, haven't you?"

"If you're allowed to."

"Oh, Steven, I'm sorry. Tom. I wasn't thinking."

"No matter. What was it Mum used to say 'Love them and let them go'. Perhaps my love wasn't as strong as yours."

Silence for a moment then Linda gathered herself together.

"This is becoming a very odd day."

"It certainly is."

"Still, let's look on the bright side. It'll be good to see Becky again."

"Yes."

"Do you know if she and Dad ever buried the hatchet?"

"Don't think so. Maybe that's what all this is about."

"He's certainly very keen to see her again."

"And at least she's coming. She could have said no after all this time."

"Glad she didn't, though how the hell Gary managed to fix it for her to come in such a short time beats me."

"Bit of a mystery, our brother. Do you think he's ever going to tell us where he's been all this time and what he's doing?"

Linda thought for a moment. "No, I don't think so." She gave a wicked grin. "But that doesn't stop us asking, does it? Come on, think it's time we went back in."

They turned towards the house finally, after all these years, relaxed in each other's company.

TUESDAY 5:03 PM

BACK IN GEORGE'S ROOM THE ATMOSPHERE WAS NOT RELAXED. George was half asleep, occasionally waking up and grunting. Kate was getting a bit concerned.

"I don't like the look of him, Pops. Isn't there something we can do?"

"I don't know. He has to hang on till Becky gets here. That was the plan."

Kate glanced sideways at her father. She loved him, admired him but was under no illusions. She was well aware that Gary had no comprehension that a plan, once made, could still go wrong, especially where people were concerned. To Gary a plan wasn't a process, it was a conclusion, a view which might work in the digital world but not often in real life.

"Perhaps he needs a drink," she suggested. "He may be getting dehydrated. Why don't you go and try and organise some coffee for us?"

"Tea. It would be tea," said Gary. "You have coffee in the morning, tea in the afternoon."

Kate suppressed a giggle. "Well, tea then. Doesn't matter. Let's get him a drink."

Glad, as always, to have something clear cut to do, Gary got to his feet.

"Right then. Tea all round. I wonder if the others will want any."

As he spoke the door opened and Linda and Steven came in.

"If you're talking about tea," said Linda, "then, yes please, I'd love some."

"Me too," said Steven.

"Right then," said Gary, "won't be long." And he disappeared.

Linda sat down beside her father and took his hand. There

was no response.

"Is he all right?" she asked.

"We don't know," said Kate, "he just kind of drifts away sometimes."

Linda stroked her father's hand. "Hi, Dad, how you doing? It's Linda here."

George stirred and slowly opened his eyes. "Who's that?"

"It's Linda, Dad. Steven's here too."

"Good. Good." Suddenly he jerked up and looked round the room. "Rebecca. Where's Becky? I have to speak to Becky."

"She's coming, Dad," said Steven, "she'll be here soon."

"I have to see Becky. I have to tell her I'm sorry."

"Don't worry, Dad. I'm sure she knows."

"But I want to see her."

Kate got up, came across the room to stand behind George and put her arms round his neck.

"Don't worry, Grandpa George. Aunt Becky's coming and she knows you love her." Slowly she began to stroke George's shoulders, the stroking gradually becoming a massage as she eased the tension out of his neck. As she worked George began to visibly relax and a smile appeared on his face.

"Goodness gracious," said Linda, "where did you learn to do that?"

Kate looked a little surprised. "It's only a basic champissage massage. We used to do it to each other in college. It eased tension in the neck after long revision sessions."

"Well, it obviously works."

"Sure it does." Kate paused and then said, "Why is Grandpa so desperate for Aunt Becky to get here? Hasn't he seen her for a while or something?"

Steven glanced across at Linda, then said. "To the best of my knowledge Becky and my father haven't met or spoken for about twenty-five years."

"Wow. You're kidding. That's a long time."

"True, but I haven't seen her since then either." He glanced across at his sister. "Have you heard from her, Linda?"

"No, she just disappeared after …"

But then suddenly she was interrupted as Dorothy burst into song:

> *You may not be an angel*
> *'Cause angels are so few*
> *But until the day that one comes along*
> *I'll string along with you*

She stopped as abruptly as she had begun. There was an awkward silence, awkward that is for everyone except Dorothy who sat back in her chair smiling.

Steven and Linda glanced at each other. "Well, clearly there's still a bit of the old mum left somewhere," said Steven.

George was now more awake and looking round. "Oh, that feels better," he said, stretching his shoulders. "Where's Gary?"

"Gone to fix some tea, Grandpa," said Kate. "Think I might just go and hurry him along."

She planted a kiss on the top of George's head, smiled at Linda and Steven and went out.

TUESDAY 5:28 PM

GARY WAS IN THE ADMIN OFFICE TALKING TO PAULINE BELFORT, the care home manager. As usual he was very direct.

"My dad thinks he's about to die," he said.

Pauline also believed in being direct. "He may well be," she said, "I hope not, but it wouldn't surprise me."

"Why not?"

"Some people just decide they've had enough. And stop."

"He says he wants to die and to die tonight

Pauline flinched. "If he did say that then I suspect that's the pain talking," she said, "but I must be honest. It may not be long. If you want my opinion …"

"Please."

"Then I don't think your father is particularly ill as such. I think he's very old and sometimes the body just winds down."

There was a pause while Gary thought this through. "And that could happen anytime?"

"Yes."

"So it could be tonight? After we've had this family gathering."

"Possibly. Tomorrow … next week … Alternatively, he might go on for years."

Gary shook his head. "No, I don't think he'll do that." He nodded. "Thank you for being so frank."

Pauline smiled. "I'm very fond of your father, Mr Redmond. Well, of course I'm fond of all our residents but I have a soft spot for George and for Dorothy too. I think it's lovely the way he spends time with her. I like to think she knows that someone who loves her is holding her hand even if she doesn't necessarily know who he is."

In spite of himself that statement gave Gary an unfamiliar feeling of emotion.

"Thank you."

"Now then," Pauline went on. "More practical matters. I gather the whole family is here with your parents today."

"Not quite all. My sister Rebecca is flying in from the States. She'll be here around mid-evening."

Pauline nodded. "And you'll want to stay with your father tonight. I imagine that's why you're all here."

"Well, yes. Dad wants the whole family around him one more time."

"I thought so. Well, we'd like to help. I've arranged for one of our Day Rooms just down the corridor to be available for you. There's two divans in there and several comfortable armchairs. That'll give you somewhere for family members to rest but still be nearby. How does that sound?"

"Very kind. Thank you."

As Gary came out of the office he saw Kate coming down the corridor.

"Hey, Pops, where you been?" she said, "they're all waiting for their tea back there."

"Oh, sorry. Got diverted. Needed to talk to the manager. I'll go and deal with it now."

"No need. All fixed. Some guy called Phil is bringing us a tray."

"Thanks, Kate."

"No sweat."

"How's Dad?"

"Bit better. I gave him a neck massage. Helped a lot, though I think Aunt Linda was a bit surprised. Don't you Brits do massage?"

"Well, yes, we do, but it's not that common in families like ours."

Kate shook her head. "Weird."

"No, not weird. Just two countries separated by—"

"— a common language. Yeah, yeah. How many times have I heard you say that?"

Gary laughed. "Well, it's true. And not just language either, habits, expectations, attitudes, all different."

"Yeah, I suppose. But you and Ma have always got on fine, haven't you?"

"Of course we have, but we like each other as people, nothing to do with nationality."

There was silence for a moment apart from the muted sound of their feet as they walked along the carpeted corridor.

Then Kate said, "You like each other?"

"Yes."

"But you don't love each other?"

Gary stopped in his tracks and Kate, surprised, stopped with him. There was a long silence then Gary said, "I don't know, Kate. I don't really know what 'love' is. I hear the word bandied around a lot but it seems to mean different things to different people. And it seems to apply to the oddest things, football teams, TV programmes, food …"

"Ice cream?"

"There you are. A good example. One of the first things you said to me when we first met was that you loved ice cream."

"I remember."

"So do I, but you were only eight. I assumed then that you were using the word 'love' as a synonym for 'like'.

"Well, yeah, I guess."

"I've thought about this a lot. I've tried to analyse my relationship with your mother, is it love or isn't it, but somehow it just doesn't compute."

In spite of herself Kate laughed. "Oh, Pops, you're so funny. Compute, that's crazy."

Gary was surprised. "What's funny?"

"You. You can't compute love. It's something you feel, it's instinctive, you can't define it or pin it down."

"Then how do you know it's there?"

"This is a very weird conversation to be having standing in a corridor."

"Oh, is it? Okay, then let's sit down. We've been given the use of a day room just round the corner. There are some chairs in there."

Kate rolled her eyes. "Well, then, let's go find them."

Once they were settled she took Gary's hands in hers. "Okay, Pops, do you remember a long time ago you told me that you didn't really understand feelings. You said they were a bit of a mystery."

"Well, they are. To me anyway."

"And that includes 'love'?"

"Guess so. As we've just said."

"Okay, then let's start at the beginning. Do you love Aunt Linda, Aunt Becky and Uncle Steven?"

Gary shook his head. "Don't think so."

"Even though they're your brother and sisters?"

"Oh, I see. You mean I must love them because they're related to me."

"No, no, I don't mean that at all." She paused for a moment in thought. "Do you think about them at all when you're not with them, wonder what they're doing, if they're okay?"

Gary shook his head again. "No, why would I? I haven't seen any of them for years until today."

"Okay, let's come at this another way. Is there anyone, anyone at all, that you think about when you're not with them?"

"You mean think about even if we're not meeting?"

"Yes, imagining what they might be doing. How they're

171

feeling, if they're happy, that sort of thing."

"Oh, I see." He thought for a minute. "Well, there's you of course, I often think about you."

"Do you?" And she blushed slightly.

"Oh, yes. And I look forward to our meetings."

"So do I." A brief pause then Kate went on. "Okay, that's me. Who else?"

"Well, Dad, obviously and Mum too. I think about them."

"Why obviously?"

"Well, they need to be looked after. And, well, they're Mum and Dad. That's what you do."

"So it's just a duty, is it?"

Gary's brow furrowed in thought. "No, I don't think so. Not duty. Sometimes it's difficult to find the time to come down here but …"

"… but you find the time."

"Yes."

"Why?"

"Well … I suppose … I suppose to make sure they're okay, I like being with them, talking to Dad. Making sure he can still be with Mum."

"I'd say that was love."

Gary's face lit up. "Would you?"

"Yes."

"Oh. Good."

"And what about Ma?"

There was a pause and then Gary said, "I do think about her. Sometimes. We had a lot of fun together …"

"I know. I'm here because of some of that fun."

For a moment Gary looked embarrassed. "I didn't mean that."

"Sorry, Pops, I know you didn't. Go on."

After a moment's thought Gary said, "We enjoy being together, your mother and I, but I think we're both people who prefer their own company."

Kate nodded. "Ma says the same."

"I'm not very good at all this stuff, Kate."

"I've noticed ..." but she squeezed his hand to take the sting out of the words. "Okay, try this. Is there anyone you'd miss if they were no longer here."

"You mean, if they were dead?"

"I guess so, yeah."

Gary thought for a moment. "That's a bit tricky."

"Well, let's start with the easy bit. I guess you'd miss Grandpa George and Nanna Dorothy."

More thought, then Gary said, "No, I don't think so."

Kate was a bit taken aback. "You wouldn't?"

"No, not really. I like being with them now, making sure they're okay and so on, but they're both old. Mum has already gone when you think about it and Dad will go soon. That's logical so why would I miss them?"

Kate took a deep breath. "Wow, Pops, you can be hard work. So there's no one, no one at all who you would actually miss?"

There was silence for a moment and then Gary said, very softly. "Only you. I would miss you terribly if you weren't here, Kate."

"Oh, Pops."

"I really don't understand about love, not in the sense everyone else seems talk about it, but if I do love anybody then I love you. Very much."

Kate nodded. "I know. I've always known. From that first day when you bought me that ice cream."

She stood up. "Come on. We need to get back to Grandpa. Our tea will be getting cold."

They walked down the corridor holding hands as they had once walked along the Embankment all those years ago.

TUESDAY 6:04 PM

HIGH ABOVE THE ATLANTIC REBECCA WAS ALSO THINKING ABOUT love. She was watching the film *Love Actually* for the umpteenth time and it had prompted her to think about how love could build, destroy, enhance or betray. Not for the first time since Gary's phone call in the middle of the night she wondered what she was doing, rushing halfway across the world to see a man who had, in pseudo Victorian style, effectively told her never to darken his doors again.

She was happy and secure in her relationship in the same way that she knew George and Dorothy had been happy and secure in theirs. Perhaps it was that strong sense of belonging and being loved throughout her childhood that had helped her find happiness and security of her own. Her parents had always believed in honesty, courtesy and good behaviour but sometimes these beliefs had been put aside in the interests of the family. One such occasion had been the Cornwall Camp Affair.

A DIFFERENT DRUM

IT IS THE SUMMER OF 1971, THE END OF HER FIRST YEAR AT Grammar School. It has not been an easy year. None of her friends from primary days have come to the new school with her and she has felt very alone. She soon realises that the academic work comes easily to her, earning a lot of praise from the teachers. Good in some ways, but not something that endears her to her fellow pupils. If she'd been a good hockey player then all might have been well, but she is awkward holding the stick and always seems to run the wrong way so she's soon the butt of many jokes.

Rebecca has always been happy in her own company,

preferring to be on her own somewhere with a book rather than part of a giggling group in a corner. As she gets older she will realise that she's not one of life's natural joiners, but aged twelve she feels her lack of need for other people is a fault within her and she worries about it.

And now the summer is here she has something else to worry about. It is time for the annual Guide camp and this year her Guide Company is going to a farm in Devon. Linda, two years older, is also going and looking forward to it, but this will be Rebecca's first camp and she is less certain. Linda had joined the Brownies as soon as she could and Rebecca automatically followed her two years later. Then last year she had moved up into the Guides where Linda was already well established.

With her rapidly developing desire to learn – anything – she finds some parts of the weekly meetings quite enjoyable. First Aid, tying knots, identifying birds and trees – all very interesting and useful. The games she is less sure about, but does her best to enter into the spirit of them, following Linda's lead.

But now she is faced with a fortnight's camp. They will be sleeping in tents, cooking their meals over a wood fire, she will actually be living with a group of girls, not just seeing them once a week. And Linda's stories of earth latrines don't bear thinking about.

She tries to express some of these anxieties to Linda but they are brushed aside.

"Sure, Becky, it's a bit weird at first. I thought that too but you soon get used to it and it's great fun."

She understands that it's fun for Linda but for her doubts still remain. She would really prefer to stay at home but she stiffens her resolve.

If you never try anything new, she thinks, *you'll never do anything.*

And so she goes to camp in Devon.

Within twenty-four hours she realises she has made a great mistake. What was bearable for a few hours on a weekday evening becomes torment when there is no escape. Endless games, endless chores, remorseless sing-songs round the camp fire which everyone else seems to enjoy, leaving her feeling totally isolated again. She tries to join in, she tries to take part, but it is a constant struggle. She is desperately homesick and there are still eleven days to go.

Tuesday evening. Dorothy answers the phone and hears a breathless Linda on the other end.

"Mum ..."

"Linda? Where are you?"

"Phone box at the end of the lane. I can't be long."

"Is anything wrong?"

"Well, no, not with me. Everything's great. But I'm worried about Becky."

"What about her?"

"I don't think she's well, Mum. She doesn't really join in and I've heard her crying in the night."

"Have you told anyone?"

"No. Thing is everyone else is having such a good time I don't think they'd understand. She also had a bit of a run-in with Skip who said she wasn't being a good team player."

"Does she have to be?"

There's a pause, then Linda says. "I guess not, but it's easier if you are."

"Is she being bullied?"

Linda is shocked. "No, no, nothing like that. Everyone is very kind but ... oh, I don't know how to put it ... She doesn't sort of ... fit. Do you think she's ill?"

No, not ill, thinks Dorothy, *just a fish out of water.* Aloud she says. "Thanks for letting me know, Linda. I need to think about this."

"Should I be doing anything, Mum?"

"No, not unless you think she really is ill. Then you must tell someone. Otherwise leave it to me."

"Okay."

Dorothy is pleased that Linda is looking out for her sister but now the responsibility has passed to her. As always with family matters she discusses it with George but he doesn't see a problem.

"She's probably just a bit homesick. She'll get over it."

But Dorothy is not so sure. She remembers the parents' day at school at the end of the summer term. She is a bit anxious about the fact that Rebecca doesn't seem to have many friends and spends so much time alone so she mentions this to the teacher, Mrs Braithwaite.

"Exactly what is it that's worrying you, Mrs Redmond?"

"I don't know really. Her schoolwork seems fine."

"It is." Mrs Braithwaite opens a file and glances down the page. "Rebecca did extremely well in the end of year exams, especially in science."

"Oh, she's bright enough. Though I suppose every mother says that."

A half smile appears on Mrs Braithwaite's face. "Yes, they do, but in this instance ..." She lets the sentence hang then closes the file and turns to face Dorothy.

"So what this comes down to is, you're worried she's spending too much time alone?"

"Yes. I am. She's not naturally a withdrawn girl. She's always very lively at home, joins in with all the things we do as a family and clearly enjoys them but it doesn't seem to go any further."

"Perhaps it doesn't have to."

"How do you mean?"

"Well, if Rebecca was withdrawn at home, not talking much, not joining in, then we might have a problem …"

"No, it's not that. She's certainly not withdrawn. She even won an end-of-the-pier talent contest once."

"Really?"

"Oh, yes. You can't stop her talking sometimes though, to be frank, I don't always have a clue what she's talking about."

Mrs Braithwaite smiled. "So she's a normal child at home but you don't think she's a normal child at school."

"That's not quite what I'm saying."

"No, but you sense she's different here. That's not necessarily bad but it can be difficult." She thinks for a moment then goes on. "I really don't think there's anything to worry about, Mrs Redmond. I know Rebecca has only been in this school for a year but she is very focused. I think she has an instinct for what she wants to do and is heading for it in a very determined way. I suspect she's probably going to be a very high achiever."

"But shouldn't she be having some fun as well? She's still only a child."

"Isn't she getting that fun at home, with her family."

"Well, yes. Yes, she is. We do a lot of things together."

"Then please don't worry, Mrs Redmond. There's a favourite quotation of mine which says: *If a man is out of step with his companions then perhaps he's marching to the beat of a different drum*. I think Rebecca is listening to her own drum."

That thought had comforted Dorothy at the time but now she is wondering if Rebecca's drum was being silenced in the guide camp.

That evening she reaches a decision and goes to find George.

"I'm going to drive down to Devon tomorrow and bring Becky home."

"Are you sure that's a good idea. Won't you just make her look foolish in front of her friends?"

"They're not her friends, not in the sense you and I understand the word and, yes, I hear what you're saying, but I have a plan."

George looks at her for a moment then grins. "And do I want to know about this plan?"

"No."

"Thought not." There's a pause then he says. "I still think we should let her work through it but if your instinct is saying that would be wrong …"

"It is saying that."

"Then go and get her. I trust your instincts way above mine."

So the next day Dorothy sets off early and reaches the Devon farm around lunchtime. She leaves the car in the farmyard and walks up to path to the camping field which overlooks the sea. The Guide Captain is surprised to see her and less than enthusiastic when she learns why she has come. Dorothy is all sweetness and charm and very apologetic.

"I am so, so sorry to disrupt things but we've had this letter which has advanced Rebecca's hospital appointment to tomorrow. It wasn't meant to be for another three weeks."

She produces a letter on hospital letterhead and waves it under the Guide Captain's nose.

"We've waited months for this and we can't afford to miss it. I know Rebecca will be disappointed but I really do have to take her back with me today."

"Well, I must say, Mrs Redmond, it would been helpful if you'd let us know if this might happen before you let her come to camp."

"Yes, I know, I'm sorry. But we thought she'd be home in good time for the appointment but as it is …" She waves the letter again.

"Yes, I see. Well, of course, she must go home if it's that important."

"It is."

"Well, then." She calls to a girl who is standing nearby. "Mary, go and tell Linda and Rebecca that their mother is here to see them." She turns back to Dorothy. "I presume you would like to see Linda as well while you're here. She will be staying, of course."

"Of course."

When the two girls appear Dorothy steps forward in front of the Guide Captain and fixes them with a steely stare. A stare that silently says, "Shut up and listen."

However when she speaks her voice is warm and gentle. "I am sorry to interrupt your camp, girls, but Rebecca's hospital appointment has been brought forward to tomorrow so I have to take her home with me now."

Rebecca looks puzzled but before she can say anything Linda, quicker on the uptake, nudges her in the ribs.

"Of course, Mummy," she says, overdoing the smarm slightly. "We understand, don't we, Becky?"

"Right then," says the Guide Captain, "go and get your kit together, Rebecca, and say goodbye to your friends."

"Come on, Becky. I'll help you pack." And Linda leads her sister across the field towards the line of tents.

"I suppose she might be able to come back after she's been to the hospital."

"That will depend on the what the hospital says," says Dorothy sweetly, "but we'll certainly keep you informed."

Half an hour later, sitting beside her mother as they head towards Exeter, Rebecca says, "I didn't know about this hospital thing. Is it something serious?"

"No," says Dorothy.

"Then why do I have to go?"

"You don't. There is no appointment."

"But you said ..."

"Yes, I know, but I had to get you out of there. You didn't want to stay, did you?"

"No, I didn't but ..."

"Well, that's sorted then. What would you like for supper?"

Rebecca is silent for a few minutes and then she says, "But if there isn't really a hospital appointment, haven't you just told Skip a lie?"

Dorothy was expecting this and meets it head on. "Yes."

"But ..."

"I know. We've always taught you to be honest and truthful. And so you should be. So we all should be, but ..." She pauses for a moment to collect her thoughts. "This is very tricky, Becky. Lying is wrong, but sometimes to achieve something important it may be necessary."

"But how do you know when it's all right and when it isn't?"

"Not easy. You have to trust your own judgement. Think of it like this. What would have happened if I'd bowled up, told Skip you were desperately unhappy and I'd come to take you home?"

Rebecca considers this. "I think she'd have been angry and the other girls would have laughed at me."

"I agree. So do you think Skip is angry now?"

"No."

"Do you think the other girls are laughing?"

"No."

"So perhaps this is the best outcome for everyone. Even though I had to tell a lie."

There's a pause and then Rebecca apparently goes off at a tangent. "How did you know I was unhappy?"

"Linda phoned me."

"Oh …" Another pause. "That was kind of her."

"Yes, it was."

After a moment Rebecca says. "So you came to rescue me but the only way you could do that without upsetting everyone was to tell a lie."

"Well, yes, I suppose that's about it. And I didn't want to make things worse for you."

"Thank you."

Several miles pass in silence then Rebecca says, "I suppose the important bit is this judgement thing. You have to decide if you're telling a lie for a good reason or a selfish reason."

My God, thinks Dorothy, *and this child is only twelve. What's she going to be like when she grows up?*

When they get home George welcomes Rebecca as though she's just been out for the afternoon. After supper, just before she goes to bed, Rebecca says to her parents. "What happens after Linda and the rest come back from camp? Do I still go to Guides each week?"

"Not if you don't want to," says Dorothy.

"I disagree," says George. "I think you should carry on going., at least for a while. If you don't, they might start thinking you've just run away. If you carry on as normal for a while and then gradually stop going – if that's what you want – then no one will notice."

"What if anyone asks what happened at the hospital?"

"Just say you're fine and leave it at that."

"Okay." She heads for the stairs and then turns back. "Thank you, Mum. Thank you, Dad. I promise I'll do my very best to make you proud of me."

AND SHE HAD. SHE CONTINUED WITH GUIDES ON AND OFF FOR A few months and then just slipped away. She eventually made a few friends of her own but had excelled at school and gone on to academic distinction, eventually becoming the first person in the family to go to university. But she never forgot the way her parents, Dorothy in particular, had stood up for her, laying good behaviour and a good principle aside in favour of protection and a solution.

Values she had always tried to follow in her own life.

TUESDAY 6:10 PM

THERE WAS AN UNNATURAL SILENCE IN GEORGE'S ROOM. THE TEA was finished. Dorothy sat in her wheelchair smiling into space, the others sat round, not knowing what to do or say. Polite small talk had run out.

There was a light tap on the door. Then it opened and one of the care home staff appeared.

"Sorry to interrupt," he said.

"Hi, Phil," said Kate, "thanks for the tea."

"No problem." He looked round the room and settled on Gary. "Mr Redmond, I wonder if I could have a word."

"Sure." Gary got up and he and Phil went out closing the door behind them.

George, who had been half-dozing, suddenly came to and sat up straight in his chair.

"Toilet," he said, "I need the toilet."

This time it was Steven who helped him across the room. Judging by the noises emerging from behind the closed door, George was having some difficulty and his strained face when he finally emerged confirmed that view.

He edged back across the room, Steven supporting him as he went. Linda took one look at him and said, "I think it would be a good idea if we got him back into bed now."

"Yes," said Steven and, with Kate helping, they gently eased George up and laid him on the bed. Dorothy watched them from her wheelchair crooning softly to herself.

Somewhere the sun is shining,
So, honey, don't you cry.
We'll find a silver lining,
The clouds will soon roll by.

185

Linda had pulled the bedclothes back and now she tenderly tucked them in around George. She put a couple of pillows behind his back so he could sit up and see them all. He was clearly very tired.

"Is that better, Dad," Linda asked.

"Feel a bit whacked to be honest." He coughed. "What time is it? Will Rebecca be here soon?"

"Not for a while yet, Dad," said Steven, "she's got a long way to come."

"I want to see Rebecca. I have to see Becky."

Linda and Steven looked at each other helplessly while Dorothy smiled into a space only she could see.

I hear a robin singing
Upon a treetop high.
To you and me he's singing,
The clouds will soon roll by.

TUESDAY 6:11 PM

"Is there a problem?" asked Gary.

"Not a problem," said Phil, "but we think it's time your mother went back to her room. We don't want her getting distressed. And we also need to give George his evening meal soon."

"Oh, I see." He scratched his head. "The thing is, we're trying to have a family reunion. My sister is on her way from the States and won't be here till later this evening."

"I appreciate that, so here's what I suggest. We take Dorothy back to her room now, let her have her meal there in her usual surroundings, and then later, when your sister arrives, we'll see if we can bring her back for a few minutes. How does that sound?"

Gary nodded. "I guess you know best. Let's do that then."

They went back into the room and Gary explained what was happening.

"She will be able to come back and see Aunt Becky, though, won't she?" asked Kate.

"All being well, yes. But Phil's right. We should get her back to her own room now."

Gary bent over his mother's wheelchair. "Come along, Mum. Time to take you back for your supper."

He began to push the chair towards the door and for a moment Dorothy looked startled. Then she began waving her arm regally and burst into song:

> *My old man said follow the van*
> *And don't dilly-dally on the way*
> *Off went the cart with the home packed in it*
> *I walked behind with me old cock linnet*

187

But I dillied and I dallied
And I dallied and I dillied
And I can't find my way home.

Her voice echoed back down the corridor and Steven shook his head. "You've got to hand it to Mum. She may be on another planet but her sense of timing's still great."

"This day just goes on getting more and more peculiar," said Linda.

"Yes, it does, but somehow ... oh, I don't know ... it feels right. Do you know what I mean?"

"Yes, I think I do."

There was a grunt from the bed and they all turned to look at George.

"Or course it's right," he said, "it's the end of a chapter. Or maybe we should call it the curtain call."

"Don't say that, Dad," said Linda.

"Just waiting for Rebecca to arrive and then it'll be time for the finale."

Steven went across to the bed and put his arm round his father's shoulders.

"She won't be long now, Dad. Once she's here we'll all have a cup of tea or something and then we can leave you to sleep."

"Don't want to sleep. Plenty of time for sleep. I want to see Rebecca. I want to see all my family together again."

He looked round the room. "Where's Dorothy?"

"She's gone off to have her supper, Dad," said Linda.

"She'll come back later, Grandpa," said Kate. "Pops has fixed it all."

"And Becky's coming?"

Steven glanced at his watch "I think Gary said her plane was due to touch down around 7:15. That's not long now. She'll probably give us a ring once she's in the customs hall."

"I must see Becky. I want to …"

Suddenly George was seized with a violent coughing fit and he bent over double.

"Becky … Becky … Oh, God, it hurts."

Linda and Steven looked at each other in consternation. Steven said quietly, "Do you think he's all right?"

"I'd better fetch someone," said Linda.

"There's nothing they can do," said Kate with calm assurance. "Grandpa has these coughing fits sometimes but they soon pass. Anyway he's already on max medication."

"Yes, but …" began Steven but then the door opened and Gary appeared again.

"What's happened?"

"Grandpa's having another attack," said Kate.

Gary moved swiftly over to the side of the bed, eased George back onto his pillows and began gently rubbing his stomach. "Water, please, Kate," he said.

He took the glass she brought him and held it at George's lips. "Just have a sip or two of this, Dad," he said, "that'll help ease the pain."

"But that's just water," muttered Linda.

"I know," said Kate softy, "but if Pops tells him it'll do him good, then it seems to work."

George was breathing more easily now. His eyes were shut but his words were clear.

"Why isn't Becky here? You said Becky was coming."

"She'll be here soon, Dad," said Steven. He exchanged an anxious glance with Linda as if to say "What can we do?"

Kate turned to her father.

"I guess you need to fix it, Pops. You know …" she lowered her voice, "it will stop him worrying."

Gary nodded.

"Fix what?" asked Steven.

Gary moved across the room to where his bag was leaning against the wall. "Kate means that Dad needs to see Becky now. It's important to him."

"I understand that but how can he? She's in an aeroplane somewhere over the Atlantic."

"No sweat," said Kate, "Pops can fix anything."

Gary, who was opening the combination lock on his case, smiled faintly.

"Well, I guess we might be able to get her on the phone," said Linda doubtfully, "though heaven knows what it will cost."

"We can do better than that," said Gary. He relocked his case then came back across the room carrying a laptop. He set it down on the small table, flipped it open and busied himself at the keyboard.

"What you doing?" asked Steven.

"Just a tick," said Gary. The screen came to life but it was turned away from the others. Keeping his eyes on the screen, Gary took out his mobile phone and punched a number.

"Becky? Hi, it's Gary. Can you turn your laptop on and enable Wi-Fi … Yes, now please. I'm going to put you in touch with Dad."

There was a moment's pause and a faint smile passed over Gary's face. "Don't worry about that. It's all taken care of, or it will be."

He ended the call and for a moment or two his hands played over the laptop's keyboard. Then he picked up the phone again.

"Logging in." He glanced at his watch. "Okay, eighteen-thirty-three G. This is 5 Queenie, Delta, 7, Rickmansworth." There was a pause then he said, "27 camels and a parrot."

The others in the room watched him in amazement.

Gary went on, "I need full visual access now to the transatlantic flight number that's in my log book." A pause. "Thank you." And he cancelled the call.

"What the hell was all that about?" asked Steven. "You been reading too many thrillers or what?"

"Just a minute," said Gary, absorbed in his keyboard.

There was silence in the room and then suddenly a voice came crackling out of the laptop.

"Hi, Dad, it's Becky."

Gary lifted the laptop and moved it across to the table by George's bed. As it moved the others caught a quick glimpse of the screen which showed an aircraft interior and Becky's face in the foreground.

"Here, Dad," said Gary, "this is Becky in her plane on her way to see you. You can see her and talk to her." Then he added, "Don't take too long, Becky, I can't hold this connection indefinitely."

George looked bewildered. "Rebecca, is that you?"

"Yes, Dad, it's me. I'm on my way to see you. Hang on in there."

"Rebecca, Becky, I can't believe it. How is it possible?"

"Don't worry about that Dad. I don't know either. Gary's fixed it so we can see each other."

"It's been so long. Oh, Becky, I'm so sorry, so sorry."

"Don't worry, Dad. That's all in the past. I'm on my way and we'll all be together again soon."

"Yes, yes, that's wonderful."

"Is everyone else there with you?"

Gary gestured round the room. "Go on, she can hear you." He swivelled the screen round and Becky's face came back into view.

"Hi Becky," said Linda, "this is amazing."

"Yes, isn't it. Hi Steven. How you doing?"

"I'm good. Looking forward to seeing you, Becky."

"Me too. And ... sorry I don't think I know ..."

"Hi, Aunt Becky. I'm Kate. Gary's my Pops."

"Oh ... Right ... I see ... Well, okay. Um ... Great. Well, hang on guys, I'll be with you as soon as I can. Gary, can I see Dad again please."

Gary turned the screen back towards George but Becky's voice continued to echo round the room.

"Dad. I'm coming. I'm coming as fast as possible. You got that."

"Yes, yes, I think so. Don't understand how this is happening."

"Doesn't matter. I'm coming. Forget the past, Dad. All forgotten. I love you."

"Oh, Becky." And suddenly George burst into tears.

"Hang on in there, Dad. I'll be there very soon. Get the kettle on, eh?"

The tears were rolling down George's face. "Oh, Becky, this is wonderful ..."

Gary was busy at the keyboard. "Think that's about it, Becky. I'm going to have to break this connection now."

"Okay. I understand. Give Dad a cuddle and I'll be with you as ..."

Abruptly her voice was cut off. For a moment there was silence in the room apart from George's sobbing, then Linda moved across to the bed and took her father's hand.

"It's all right, Dad. Everything's okay. We're all here and Becky's coming."

With an effort George controlled his tears. "Was that really, Becky? Was she really talking to me?"

"It really was Becky, Dad," said Gary.

Steven said tentatively. "How the hell did you do that?"

Gary shrugged. "Doesn't matter."

Steven looked at him for a moment. "Still good with computers then," he said.

Gary smiled and nodded.

"On the side of the angels now, are you?"

Gary's face went blank but Kate turned towards Steven, her face angry.

"That was uncalled for, Uncle Steve."

Steven had the grace to look embarrassed and Linda rushed in to try and fill the awkward gap. "Um ... if you're still handy with computers, Gary, I wonder if you could give me some advice."

"What sort of advice?"

"I'm having trouble with my computer at home. It seems to be running very slow and sometimes it just freezes. I took it into a shop in town but they said it wasn't worth repairing. Chuck it and buy another one, they said, but it's not that old. Any ideas what I could do?"

Gary sighed. "Give me your email address and I'll email you a link, download it, leave your computer on for an hour and I'll fix it."

"Then what?"

"Then I'll remove the link and put a message on your screen to say it's sorted."

"How do you know you can sort it?"

Gary sighed again. "I can sort it. Okay?"

"Okay. Thanks. It'll be good to have an email address for you too."

"You won't. I'll use a proxy address and I'll cancel it after I've done the job. Believe me, it's safer that way."

Steven stepped in. "What is all this? Are you in danger?"

"No. But it's best if you're not in direct contact with me."

Steven looked disbelieving. His expression clearly said

Exaggerated nonsense.

Instead he said, "What exactly is it that you do, Gary?"

There was a long pause. Linda and Steven looked at Gary. Gary looked down at the floor. George had his eyes shut. Only Kate seemed relaxed, a half smile on her face.

"He won't tell you," she said cheerily. "He won't even tell me. All I know is that he fixes stuff."

Steven still looked dubious. "What kind of stuff?"

"Any stuff," said Kate. "Pops is great. Take him a problem and he finds the answer."

Gary looked embarrassed. "Look, can we leave it. None of this matters. Today is about family. Dad especially."

Linda moved across and sat down next to Gary. "We don't want to upset, you, Gary, but you must realise this is all a bit of a shock to Steven and me. You suddenly appear again after all this time. We find out you've been seeing Dad regularly and on top of that we find you have a daughter." She turned and smiled at Kate. "A grown up daughter as well. You can't blame us for being curious."

Gary nodded. "No, I can see that, but I mean it when I say it doesn't matter."

Steve chipped in. "Is it legal?"

"Don't be so rude," said Kate angrily. "Pops wouldn't do anything wrong."

Steven opened his mouth to say, "He wasn't always so righteous" but he caught Linda's quick shake of the head and shut it again.

"Okay," said Gary, "I'll just say this and then that's it. Think of me as poacher turned gamekeeper."

There was a silence as his brother and sister contemplated this answer.

Steven spoke first. "So are you saying …?" But Gary

interrupted him.

"I'm saying that none of this matters today. What matters now is Dad, sorting out what he wants. Okay?"

"Well, yes…"

"Good. Now look, there's some practical stuff to arrange. Let's go somewhere else and fix the details. Kate, Dad's meal will be here soon. Can you deal with that and look after him for a few minutes?"

"Sure."

"Come on then," and without further ado Gary stalked out of the room.

AN OFFER YOU CAN'T REFUSE

POACHER TURNED GAMEKEEPER. HE REMEMBERS THE FIRST TIME he heard that phrase – it's the day he is released from prison. The prison authorities have explained that they will give him some money and a travel voucher and set him loose.

He doesn't really want to be let out. He hasn't been unhappy the last few months. The routine, the certainty, the structure of each day, have been very comforting. He doesn't know what he is going to do when he's released.

The prison authorities seem to assume he will just go home but he isn't really comfortable with that. Apart from one short visit from his mother and Linda he has seen no one from his family since he was arrested. He's had a number of letters from Rebecca but he understands she is now living abroad. He would prefer to stay where he is but realises that is not an option.

He hasn't told anyone in the family that he is being released but when he walks out through the gate he is met by two people, a man and a woman, both formally dressed and both smiling. He is not entirely comfortable with those smiles.

The woman takes the lead, holding out her hand. "Hallo, Gary. My name's Fenella and this is Marcus. Do you fancy a coffee? There's a café just down the road."

Slightly warily Gary goes with them. Fenella orders coffee and cake and they sit in one of the booths, Gary on one side, Fenella and Marcus on the other.

Gary, never one to resist a bit of cake, tucks in but he is still puzzled. Who are these people and what do they want with him? Then he has a thought. Maybe they work with a charity. Direct as ever he says, "What's all this about?"

The woman doesn't answer him directly but says. "Do you have any plans, Gary, now you've been released?"

He shakes his head. "I don't know. Why?"

"Well, if you're interested we have a suggestion."

He looks from one to the other, not sure where this is leading. "What sort of suggestion?"

"We would like you to come and work with us. We can't tell you much about the job at this stage except to say it has to do with computers."

At the mention of computers his eyes light up. Not having a computer to play with has been one of the hardest parts of his prison sentence.

"Why? I don't have a computer any more. The police took it away. My probation officer said ..."

"Yes, we know, but that's not a problem. We're interested in your technical skills, Gary, so we'll sort all that. You'll have access to state of the art equipment."

It all sounds too good to be true but. he is still cautious. This certainly isn't a charity. "Is this an IT support job?"

"Not exactly."

"Who do you work for? Microsoft? Google? Facebook?" He's heard that some of the big multinationals run programmes that give reformed criminals a second chance. It seems unlikely, but maybe this is something like that.

"You will be asked to sign a non-disclosure agreement."

"Is the work legal?"

Fenella gives a half smile. "It's legal, Gary. There's no risk of your going back inside."

He nods. "Okay, but can't you give me some idea?"

Fenella looks at him for a moment. "You know why you were arrested and convicted, don't you?"

"Of course I do."

"Well, let's say we would like to harness those natural skills of yours. You could think of it as poacher turned gamekeeper it you like."

He turns that thought over in his mind. "Where would I be working?"

"In London. That's all I can say. We will also arrange accommodation for you. Initially it will be a flat which you will share with Marcus here ..."

Marcus nods and smiles.

"Then later, if everything works out, as we hope it will, we'll find you a place of your own."

"You'll give me somewhere to live?"

"Yes, but there is one more condition. The NDA is very specific. You won't be able to talk about any aspect of your work with anyone else, not even your family. How do you feel about that?"

Gary thinks about it. He likes the idea of a London flat much more than the thought of going back to the little bedroom in his parent's house. And he likes the thought of having state of the art computer equipment. But he's never signed an NDA before. It sounds very much like an instruction not to see his family again.

"Sounds good, but there has to be a catch."

"No catch. Not in the sense you mean. You will have a proper employment contract, pension, all the usual. The thing is, if you live up to our expectations, then the work you'll be doing is highly confidential, hence our concern about your discretion."

"Don't talk to my family. Got it."

"Your family and friends."

"I don't have any friends."

Fenella and Marcus exchange a glance. "Just your family then. I realise this will be hard but there really is no option. What do you say?"

Gary thinks about it. If he says *yes* then he gets to work at the one thing he knows he is good at. If he says *no*, then what is he going to do instead?

He thinks of his parents, the mixture of sadness and shame on their faces as the police led him away. He thinks of his brother and sisters, all much older than him, they had never really been close. He realises that the idea of family, an idea he has always cherished, is much stronger in the abstract than it ever has been in reality. What difference will it really make if he never sees them again?

But he still has a qualm about his parents.

"Okay," he says at last, "I'll come and work for you but I have one condition too."

Fenella's face hardens. "I'm not sure about conditions, Gary."

"It's quite simple. I'll agree to the NDA but I want someone to keep an eye on my parents and make sure they're okay. If at any stage they're not, then I must be told and I reserve the right to renegotiate our deal."

There's a moment's pause, then Fenella says. "I think we can agree to that."

"Good. Then I'll come."

AND SO IT WAS THAT WHEN HE CAME OUT OF PRISON AS FAR AS HIS family were concerned, Gary Redmond simply vanished.

TUESDAY 6:40 PM

GARY LED HIS BROTHER AND SISTER DOWN THE CORRIDOR TO THE day room where he'd had the conversation with Kate.

"Now then," he said, "practical matters. I presume the two of you are staying until the end."

"What do you mean, until the end?"

"Well, until Dad dies, of course," said Gary surprised.

"Until Dad dies? But that could be weeks."

"No, he's going to die tonight. He said so."

"But Gary," said Linda gently, "people can't just choose the moment they die. It's something that just happens."

"But he told me," said Gary, "that's why we're all here."

Steven cut in. "Look, let's not get sidetracked. Dad's clearly not in a good state and we're both staying for the time being." He glanced at Linda and received a confirming nod. "And in any case we're not going anywhere until Becky arrives. Does that satisfy you?"

Gary still looked puzzled. "Well, yes, that's what I was asking. That's why I've made the arrangements."

Steven sighed. "More arrangements?"

"Yes. The manager here has been very helpful. She's arranged the use of this room for us so with the divans and some armchairs we can get some rest. She's also happy for us to bring some food in so I thought we could organise a takeaway."

"That makes sense," said Linda.

"Well, if it's going to be an all-nighter I'd better give Hazel a call."

"Yes, and I need to ring Dennis. I left him some sausages but I suspect he'll just go down the pub." She paused then added. "I hope he does actually. Last time I left him alone I had to replace the frying pan."

Steven smothered a grin as Linda went on. "Do you really believe Dad will die tonight, Gary."

"Yes, I do. And it's what he wants."

"It can't be," said Steven, "no one actually wants to die."

"Dad does. Why not ask him?"

Faced with such certainty Steven backtracked a little. "Well, okay, just supposing you're right. All seems a bit ghoulish, us all hanging round his bed waiting for him to pop his clogs."

"Steven, for heaven's sake ..."

"I'm only saying ... I'm not very comfortable with this."

"Nor am I, not really. But this is our father we're talking about. Show a little respect."

"Yes, sorry, you're right."

Gary looked from one to the other. "I don't understand all this. It's Dad's decision and if he wants to die surely it's best if he does so with all his family round him rather than alone amongst strangers."

Suddenly Linda flung her arms around Gary. "Of course, it is, Gary, and thank you so much for arranging it all."

Gary was clearly uncomfortable with the physical contact and gently eased himself away.

"It's nothing," he muttered, "just doing what Dad asked, that's all."

TUESDAY 6.52 PM

STEVEN WENT OUT INTO THE CAR PARK TO PHONE HAZEL. ADRIFT on a confusing day of a rediscovered brother, an undreamt of niece and uncertainty about his father's health, he turned to his wife for a sense of security and reassurance.

. Hazel had come into his life when he had just about given up on personal relationships. The depression that followed his divorce and the breakup with Vanessa, meant he struggled with any kind of company, especially female. Then, as he gradually began to find his feet again following Rebecca's intervention, he started to realise just how lonely he was. The problem was that aged thirty-five he wasn't doing anything outside work that brought him into regular contact with other people, especially women. He had a brief fling with a woman at work, Maisie, but inevitably it was awkward and before long just fizzled out.

In desperation he tried a dating agency, *'We will help you find your life partner ...'* but although that resulted in a few pleasant evenings he met no one he liked enough to want to meet again. He eventually came to the conclusion that the fault lay within him.

One woman, Jennifer, a gentle brunette, actually said to him at the end of their evening together, "You could be a lovely man, Steven, but you're far too gloomy for me. I want someone who's fun."

He had smiled pleasantly but deep down that had hurt. *What happened to the fun,* he thought to himself. *There was a lot of fun about when I was growing up so where did it all go?*

And then he met Hazel.

I'M NOT HALF OF ANYBODY

ONE OF THE YOUNGER MEN IN THE OFFICE HAS JUST GOT ENGAGED and invites some of his colleagues to have a night out and go ten-pin bowling. Steven is persuaded to join them and, slightly to his surprise, finds he is enjoying himself. In the next lane is a group of women and inevitably banter begins to flow.

After a while they agree to have a competition, they'll split into two groups, each a mixture of men and women, and the two teams will compete against each other. There is much laughter as the teams sort themselves out and then the bowling begins.

Steven is not very good at bowling and it's as much as he can do to get his ball down the far end of the lane without it running off into the channel at the side. His efforts cause a lot of hilarity but finally one of the women on his team takes pity on him and shows him how to hold the ball, how to stand and the moment to let go. When he still seems uncertain she takes his hand and guides it as he bowls and to his amazement it reaches the far end and actually knocks over three skittles.

His team loses, quite spectacularly, but he realises that for the first time for a long while he is actually having fun. Afterwards they all go to the bar and his bowling instructor comes and sits beside him.

"Not done a lot of bowling, then?" she says.

"Was it that obvious?"

"Just a bit. So what do you do for fun?"

He looks away, embarrassed. "Not a lot. Work's pretty busy. You know how it is."

"No, not really. You've got to switch off sometime. I'm Hazel by the way."

And that's the way it begins. She introduces him to table tennis, real ale festivals, fringe theatre in tiny rooms above pubs, guided wildlife walks where, to his delight, he actually gets to see a water vole. They even try line dancing but after he's fallen over for the third time they agree to give that one a miss.

Hazel is full of life and in her company he blossoms. After so many false starts he is now certain he's in love and after six months or so he suggests they should find a place together. However, she is initially doubtful.

"I'm not sure, Steven. That would make it serious wouldn't it? Us, I mean."

"I thought we were serious. I love you, Hazel."

"Yes, I know. And I could love you too, Steven, but if it's going to work between us there's some stuff to sort out."

"What sort of stuff?"

"Little things. Silly stuff, maybe, but it's those silly things that can so easily break a relationship."

"Like what."

"if we're going to be together then we need to be together as equals."

"We are equals."

She smiles. "That's the man's point of view." She pauses for a moment. "Okay, then, the other night in the pub, when we met those people from the art group, you introduced me as 'your other half'."

"Yes, but you know what I mean. It's just an expression."

"Not to me, Steven. I'm not half of anybody. I'm me. You're you, and that's the way it has to be."

He is silent. In his heart he thinks she is making too much of it but the new Steven, happy with Hazel, is prepared to do anything to keep this happiness.

He says. "I understand. I promise never to use that expression again. Or at least" – he feels he needs a bit of insurance – "I will do my best not to and feel free to clout me if I inadvertently do so."

Hazel laughs. "Don't worry, I will."

Another thought occurs to him. "But I can't stop others saying it. A lot of people do."

"Of course they do. And that's fine. I know it's not said with malice but people, men especially, don't think about the broader implications. The thing is, Steven, if we're going to have a future together I need us both to accept we're equals, not some kind of man, little woman thing."

"No, I understand."

"Oh, and I'm not doing your ironing. Okay?"

BACK IN THE CAR PARK STEVEN'S SPIRITS LIFTED AS THEY ALWAYS did when he heard Hazel's voice.

"How's it going?" she asked.

"It's being a very odd day." He paused, then decided that standing in the car park on a mobile phone was not the moment to tell Hazel about Gary, let alone raise the question of Kate.

"Dad's not looking good. I'm glad I came."

"I thought you would be." There was silence for a moment then Hazel said, "Is Linda there too?"

"Yes."

"And how's that?"

"It's okay, yes, it's okay. We had a good talk. Think we're friends again."

"Good, I'm glad. About time. So what happens now?"

"Not sure. We wait, I guess. My sister, Becky's flying in from the States. Should be here sometime this evening."

"Wow. It really is a family gathering then."

"Yes. Look, Hazel, I don't honestly know if Dad is going to die soon or not. I do know he wants to see us all together so I can't get away for a while."

"Of course you can't, this is family stuff, Steven. Do whatever you need to do, just let me know what's happening. Okay?"

"Okay. Better go. Love you."

TUESDAY 7:01 PM

REBECCA COULD SEE THE SILVERY THREAD OF THE THAMES slipping under the wing as her plane came onto the final approach for Heathrow. She had managed to sleep for quite a lot of the journey which, she suspected, was just as well as the next few hours could be quite emotional.

She had tried to think what she would say to George after all these years but she still had no idea. And there was Linda and Steven, it was over twenty years since she had seen them so that wouldn't be easy either. As for the unexpected young woman she'd seen on the videocall – was she really Gary's daughter? That was a conundrum too far.

Play it by ear, I guess, she thought to herself.

She was heartened by the brief conversation she'd had with George. Her father was obviously desperate to see her and she took comfort from that. She was determined to try to forget that last upsetting meeting and instead to concentrate on all the positive family memories of her childhood. Was it just the telescoping of time that made them seem like golden days? The birthday parties, the days out, walks in the park, toasting bread over a coal fire, the death of her guinea pig and the funeral service as they buried him under the damson tree. Dozens of little snippets that made up a childhood mosaic.

She knew these memories, although true, were not an accurate record of the past. She was only too well aware that memory tends to eliminate bad times and magnify the good, but surely it was this that made life bearable. However, she had never liked loose ends and she was relieved that at last she was about to deal with the major piece of unfinished business in her life.

She began gathering her bits and pieces together ready for landing.

TUESDAY 7:14 PM

THE DAY WAS STILL WARM EVEN THOUGH EVENING WAS COMING on. The remains of George's meal, hardly touched, sat on a table. Through the open window came a smoky smell.

Linda sniffed. "Someone's having a bonfire somewhere."

George lifted his head. "That'll be one of the gardeners, down the other side of the vegetable patch. I often smell it when the wind's in the right direction." He coughed slightly. "Reminds me of our family firework parties."

Steven laughed. "Ah, yes. They were fun. D'you remember the last big one we had, the night Mr Demetriou's wooden horse went up in flames?"

"Horse?" said Linda, "what horse?"

"Oh, come on. You must remember. The neighbours were delighted. We did them a favour."

"An unintentional favour," said George. "I had that bonfire well under control before that gust of wind came."

Gary suddenly became animated. Here was an actual memory he could share. "I remember that. Everyone came from along our road, there were sausages and lots of fireworks and you burned that man you didn't like on the fire."

"You burned a man?" Kate was horrified and Linda hurried to reassure her.

"It was an effigy, Kate. It's an English tradition to burn what we call a *guy* on a bonfire on 5th November because a man called Guy Fawkes tried to set off a bomb under the Houses of Parliament."

"Pity he didn't succeed," muttered George.

"Okay, I get that … I think. So you were burning this Guy Fawkes dude?" She paused. "Gee, it still sounds rather odd."

"Well, no," said Steven, "on that occasion we brought the practice rather more up to date and burned an effigy of one of our Town Councillors, Mr Throgmorton."

"I don't get it."

"Councillor Throgmorton was a thief and a crook," said George. "He forced through closures of the local youth club and the arts centre to save money. Then it transpired that he'd been fiddling his expenses for years. He'd taken the Council for about fifteen thousand pounds since he'd been elected."

"What a creep."

"Got it in one," said George.

"Did he go to jail?"

"No, he didn't," said Steven, "At first he denied it, then he said he must have made an accounting error and he'd pay the money back."

"He had friends in high places," said George, "so no comebacks. He was told he was a naughty boy and not to do it again. That's why we decided to burn him. Just for a bit of personal satisfaction."

"Must have been one of our last big family events," said Steven. "Would have been, what 1971, 72, I think. Yes, must have been 'cos I'd just started that course at the Tech. Life was a bit interesting around then."

STEVEN LIGHTS ROMAN CANDLES AT BOTH ENDS

HE HAS ENROLLED AT A TECHNICAL COLLEGE TO DO AN HNC IN Business Studies. He's expecting it simply to be an extension of school but it isn't. So long as he attends the necessary lectures and completes his assignments on time he's free to come and go as he pleases. The workload is pretty heavy and he doesn't have much money, but he is freer than he has ever been before.

During his last year at school he was going out with a local girl, Wendy, who is not impressed that he now has very little time to spare. It's partly to appease her, and partly one last tug at the family connections, that he's come home early for this Guy Fawkes Night party.

He helps his father get the bonfire going and, as the eldest, also helps with the fireworks, making sure the younger children stay well back. His mind is only half on the job. He is remembering the few exciting minutes with Wendy at the bottom of the garden behind the shed before the party begins. The snatched kisses, the fumbles, the promise of more to come. He wishes the party was over so he and Wendy could find a quiet corner somewhere and …. what?

He doesn't allow his imagination to go any further. Also at the back of his mind is the thought of Tamsin. She is on the same college course as him and recently they've been meeting during the week for a drink. He feels this is a relationship that could develop but is confused about what he should do. He is not yet mature enough to think about the girls themselves, just what would be best for him, but even in his immaturity he realises the difficulties of trying to run two girlfriends simultaneously.

He is thinking about all of this as he sets off fireworks, launches rockets and pokes the bonfire. He shares his father's view about Councillor Throgmorton and thinks it is a good wheeze to burn him on the fire. He doesn't give a moment's thought to the wooden horse in Mr Demetriou's garden next door and neither is he aware of the steadily increasing wind. His mind is bouncing between Wendy and Tamsin but mostly Wendy as she is actually here with him now.

Bird in the hand, he thinks, without really understanding what a cruel and selfish thought that is.

"I DON'T REMEMBER ANY COUNCILLOR," SAID LINDA, "I THOUGHT it was just another guy. I'm sure I helped make it."

Kate shook her head. "Sounds crazy to me. But what was that about a horse?"

"No horse," said Gary, "just lots of fireworks and rockets and bangers and roman candles and sparklers and cooking sausages on sticks over the fire." He sighed. "It was all such fun."

Kate was looking at him fondly. "Happy memories, eh, Pops?"

"Oh, yes."

GARY GOES OUT WITH A BANGER

HE IS HAVING A WONDERFUL EVENING. ALTHOUGH HE HAS HEARD endless stories about big family events, he hasn't had the chance to actually participate in many of them. He likes the idea of friends and neighbours being there but feels no need to mix with them. Just knowing they're there is enough. He is not comfortable with other children on a one-to-one basis but doesn't mind being part of a crowd.

He would like to light some of the fireworks himself but he knows his father won't allow it. The best he can hope for is one or two of the sparklers to hold at the end of the evening. However, when no one is looking, he does manage to remove two bangers from the box and secretes them away in his bedroom. He'll let those off somewhere in the next few days when he's on his own. In the meantime, there are sausages to cook, fireworks to watch, the fire to admire and the excitement and the noise all around. Gary is content. One of the rare family occasions which actively involve him, rather than those before he was born which he can only enjoy vicariously.

"WELL, I CERTAINLY DON'T REMEMBER A HORSE," SAID LINDA, "but I do remember the Gibsons from number 19 brought their dog and it got off the lead and wrecked the snacks that Mum and I had spent so long making."

Steven frowned. "I don't think that was the firework party," he said, "Wasn't it that barbecue the summer before I got married. I'm sure Sandra was with me when the dog ran riot."

"Course it wasn't," said Linda, "if we were having a barbecue we wouldn't have made all those fiddly little snacks?"

"I don't think it was the Gibsons who had the dog," said George, "wasn't it Albert Smithson? He had that nasty little yappy thing. Rat on a string, I used to call it."

"Well, I thought it was the Gibsons," said Linda, "and the dog I'm thinking off wasn't a yappy little thing. Much bigger. Labrador or something like that."

Kate shook her head. "I think I'm losing the plot," she said. "Are you sure it wasn't the horse that wrecked the food?"

"There wasn't a horse," said Linda, "I would definitely have remembered a horse."

"There was a horse, Kate," said Steven, "but not a real horse any more than it was a real man."

"No horses were harmed in the making of this memory," muttered George.

"I think you're making this up," said Linda.

"Oh, come on, you can't have forgotten. Mr Demetriou next door had built this very large replica of the Trojan Horse in his garden. Huge bloody thing it was. He made it from old packing cases or something. It was not a pretty sight."

"He built a horse?"

"He did. Wasn't popular with the neighbours, especially the Turkish family whose garden backed on to his. Think they took it personally or something. Anyway there was a serious row brewing. Some of the neighbours said he needed planning permission for a construction that size. He maintained it was just a hobby, like a model railway, only bigger."

"I really don't remember this," said Linda, "what happened?"

"The wind happened," said George. "It started gusting quite strongly and then suddenly a whole shower of sparks were carried over the fence and set fire to the horse. It went up like a … like a …"

"Like a horse on fire …?" suggested Kate and Gary started laughing.

"But this is silly," said Linda, "I'm sure I'd have remembered something like that."

"You were probably inside helping your mother," said George.

"Either that or you were off in a dark corner with that Roger from down the road," said Steven grinning.

Linda blushed. "It's all such a long time ago," she said.

LINDA SPINS ON A CATHERINE WHEEL

SHE ISN'T THINKING ABOUT THE FIRE OR COUNCILLOR Throgmorton or wooden horses. At fifteen she's not concerned with politics or councillors or much at all outside her own areas of interest. Tonight she is revelling in unexpected freedom. As the older daughter, the one with the mothering instinct as Dorothy puts it, she's the one who usually has to look after Gary, who is only 4, but for some reason this evening that chore has been given to Rebecca. Even so she instinctively glances across at her younger brother, watching him edging closer and closer to the fire, a sausage impaled rather uncertainly on a pointed stick.

She half wonders whether she ought to intervene but then Rebecca is there, quiet and efficient, taking Gary's hand and speaking softly to him.

"Gary, be careful ..." she hears Rebecca say as she takes the stick, pushes the sausage more firmly onto it and then helps him burn it to a state where he can safely eat it, unappetising though it looks.

Linda smiles to herself and turns back to the fireworks. Another rocket goes up, showering the sky with coloured, streaming sparks. She glances round the garden. Several of the neighbours with children are there, invited by Dad to join in the fun. Steven and Wendy have their arms round each other. George is rummaging in the box for more fireworks, Dorothy is singing softly to herself as she so often does but her eyes are constantly ranging over her family. A lovely occasion.

She sees her father fastening a Catherine Wheel to the fence and moves closer. She loves Catherine Wheels, the way they start slowly and then spin faster and faster. There it goes, turning gently and then suddenly it is off, sparks flying everywhere.

One lands in her hair and for a brief moment she panics. Then she feels a hand brush the spark away and, turning, she sees Roger from two doors down smiling at her.

"No harm done," he says, smiling, "I knocked it away in time."

"Thank you," she says shyly. Roger is about her own age and she feels awkward in his company.

"Happy to help," he says and then, to her surprise, he leans forward and kisses her gently on the cheek before turning and vanishing into the throng. She touches her cheek, her mind spinning like the Catherine Wheel that has just come to a red-glowing halt.

"WE GOT THE HORSE DOWSED PRETTY QUICKLY," SAID GEORGE. "I had the garden hose handy as a precaution anyway. Wasn't much left of it though."

"Do you remember what Mr Demetriou called you?" asked Steven grinning.

"Oh, yes. Not at all appropriate for a party with children present."

"And then he said he would report you to the RSPCA. That was hilarious."

"The RSPCA?" said Linda, "for a wooden horse?"

"The man was beside himself. Understandable in a way, he'd been working on that horse for over a year and then suddenly, poof, it's gone."

"Neighbours were pleased though," said Steven, "there they were, gearing themselves up for a legal dispute and then suddenly problem solved at a stroke."

"And Mr Demetriou never spoke to us again. Especially not after the story in the local paper."

GEORGE SETS OFF ROCKETS

HE HAS ORGANISED A NUMBER OF FIREWORK PARTIES OVER THE years but this last big family one is the most memorable of all. Dorothy raises a quizzical eyebrow when he announces his intention of burning Councillor Throgmorton but raises no objection. He makes sure only to invite those neighbours who are unlikely to take offence but the gesture seems to be generally appreciated.

When the reporter from the local paper arrives he is careful to express the same surprise as everyone else.

"How did you hear about this?"

"We had a tip off," the reporter says, "anonymous phone call."

"Oh. Well, now you're here do you want a drink?"

"Wouldn't say no."

They find him a beer and he and George stand for a few minutes watching the fire.

"So that's Councillor Throgmorton going up in flames, is it?" the reporter asks.

"It can be whoever you want it to be," says George. "'Scuse me, I need to let off some more fireworks or the kids'll start getting restless."

Three rockets, four Roman Candles and one Golden Rain later the reporter edges close to George again.

"Would it be true to say that you're not a supporter of Councillor Throgmorton's party, Mr Redmond?"

"Not a great supporter of any of them," says George, "I suppose there must a few that are well intentioned but in my experience most people elected to public office don't give a stuff about the people who put them there – they're only interested in themselves and what they can get out it."

"Strong words. Are you saying you think the system is corrupt?"

"Of course it is," says George, "power and absolute power and all that. It's not always money of course, sometimes it's just 'cos they like seeing their picture in the paper, having a title without needing to work for it."

"That's a pretty cynical view."

"Maybe. Maybe not. But let me ask you this. If you or I had been caught with our hands in the till like he was …" and he gestures with his beer glass towards the charred remains of what might or might not be an effigy of Councillor Throgmorton, "would we have got away with an apology and a promise to pay back what we'd stolen? I don't think so, do you?"

At that moment Steven sets off three giant golden rain fireworks, and as the colours and stars burst into the night sky, Dorothy's voice rises above the hum of the crowd.

I dreamt I saw a shining star
That shone on you and me.
It touched our hearts
It touched my soul
Your love has set me free.
Our dream came true
It's me and you
For all eternity.

George and the reporter look at each other in a moment of complete understanding.

"Good to have dreams, isn't it?" says the reporter.

"Even better to realise them," says George.

TUESDAY 7:43 PM

ANOTHER SILENCE HAD FALLEN IN GEORGE'S ROOM. GEORGE himself sat propped against his pillows. From time to time he smiled round at them but they could see his concentration was mostly directed inwards. The rest of them sat around like a small audience at a bad play, casual conversation long since exhausted.

Linda had no idea how the rest of the day would go. She had finally managed to get hold of Dennis on his mobile to discover, as she'd suspected, that he had abandoned the sausages and gone down the pub. She hadn't told him anything about the day, only said she didn't know when she'd be back.

"No probs, old thing," he'd said. "Take whatever time you need. I'll be fine. They do a good breakfast down the Pig and Whistle these days."

Dear Dennis. So long as the inner man was catered for and he could potter around in the open air making hopeful swipes at golf balls, then he was happy.

She glanced round the room, reminded of Steven's recent comment about being ghouls, sitting there waiting for their father to die. She still didn't know what to think about that, Gary seemed so certain but then Gary only ever dealt in certainties. Shades of doubt and subtleties were completely foreign to him. However, she did know she couldn't stand this atmosphere much longer so she got to her feet.

"Time to get that takeaway you mentioned, Gary. I don't know about the rest of you but I'm starving."

"Good idea," said Steven, "what we going to get?"

"Pizza's easiest," said Gary, "there's a good place just the other side of the village."

"Is that back towards Southampton?"

"Yes, that's the one."

"Okay, then. What does everyone want?"

Gary shrugged. "Anything. I'm not fussy."

"I'd go for a selection, Aunt Linda," said Kate, "then we can mix and match if we want to."

"Fine by me," said Steven.

George roused himself briefly. "No anchovies for me. Can't stand the things."

"You don't have to, Dad. You've had your supper. This is for us."

"Hey, Grandpa," said Kate, "what does an aardvark like on its pizza?

"No idea," said George.

"Ant-chovies," said Kate and collapsed into giggles.

"All right," said George not to be outdone, "why do people go into the pizza business?"

"To make a lot of dough."

George gave a stage sigh. "I dunno, be kind to them and they nick all your best gags."

Steven and Linda rolled their eyes heavenwards.

"I hate to break this up," said Linda, "but I'm still hungry so, jokes, aside, I'm going pizza hunting now."

"You'd better pack your pizza pistol," said Kate.

In spite of herself Linda laughed. "Just for that, young lady, you can come along and give me a hand."

"Oh, okay," and, with a quick glance at Gary, Kate followed Linda out of the door.

TUESDAY 7:49 PM

THE TWO WOMEN WALKED OUT TO THE CAR PARK IN SILENCE BUT once they were settled in their seats Kate said, "Okay, now we're on our own, what is it you want to ask me?"

"How do you know I want to ask you anything?"

Kate smiled. "Oh, come on, Aunt Linda, you've been bursting with curiosity ever since I arrived. It's no big deal for me but I should warn you, I probably can't help."

Linda glanced sideways at her. "Truly your father's daughter, is that it? Just appear out of nowhere and refuse to answer any questions?"

Kate's smile faded, then with the brutal directness of the young, she asked. "Do you resent me? Is that it?"

Linda was horrified. "Resent you? Good God, no. The little of you I've seen I like very much. It's just that ..."

"You didn't know I existed."

"Quite. It was pretty startling to suddenly hear from Gary again after all these years and then ... then ..."

"Then to discover you had an American niece? Yeah, I can see that's a bit out of left field."

"I've no idea what a 'left field' is but it was certainly one hell of a surprise."

"Well, I don't mind telling you what I can but, as I said to Uncle Steve, it's not much."

Linda started the engine. "Come on. We'd better go and get these pizzas or they'll be wondering what happened to us. Anyway my stomach thinks my throat's been cut."

Kate laughed. "I do so love the British sense of humour."

As they drove out of the car park and turned towards Southampton Linda said. "Okay, what can you tell me?"

"Where d'you want me to start?"

"Well, you could tell me a bit about Gary. I know he's my brother but it's years since I've seen or heard from him. I don't know where he lives, what he does, his relationship with you and your mother. How come he has been looking after our parents all this time and none of us knew. What does …"

"Hey, hey, slow down. I can't handle all that in one go."

"No, of course not. Sorry. It's just that …"

"Yeah, I know. No sweat. Okay," She took a deep breath. "First, and this is gospel, I can't tell you much about Pops 'cos I don't know."

"But you've obviously got a good relationship. You spend time with him. You must have got to know him."

"Well, kinda. But there's more than one Pops, you see. There's the day-to-day Pops – I know nothing about him. Then there's my Pops and I think he's great. And yeah, I know that sounds odd but that's how it is."

"Which … er … Pops … does your mother know?"

Kate wrinkled her nose. "That's kinda tricky. I figure she's got a boot either side of the trail but I don't know for sure."

"But she must have said something over the years."

"Not much about Pops. I know he and Ma like each other a lot but they're not married and never will be. Pops lives in London. Ma lives in Philadelphia – so do I when I'm not studying in London."

"Do you live with Gary when you're over here?"

"No, I have a little apartment in Streatham. He comes and stays with me there sometimes."

"So where does he live?"

"London."

"Yes, but where?"

"No idea. He never says."

"But you must have asked?"

"Of course. At the beginning. But guess what …"

"He didn't answer."

"Got it in one."

There was a brief pause as Linda considered this. "So you don't know what he does either?"

"Not specifically, nope."

"Not specifically?"

"Well, he's a real whizz with IT stuff, as you've seen."

"Yes. He always was. That was what …" she broke off in confusion.

"What sent him to prison, yeah, I know all about that."

Linda breathed a sigh of relief. "Good. But you think he's put all that behind him?"

"Depends which bit you mean. He's certainly still in the IT game, that's for sure. So's Ma, in a kind of specialist way. But what Pops does these days is definitely kosher."

"Poacher turned gamekeeper, that's what he said, wasn't it?"

"It figures."

"So what does your mother do?"

"No idea. Well, again not specifically." She paused for a moment and then said. "My best guess would be that they're both, in some way, in the spook business."

"Spook business? You mean spying, MI6 and all that."

Kate laughed. "More of the 'all that' I reckon. For a while I wondered if Ma might be CIA but I don't think she is. My guess would be that she, and probably Pops too, are more like a factory ship attached to a whaling fleet."

For a moment Linda struggled with this unexpected analogy. Then she said, "You mean, they're not actually in MI6, CIA, whatever but maybe supply support services."

"Quite possibly. But you can bet your bottom dollar they

won't confirm or deny it. Neither of them."

They reached the pizza place and Linda pulled in by the kerb. "So when you meet Gary in London …"

"We do stuff. Have fun. Sometimes he can't make it. Sometimes he cancels at the last minute, but on the whole we have a ball."

"But you didn't meet him until you were eight years old, or so he told me."

"That's right, but we clicked from the start."

Linda sighed. "That's the bit I still don't understand. Didn't you feel cheated in some way, that you hadn't known about him before?"

"No, not really. You could see he and Ma were cool together and believe me, that's better than the parents of most people I know back home. I thought he was great. He bought me my first ice cream cornet."

"Good for him, but there's a bit more to parenting than that. How often did you and Gary meet while you were growing up?"

"Not a lot. I was twelve before Ma came back to London again."

"So you didn't see him for another four years?"

"No, but we did exchange emails all the time. He set up a special email address just for me to use. I'd tell him all about school, college, about my friends. He'd tell me all about his childhood, all the things you did as a family while he was growing up."

"And some that we did as a family long before he was born, I suspect."

"Could be. But it was when I was sixteen that we really bonded."

"What happened then?"

"Ma arranged for me to come to London for a month in the summer vacation. I stayed in a hotel near Russell Square and

Pops would come round each day and we'd do stuff. Then one day he suggested we should take a trip together, see something of England other than London, as he put it. I was all for it …" Her voice tailed off as the memory began to kick in. "It was the most wonderful trip I've ever had."

HEY, HO FOR THE OPEN ROAD

SHE IS CONVINCED THAT, EVEN IF SHE LIVES TO BE 100 THE memory of that travelling time with her father will never fade. One of the greatest joys, not understood at first but learned as the journey progresses, is that it isn't just a trip of exploration for her, but for Gary as well.

How he had first conceived such a trip she never learns, though she suspects her mother's influence somewhere along the way. It soon becomes apparent that Gary has hardly ever stirred out of London so they share the pleasure of discovering new places, new things to do, together.

Remembering her interest in birds he has done his home-work and their journey begins with a visit to Weymouth and the RSPB reserve at Radipole Lake. From there they wander westwards, a brief stop at Exeter, a drive across Dartmoor and on into Cornwall.

They stay one night in a small inn on the edge of the sea in a Cornish cove. After they have eaten they wander out onto the beach and sit on the rocks watching the light fade over the sea. Later, in her diary, Kate writes, '*There was total silence apart from the soft sound of the sea on the sand, the velvet black night, the myriad of stars high above,*' though even as she writes she's aware it's not original, it's borrowed imagery. But the moment is still magic.

As the dusk deepens and their faces became less distinct to

each other Gary begins to talk softly. Later, she's not sure whether he is really talking to her or to himself.

"Families matter," he says, "they create a bond that's stronger than anything else. Even when a particular family relationship doesn't work very well, for whatever reason, that bond is still there. And the key to that bond is memories, shared memories, memories of the good times, but also of the bad. The good memories are your comfort as the years pass, the bad ones remind you of what you have come through. Regrets are pointless. You have to deal with stuff as it is."

In the dusk she reaches out and takes his hand. "Do you have regrets, Pops?"

"I try not to."

She says nothing and after a moment he goes on. "Memories are comforting. Memories are facts."

Kate is doubtful about this statement. Even at sixteen she is aware that no two recollections are ever quite the same. She feels that most memories are more likely to be a subjective, possibly polished, recall of the past.

She says none of this to Gary, not wanting to break the spell.

"You're safe with memories," Gary says, "you know where you are. Less confusion."

A slight breeze off the sea ruffles Kate's hair. In the background she is conscious of the rise and fall of the waves. Then she says softly. "Did anyone ever hurt you, Pops?"

"No, not really, no one ever hurt me. But I was very alone."

"While you were growing up?"

"Yes. I was the youngest, you see. Rebecca was already eight when I was born and the others were older still. Childhood was over in that house before I even came along."

Instinctively, she puts her arm around his shoulders and holds him close. "What about school? Did you have any buddies there?"

She feels him shake his head. "No, not really. I didn't understand what they were talking about and they thought I was stupid. Home was security. They didn't laugh at me at home. I could share all family stories, the memories, even if they weren't things I'd actually done. I felt safe there."

Kate says, "It was different for me. I never felt alone when I was growing up, even though it was only me and Ma, but I did feel a bit of an outsider at school."

Gary turns to her in surprise. "Did you?"

"Yes. Oh, I had lots of friends but somehow I felt different. I never really knew why. When I was very young I wondered if it was because I didn't know who my father was. Lots of my friends had parents who were divorced but at least they knew each other. I only knew Ma, and she was great, but it was just her."

"Oh, Kate."

"Then I met you and I realised that I was actually luckier than many of my friends. A lot of them had parents who seemed to squabble a lot but you and Ma never squabbled. Oh, I know you didn't meet that often but when you did you were so obviously good together that it gave me a warm feeling."

A rogue wave, perhaps driven by the wind, comes up to the rocks and splashes their feet.

Kate turns and faces her father. "Do you feel close to Grandpa George and Nanna Dorothy?"

"Well, I think I must do. They're my parents. I owe them everything."

"But you never see them."

"No." There's a pause then Gary says. "But I know where they are. I keep an eye on them. One day they might need me and then I'll be there."

"Perhaps they need you now."

She senses, rather than sees him, shake his head. "No, they

have each other. They don't need me."

There's a long pause and then Kate says, "I need you, Pops."

Gary pulls her close and hugs her. "And I need you too, Kate."

They sit in silence for a moment, a silence broken only by the sound of the sea on the pebbles.

AT THE WHEEL OF HER CAR OUTSIDE THE PIZZA PLACE LINDA stirred in her seat. "Sounds like you really got to know each other on that trip."

"Yes. Yes, we did. I don't think Pops finds it easy to open up to other people but we seem to get along just dandy. And he's always talking about the family, memories, things you all did. I feel I know you all so well just from those conversations."

"Don't you think it's all a bit odd, him remembering stuff we've talked about, not stuff he actually shared."

Kate's response was terse. "Didn't get much chance to share it, did he?"

Linda was silent. After a moment Kate said. "I've answered all your questions, Aunt Linda. Now can I ask you one?"

"Yes, of course."

"Did you and Uncle Steve and Aunt Becky treat Pops badly when he was a little kid?"

Linda was startled. "Treat him badly? Well, no, no we didn't."

"Well, I get the feeling that he doesn't think he properly belongs to your family but he wants to belong, desperately."

"Well, I don't know. He was so much younger than all of us, of course, so I guess he was rather on his own. I've never really thought about it before."

"I think he has, but I didn't really understand, not until now, meeting you all, seeing you all together. Been a strange sort of day, hasn't it?"

"Yes. Yes, it has been a very strange day but I'm starting to think an important one. Now come along. Let's grab those pizzas and get back. They'll be starving back there."

TUESDAY 8:05 PM

SHE WAS STIFF FROM SITTING SO LONG, EVEN IN A FIRST CLASS seat, so the walk through the corridors to the arrivals hall was very welcome. In passport control she paused to judge which queue to join when she felt a touch on her arm and found a young man standing beside her.

"Dr Redmond?" he asked.

"Yes."

"Dr Rebecca Redmond?"

"Yes."

"Would you come with me, please, ma'am."

"Is there something wrong?"

He smiled. "Not at all. I have instructions to meet you and make sure you reach your father's care home as soon as possible. There's a car waiting outside. If you'll just let me have your passport …"

He led a bemused Rebecca through one of the unmanned passport control channels, flashed a pass at someone the other side and headed straight for the green channel in the customs hall.

"What about my luggage?"

"All taken care of, ma'am. It will be in the car almost as soon as you are."

Sure enough there was her case being loaded into the boot of a light blue BMW and she found herself helped into the back seat.

Gary, you are amazing, she thought as the young man got into the passenger seat beside the driver and the car pulled away heading for the motorway.

Aloud she said. "Well, thank you very much for all this. It's very kind of you."

"No problem, ma'am. We'll get you to your father as quickly as we can."

"Well, I'm very impressed. Do you work for my brother?"

The young man turned round in his seat and smiled. "It's not quite as straightforward as that, ma'am. We're doing what we've been asked to do. We can talk if you wish, or not if you prefer, but we cannot answer any questions. I trust you are happy with that."

Rebecca nodded. "Almost happy," she said.

Immediately the young man's smile vanished. "'Almost'," he said, "is there something else we can do for you?"

"Too damn right," said Rebecca, "you can stop calling me ma'am. Makes me feel like the Queen. My name's Rebecca, Becky to friends. And I guess the service you're giving me makes us friends."

The young man smiled. "Okay, Becky," he said, "and you can call me Joe."

"Which I guess isn't your real name."

His smile stayed intact. "It's a name, it will do. Now in that box on the seat beside you there's a bottle of water and some biscuits. Just help yourself."

"Thank you, Joe." And Rebecca sat back in her seat and let this strange day continue to unwind.

TUESDAY 8:19 PM

<small>WHEN LINDA AND KATE GOT BACK TO GREENACRES THEY WERE</small>
met by Steven.

"Slight change of plan," he said, "the carers are in with George just now, giving him a wash, preparing him for the night and so on."

"Oh, okay."

"Gary's arranged for us to use the residents' dining room to eat in. It's just along here."

It was a large room but they had it to themselves and they sat round the table, sharing out slices of pizza.

After several hours in each other's company with nothing in common apart from a shared history, the conversation had descended into the trivial.

Steven, in a desperate attempt to sound normal, started talking about one of the delegates on the course he had just been running.

"I tell you, he carried obsession to degree level. Over coffee one morning he confided that his main ambition was to photograph every lighthouse round the British coast and label it with its name." He laughed. "What's the point of that, I ask you?"

"What's wrong with it if that's what he enjoys?" said Linda. "I seem to remember that you used to collect beer mats and pin them up on your bedroom wall."

"Yes, but I was sixteen then. I threw them all away when I got married. Just so much rubbish."

"No," said Gary, "I rescued them. I still have them."

"Good God, what for?"

"Well, they're shared memories, aren't they? Part of our family home. I couldn't understand why you wanted to get rid of them."

"So you kept them?"

"Yes and also …" he broke off and his face went blank.

"And what?" said Steven and then he suddenly realised. "You've got other stuff as well, haven't you?"

"Yes, but …"

Suddenly Kate broke in. "Hey, what's the big deal here? Sure Pops has got loads of stuff, family stuff that no one else wanted. He's shown me some of it. It's great."

Steven was not convinced. "Tell me this, Gary. Why don't you remember your own childhood, not ours?"

For a moment there was an uneasy silence and then Gary muttered, "Because you guys had all the fun. My childhood was spent alone. You'd done all the good stuff together before I was born."

There was an embarrassed silence then Linda leaned across the table and took Gary's hand.

"We hadn't thought of it like that, Gary, but it's not our fault you know."

Gary just sat there, eyes downcast. Kate took his other hand.

"Come on, Pops, hang loose. It's cool. There's nothing wrong with treasuring the past."

"Yes, but whose past?" muttered Steven but was silenced by a glare from both women.

"Tell them about your memory box, Pops."

"Memory box?" asked Linda.

"Yeah. It's this kinda large trunk. Pops keeps all his family bits and pieces in it. He brings it over to me sometimes and tells me the stories behind them."

"What sort of bits and pieces?"

"Wow, you wouldn't believe, tons of stuff." Kate thought for a moment. "There's Grandpa's old Air Force pay book. There's an ashtray printed *A Present From Torquay*. That's where Grandpa and Nanna Dorothy first met, you know."

"Yes, we know," said Linda.

"Then there's a Christmas tree decoration – a reindeer wearing a bobble hat. Oh, and an old watch, quite old fashioned, hard to read, not an antique or anything. Think it belonged to some relative who passed it on."

"Hang on," said Steven, "was that my watch? The one that one of our old uncles gave me?"

Without lifting his head Gary nodded.

"I remember that watch. I was very proud of it but Mum wouldn't let me wear it to school. Don't know why, but I do know a couple of years later when Linda got her first watch they did let her wear it to school. I thought that was very unfair."

Linda stared at him. "And you've remembered that all this time?"

Steven had the grace to blush. "Yes, crazy isn't it. I know that, but it was one of those silly things I've never forgotten. Perceived injustice, I guess."

"Well, I don't know. I don't remember that at all."

"I think it's cool," said Kate, "all these little pieces of the past."

"Bit of a magpie, aren't you, Gary," said Steven. "Okay, you've got my old watch – and you're welcome to it by the way. I've moved on from then, unlike some apparently."

"Cool it, Uncle Steve," said Kate with a sudden authority. "These things make Pops happy and they don't do you any harm, do they?"

Once again Steven was embarrassed. "No, I suppose not. Okay, then, Gary, I bet you've got something in there of Linda's, haven't you?"

Linda gave a sudden gasp. "Nellie," she said.

Kate was puzzled. "Who?"

"Nellie. My little felt elephant. You gave her to Dad, didn't you, Gary?"

233

Gary finally raised his head and looked round the table. "Yes, I did," he said with a touch of defiance. "Dad was lonely, Mum having lost it, no one except me ever visiting. I wanted him to have something that reminded him of our family when we were all together."

There was a wobble in Linda's voice. "That's lovely, Gary," she said, "I'm so glad you rescued Nellie and now she couldn't be in a better place."

Gary gave a shy smile. "I've also got some furniture from your doll's house," he said, "I didn't have room for the house itself but there's the little bookcase and a chest of drawers and the kitchen stove and one of the beds."

In spite of himself Steven was getting interested. "Anything else of mine?" he asked.

"Yes. There's one of the racing cars from your Scalextric set, the plastic Spitfire kit that used to hang in your bedroom and the pack of trick cards from your conjuring outfit."

"Good God," said Steven, "I'd forgotten all about that pack of cards."

"What sort of trick cards?" asked Kate.

"Oh, it was great fun. If you riffled through it one way it looked like a normal pack, riffle the other way and every card was the three of diamonds." He looked at Gary with mock severity. "I do hope you never used them in a card game for money, Gary."

Gary missed the joke completely. "I've never used them at all," he said, "I never do anything with any of this stuff, just sit and look at it …"

"And remember your family, yeah, Pops?" said Kate.

"Yes," said Gary.

"What about family photos?" asked Linda, "do you have any of them?"

"I've got a few, very old ones," said Gary, "but I don't know who everyone is. When I first started visiting Dad, he and I went through the pictures together and he told me who some of them were, but he didn't recognise all of them either."

"Have you kept a note of who's who?"

Gary looked surprised. "Yes, of course. Every picture is now labelled with all the information available."

"Every lighthouse identified," muttered Steven.

"There aren't any lighthouses," said Gary. "Why would Mum and Dad have pictures of lighthouses?"

Steven glanced across at Linda. "No, of course not," he said, "I wasn't thinking."

"Were there any other albums?" asked Kate.

"There must have been," said Steven, "I can remember lots of pictures of us as kids, birthday parties, family holidays. No idea what happened to them though."

Linda looked thoughtful. "Do you know," she said, "I think I might have them. I'm pretty sure I've still got a box in the loft with stuff in from the old house before it was sold. I'll have a look when I get home."

Gary's eyes lit up. "If you find them, could I have them?"

Linda shrugged. "Don't see why not. You okay with that Steven?"

"Sure. I'd forgotten all about them till just now."

"I'm pretty sure they'll be there, Gary, so I'll dig them out for you. Where shall I send them?"

There was a silence. Gary's face went blank.

"I've got to send them somewhere, Gary," said Linda gently.

"Send them to me in London," said Kate, "I'll see Pops gets them."

"I still don't get all this secrecy," said Steven, "why can't you just give us an address Gary. We'll be staying in touch anyway, after today."

There was a pause then Gary said.

"Send the stuff to Kate."

In the awkward silence that followed the door opened and one of the carers came in.

"George is all settled now," she said, "you can go back in whenever you're ready."

TUESDAY 8:53 PM

AFTER THE CARER HAD LEFT THE ROOM GEORGE LAY BACK ON HIS pillows. He was exhausted but he was determined not to sleep, he had to be awake for when Rebecca arrived. He let his mind drift and, as always, that meant memories of Dorothy. What a wonderful life they had had, mostly. When he saw what happened to some marriages these days he felt very happy that they'd remained firmly in love until change, fate, call it what you will, had decreed that Dorothy would finally set out on a private journey without him. They had been married now for over 60 years and he wouldn't change a thing – except to wish that Dorothy was still with him.

Over 60 years and never a harsh word between them. As this thought occurred he actually chuckled grimly. He must be going senile – these were teenage romantic memories he was conjuring up. Of course there had been harsh words, not many of them, true, but no path every runs as smoothly as memory would have us believe.

They'd had a good marriage, him and Dorothy, but there had been moments. As though deliberately poking at a wound he set himself to remember some of the less than smooth times. He had no patience with self-delusion. Bad stuff will always happen, it's how you handle it that matters. Or so he had always believed. Until Rebecca. What a fool he had been there.

What else? Their uneven start of course – saved by her father. The time he had lost his job and hadn't trusted her enough to tell her. Steven's divorce and how she had understood why it happened in a way that he could not. And the trivial things. That argument over what colour to paint the bathroom. How childish can you get but that had rumbled on for days before Dorothy, inevitably, got her own way. His refusal to have a dog, although the children begged and begged. Dorothy had sided with them but more, he always thought, as a gesture of solidarity. He suspected she was as relieved as he was when they settled for a guinea pig instead.

And then of course there was the job row. Looking back he realised that this had always been inevitable but at the time the quarrel – like most quarrels – came right out of the blue.

A WOMAN'S PLACE…

FOR ONCE HE IS HOME EARLY AND THEY'RE HAVING A QUIET CUP of tea together at the kitchen table. He is feeling quite relaxed. He has more or less decided to take Dorothy to Scarborough for a few days for her birthday; the job is going well, the owner of the removal firm, Ray Dobson, has become a good friend and often says he appreciates what George does; they've had a card from Linda who is currently in New Orleans; the rest of the kids all seem happy. All is well with his world.

Then Dorothy drops her bombshell.

"I've decided I want to get a job," she says.

He's completely taken aback. "What do you want a job for?" he says, "you don't need a job. I'm making quite enough for both of us."

Dorothy sighs – he remembers those sighs so well – they were more expressive than many people's long statements.

"That's not the point," she says.

"Well, what is the point?"

"I need a challenge. I need to put my mind to work. I'm just vegetating here."

"Vegetating? With four children to look after."

Another Dorothy sigh. "Don't be so patronising, George," she says, "and in case you hadn't noticed, two of them are off our hands and Rebecca is fifteen. Tell her she needs looking after and she'd laugh in your face."

"Gary's not grown up. He's only, what, seven?"

"True. But I can have a job and still cope with one child. Or do you think that's beyond me."

"No, no, of course not. That's not what I'm saying."

"Then what are you saying? That a woman's place is in the home? You'd better not be saying that."

He says nothing, but that is exactly what he's thinking. He is the man. It is his job to provide for his family. But he knows his Dorothy and treads very carefully.

"No, that's not what I'm saying. But you don't need to get a job. There's plenty to do here."

Dorothy snorts and her snorts are nearly as good as her sighs. "Plenty do round here? You mean making beds, dusting, washing up ..."

"I do the washing up ..."

"That's not the point. Are you telling me my role in this marriage is housework."

"Well ..."

"Forget it, George. I need more than a dishcloth and a hoover in my life."

He tries a different tack. "What sort of job do you want?"

For the first time she looks uncertain. "I don't know. I haven't thought about it. I just need a challenge."

"So you keep saying. But what sort of challenge."

"Oh, for heaven's sake, how should I know. Something that'll stretch me. Get me out of the house."

Her uncertainty gives him an advantage – or so he thinks. "Well, then, why don't you have a think about the kind of challenge you want and then we can talk again."

She opens her mouth to respond but then the door bangs and

Rebecca comes in full of her day at school and the conversation stops.

He waits for Dorothy to resume the conversation but she doesn't do so. He congratulates himself on a problem averted, forgetting that Dorothy silent, is Dorothy dangerous.

NOW, LYING IN BED, THE LITTLE FELT ELEPHANT WATCHING HIM from the chest of drawers, George shook his head.

"She had me fooled, didn't she, Nellie?" he said. "All those years together and I still hadn't worked it out. I should have known that Dorothy would apparently give in and then go off and do what she'd always planned to do anyway."

The little elephant gazed passively back at him as though saying, "She always knew her own mind, mate."

"True," said George, answering the unspoken statement. "But it all came out in the wash and we always knew how we felt about each other."

That particular quarrel – long since forgotten – had reached its final conclusion on the occasion of George's 50th birthday.

DON'T DILLY DALLY ON THE WAY

SPRING 1974. THEY HAVE RECENTLY MOVED TO A BIGGER HOUSE about fifteen miles from Southampton on the edge of the South Downs so they decide to hold a joint 50th birthday-cum-house warming party in the garden. All the family are coming, old friends, new neighbours, work colleagues. A big affair.

George hires a large marquee which is put up in the garden but in the event the weather is kind to them. A catering firm is brought in to run a barbecue and Steven, now aged twenty one and with his latest girlfriend in tow, is master of ceremonies. The day is due to start at midday with toasts.

By late morning there is a crowd of people in the garden but as midday approaches George realises there is no sign of Dorothy. He goes into the house and calls her name but there's no response.

He goes back out into the garden and grabs hold of Steven. "Look, it's almost time for the toasts and there's no sign of your mother. Any idea where she is?"

"Sorry, Dad, no. Don't worry, she'll be around somewhere."

George is not reassured so he goes to find Linda but she is occupied with a group of friends and seems completely unconcerned.

"Don't worry, Dad. She'll be here, you know Mum."

He is not really worried but he can't understand where she has got to then suddenly he hears Steven calling the assembly to order.

"Ladies and gentlemen and … family …" He pauses for the inevitable laugh. "Thank you for joining us here today to welcome my parents to their new home in this beautiful village and to celebrate my father's 50th birthday." He turns to George. "You're looking good on it, Dad, not a day over 60, I'd say."

More laughter. George joins in but there is still no sign of Dorothy.

"Okay then," Steven goes on, "if you haven't got a drink yet then now's the time to rectify the omission. In a few moments we'll have the formal toasts and then you'll be free to have a mad scramble round the barbecue. But first we all need to sing, and you all know what you've got to sing, don't you?"

"Yes …" roars the crowd.

George sighs gently as he waits for the inevitable rendering of *Happy Birthday To You* but that's not what happens.

"Right you are then," calls Steven, "one, two three …" and everyone bursts into song.

My old man said follow the van,
And don't dilly-dally on the way.
Off went the van with my home packed in it,
I walked behind with me old cock linnet ...

George is bemused. What on earth is going on? Then suddenly, over the singing, he hears the throaty roar of a diesel engine and sees one of his firm's large removal vans coming up the drive. "What the hell ..." he says but the singing continues.

But I dillied and I dallied.
I dallied and I dillied.
Lost the way and don't know where to roam.
Oh, you can't trust the specials like the old time coppers,
And I can't find my way home.

The van comes to a halt at the same time as the song ends and to George's total and utter amazement he sees Dorothy climbing down out of the driver's seat.

A huge cheer goes up from the crowd as Dorothy, dressed in the working overalls of one of the firm's drivers, walks towards George singing as she comes.

I didn't dilly or dally.
Or dally or dilly.
I found my way and never want to roam.
You can trust your friends, and your brand new neighbours,
And now I've found my way home.

And she enfolds George in a huge embrace as the cheers grow louder.

After that the toasts, warm and sincere though they are, seem something of an anti-climax. When they're over and the queue is forming at the barbecue, George and Dorothy find themselves alone.

"Happy birthday, darling," says Dorothy, "now I'd better go and change into something more suitable for a party." And she pats her brown overalls.

"Oh, no you don't," says George, holding onto her arm, "you're not going anywhere without some explanations."

"What sort of explanations?" asks Dorothy, wide-eyed and innocent.

"Well, you can start by telling me how you come to be driving a truck that size," says George, "you need a PSV licence for that, you know."

"Of course, I know," says Dorothy, "And I've got one. I'm not completely irresponsible, you know."

"But how … when …" George is lost for words.

"How is easy," says Dorothy, "I took lessons and then I took the test. *When?* Well, I passed the test about three months ago. The examiner said I was a natural."

"You kept it pretty quiet," says George.

"Yes, I did, didn't I?" says Dorothy, "just as you did all those years ago when my father put you up to doing the same thing."

Suddenly George sees the funny side of it and bursts out laughing. "You never cease to amaze me, Dottie," he says, "but I hope you're not going to apply for a job driving a removal van."

"Of course not, dear," says Dorothy, "I think the driving's a lot of fun but I have no desire to spend all day humping wardrobes and pianos around the place."

Suddenly they realise they've been joined by the rest of the family.

"Happy birthday, Dad," says Steven. "Enjoy that did you?"

"Cunning so-and-sos," says George, "I presume all the guests were well briefed."

"Of course," says Linda, "we even gave some of the younger ones song sheets in case they didn't know the words."

Gary was bouncing up and down in excitement. "And I went round on my bike and delivered them all."

"Then last week we organised a short rehearsal for a few people," says Rebecca, "so we'd be sure to have a core of singers at least. We knew it would need to be loud to be heard over the sounds of Mum's engine."

"You're a conniving load of conspirators, "says George but inside he was glowing with the realisation of the trouble they had all gone to for his birthday. "So come on, all of you, let's enjoy the party."

"There's just one other thing before we do that," says Dorothy and turning she waves at Mr Dobson who is hovering on the edge of the family group.

"Come on, Raymond," she calls, "time for your contribution."

"What now?" asks George but Ray Dobson is already advancing, hand outstretched.

"Happy birthday, George," he says.

"So you were in on all this, were you?" says George.

"Of course he was," says Dorothy, "I didn't nick the lorry you know."

"Wouldn't put it past you," mutters George but then does a double take as he hears what Ray is saying.

"It was a great day for my company when you first walked in the door, George. I don't think we'd have been so successful so soon without your help."

I think you were going down the pan without my help, thinks George, but clearly this is not a thought to be expressed aloud.

"So, in view of that," Ray goes on, "your birthday seemed an appropriate moment to confirm you as Deputy Managing

Director of Dobson Removals."

"What?" George is dumbfounded.

"It means a pay rise of course, which you'll have to earn incidentally by bringing in more business. But you might find your new employee will help with that."

"New employee? What new employee?" And then suddenly the penny drops and he turns to Dorothy. "But you said you didn't want to drive a removal van."

"Neither do I," says Dorothy, "but I am going to drive a coach."

"A coach?"

"Yes, remember them, George? They carry people around the place."

"But we don't have any coaches."

"We do now," says Ray, "took delivery last week. I promised Dorothy that if she passed her PSV test I'd invest in a coach and we can start running outings for schools, old folks' homes and the like. Your first job as Deputy will be to find some business for her to do but I'm told you have experience in that field."

George is lost for words but the surprises aren't over yet.

"Time for your present, Dad," says Linda, "we all contributed something towards it."

"Yes, and it's a …" Gary's excitement is cut short as Rebecca clamps a hand over his mouth.

"It's a secret, Gary," she says, "we have to show it to Dad together."

"Oh, yes, of course. Sorry."

George looks round at them all. "I sense another conspiracy."

"Come on, dear," says Dorothy and takes his hand. Followed by their four offspring she leads him round to the back of the removal van still standing in the drive.

"Steven, will you do the honours," she says.

Steven lowers the tailgate, stands on it and beckons George to join him. Together they raise it up and then Steven opens the back doors of the van. There inside is a new, beautifully shiny, ride-on mower. George doesn't know what to say.

"We thought this would be a good present for you, Dad, now you've got this new house with a fair bit of lawn. Don't want to go on pushing a hand mower round that lot, not at your age."

"Cheeky bugger," mutters George automatically but inside he is brimming over with love for them all.

TUESDAY 9:06 PM

THE CAR PULLED INTO THE GREENACRES CAR PARK AND STOPPED. Joe got out and opened Rebecca's door.

"We're here, Becky," he said, "and it looks as if you've got a welcoming committee."

She looked across and there in the doorway stood three figures, Steven, Linda and Gary, all looking older than she remembered. She felt a rush of emotion. It had been such a long time.

Steven came across and gave her a big hug. "Welcome home, Becky."

Then another hug from Linda. "Oh, Becky, it's been so long."

"Don't. You'll make me cry."

"Me too."

"Give me that." Steven took the suitcase that Joe had produced from the boot and the three of them turned towards the door of the home.

Then Gary was there. Rebecca made a move towards him but he very slightly recoiled so instead she held out her hand. He shook it formally.

"Glad you made it," he said.

"Thanks to your very efficient arrangements," said Rebecca.

Gary smiled faintly. "You go with the others," he said, "I'll just sort things out here."

He turned away and, as she walked towards the door with Linda and Steven beside her, she heard him say.

"Everything all right, Joe?"

"No problems, Mr Redmond. All went very smoothly."

And then they were inside the building and moving out of earshot.

Linda took her arm. "I think you need a few moments, Becky.

Would you like to have a quick wash and brush up before we go along and see Dad?"

"Yes, yes, please and I could murder a cup of tea."

"I'll fix that for you." And suddenly Rebecca was face to face with the young woman she'd seen on the videocall. The woman held out her hand. "Hey, it's great to meet you, Aunt Becky."

"You're Gary's daughter?"

"Sure, I'm Kate."

"Then we can do better than a handshake." And Rebecca gave her a big hug. "Lovely to meet you too, Kate. There's a lot here I don't understand but …"

"It'll keep," said Steven, "now Linda, you take Becky along and Kate if you can …"

"Tea, yeah, sure. I'll bring it along to the pizza room, shall I?"

Gary appeared behind them and looked at Steven. "Now we're all here d'you think I ought to go and get Mum?"

Steven shook his head. "I don't think so, not yet. I think Becky and Dad need some time together first."

"Oh, okay." And for the first time that day Gary looked as though the initiative was drifting away from him.

TUESDAY 9:10 PM

"Dad. Dad. Wake up."

"Eh? What? What is it?"

He opened his eyes and saw Linda smiling down at him.

"Rebecca's here, Dad. She's just arrived."

"Becky? Becky's here? Where is she?"

He struggled to sit upright in his agitation but Linda smoothed him down. "She's just popped to the loo. It's a long drive from Heathrow. She'll be here in a tick."

"Oh, I must sit up, yes, sit up …"

"Come on then." Gently Linda helped him up against the pillows. "There's how's that."

He looked round the room. Kate was beside the bed holding a brush. "Shall I just fix your hair for you, Grandpa. Need to look smart for this reunion don't you?"

He nodded, too choked to speak and Kate gently brushed his few remaining hairs neatly to either side.

"There. Now you look really cool."

Steven appeared in the doorway. "Becky's just coming. Big moment, eh, Dad?"

George nodded, his heart was too full to speak. At last, after all these years, he had a chance to make amends.

AN UNEXPECTED OUTING

HE REMEMBERS THE OCCASION AS IF IT WERE YESTERDAY. HE AND Dorothy have just come back from a week in Torquay, a giggly reminiscence sort of week. They had even been on a coach trip to Widecombe.

Rebecca rings from her flat in Cambridge where she's been living since returning from Berlin six months ago. She says she has some news for them, could she come down and see them that weekend.

"Tell her to come for Sunday lunch," says Dorothy but Rebecca pleads another date and says she'll arrive mid-afternoon. Both George and Dorothy look forward to it. They haven't seen much of Rebecca since she got back. Her job, not that they understand exactly what it is she does, is obviously very demanding.

Dorothy bakes a chocolate cake and when Rebecca arrives they sit round the table on the patio in the shade of the apple tree. Rebecca asks after their holiday and hears again how George and Dorothy first met in Torquay. The family memories, so familiar to all of them, flow along their usual course, but at last they peter out and Dorothy looks expectantly at Rebecca.

"So come on. What's this news you've got for us?"

Uncharacteristically Rebecca hesitates and George chips in, grinning. "Don't tell me. You're pregnant. Is that it?"

"George. Please don't make jokes like that." Dorothy is indignant.

"Keep your hair on," says George, "it wouldn't matter if she was. Wouldn't mind a couple more grandchildren and I like to think I'm pretty broadminded."

"I'm not pregnant," says Rebecca flatly.

"Of course you're not, dear," says Dorothy. "Anyway I'd've known if you were."

George rolls his eyes upwards. "Okay," he says, "poor taste. So what is it? Spit it out."

Rebecca looks at her parents. "Well, the good bit is that I'm being headhunted."

"Headhunted? You mean …"

"Yes, I've had several job offers, all for better positions and more money. I did some good work in Berlin and I've progressed that since coming back to Cambridge. Now I've been contacted by several different companies and three of them have offered me a job."

"What sort of companies?"

"Plant life research labs, universities, pharmaceutical companies, all places that can use my expertise."

"Are all these in Cambridge?"

"Oh, no, they're all over the world."

"Oh." Silence for a moment then Dorothy asks, "So where exactly?"

"Well, one is in the UK, in Lancaster. Another is in the States in New Jersey and the third one is in Sweden."

George looks at her. "And I'm guessing that with all this shilly-shallying you haven't chosen Lancaster."

"No, Dad. I've accepted the offer from the States. They were all tempting, but I've made my choice. It's an amazing job, the sort of thing I've always dreamed of."

"What sort of work will you be doing?"

Rebecca smiles. "I could tell you, Mum, but it's very technical. Simplest answer is scientific research. Plant research."

"Well, I can see why you're tempted," says George, "what with your high-powered qualifications and all that. I'm just sorry you're going to be so far away. Your mother and I aren't getting any younger you know."

Dorothy is looking down at her plate. Then she says. "I imagine this means you'll be moving over there."

"Oh, yes."

"How long for?"

Rebecca shrugs. "I would think for a good while. This could just be the first step. There's so many more opportunities out there for people like me."

"Will you be able to come back home occasionally?"

"Not often," says Rebecca. "It's going to be pretty full on for some time and companies in the States don't give their employees much annual holiday."

There is silence in the garden for a few moments. Below the table an entrepreneurial sparrow conducts a commando raid on some fallen crumbs from the chocolate cake.

George drains his cup. "And this job really is better than the Lancaster one, is it? I'm thinking that at least if you were up there you could get home from time to time."

"It has to be the American one, Dad. In career terms there really isn't any choice."

Dorothy rouses herself then stretches across the table and puts her hands on Rebecca's.

"Thank you for telling us, dear. I'm really glad about the new job, for your sake." There is a pause and then she goes on, "I suppose we won't be seeing much of you from now on."

"No, I don't think so. Sorry, Mum, but if all this works out as I hope, I might settle out there permanently."

"Permanently?"

"Yes. There's so much interesting work going on in the States in the areas that interest me. I may even take out American citizenship at some stage."

George can't believe his ears. "What? Become an American citizen? Stop being English and become a bloody Yank?"

"What's wrong with that, Dad?"

"What's wrong with it? Everything's wrong with it. You're English, that's something to be proud of. It's not something you can casually throw away."

"Dad, please understand. I'm not throwing anything away. It's just there's likely to be more opportunities in my line of work if I become an American citizen. Anyway, that's for the future. I'd have to work there at least five years before it would be possible, and only then if my company is prepared to sponsor me."

"Well, I must say this is a all bit of a shock. We understood why you went to Germany but we thought you were home for good now."

"I've got to go where the work is, Dad."

"We understand that, dear," says Dorothy, "but from our point of view we're just a little disappointed you won't be around."

George nods. "True enough. So when do you actually leave?"

There's a moment's silence. Then Rebecca says, "Next weekend actually. I've come to say goodbye."

"Oh, Becky, that soon?" Dorothy is quite upset.

"Cutting it a bit fine, weren't you?" says George.

"Yes, I know. I'm sorry but in the end it all happened rather fast."

"I hate to think of you going all that way on your own."

"Oh, come on, Dottie," says George, "she's a grown woman. She'll be fine."

"Yes, I will." Rebecca hesitates then, as though signalling an announcement, a church clock somewhere in the distance strikes four.

Suddenly George's natural instincts kick in and he turns to look at Rebecca. "There's something else, isn't there? It's not just the job."

"Yes, there is something else. I won't be alone. My friend, Chris, is coming with me."

George looks at her. "And by 'friend' you mean …?"

"Yes, my partner, Christina."

There is a long silence broken only by the chittering of an angry robin defending its territory.

Finally, Dorothy says, "Oh, I see."

Rebecca looks across at George. "Dad," she says tentatively.

George shakes his head. "Well, that I wasn't expecting."

"Just be happy for me, Dad, I've found someone I care about and who cares for me."

"But it's not a real relationship, is it?"

"It's real enough for me."

George looks away, out across the garden. "Well, I think you could be making a big mistake?"

"No, I don't think so."

Dorothy says tentatively. "Are you sure, dear, about all this?"

"You mean, am I sure about Chris? Yes, yes, I am. She's the best thing that ever happened to me."

"Better than your family, you mean?" says George.

"Not better, Dad. Different."

George is silent.

"Dad," says Rebecca gently. "I'm going away. I'm going to be living and working on the other side of the world. I could have lied to you."

She glances across at Dorothy. "But years ago Mum taught me there's good reasons or selfish reasons for lying. If I'd lied to you now, even by omission, it would have been a selfish lie. I couldn't do that. I want to be honest with you before I go."

George does not smile. "Well, as I said, you're a grown woman. You have to do what you have to do. Just one thing though. When did you decide all this?"

"All what?"

"Deciding you … you feel like this."

Rebecca paused for a moment. "As far as my feelings go, I think I've always known. It's something I accepted years ago, long before I met Chris."

"Well, all I can say is that you kept it pretty quiet. We had no idea, did we, Dorothy?"

Dorothy doesn't reply and suddenly realisation dawns on

George. "You knew about this, didn't you?" he says.

"Not exactly," says Dorothy, "I didn't know as such, but I did wonder."

"And you didn't think to say anything to me?"

"No. I wasn't sure, and anyway it's not really our business. As you said, Becky's a grown woman."

There is a long silence. George looks out across the garden. Finally he nods. "Yes, a grown woman. Okay, Rebecca, you've told us. It's your life. You'd better get on with it, though I think you're being very selfish."

"Selfish?"

"Yes. Not much chance of any more grandchildren now, have we? Your mother was looking forward to that."

Dorothy sat bolt upright. "Now just a minute, George."

Rebecca was outraged. "Selfish? What happened to 'we're very proud of you, Becky. First member of the family to go to uni' and all that."

"We were proud of you but now it's different. Chances are we'll never see you again. You might have the posh education, but you don't mind disappointing your mother, do you."

Dorothy is getting angry now. "Don't you go putting words into my mouth, George Redmond. Yes, I'm sorry Becky's going so far away but she'll come back and see us, won't you, Becky?"

"Of course I will, Mum."

"Though, as you've said, it won't be often," says George.

"No, it may not be often, but I'll come when I can."

"Fair enough, but let's get one thing straight. This will always be your home, Rebecca, but if you come to see us, you come alone. Is that clear?"

There is a long silence. Rebecca looks at her parents. Then finally she says, "Do you mean that, Dad? If Chris and I visit the UK, I could come and see you, but I couldn't bring Chris?"

"Always happy to see you, Rebecca, but only you. Okay?"

"No, not okay, Dad. I knew this would be a bit of a shock but I thought that once I'd explained you'd understand."

"All I understand is that you've decided to abandon your own family."

"I am not abandoning you. I'm trying to explain that I'm starting a new life with an exciting job and I am going to share that life with someone I love."

George is silent and after a moment Rebecca goes on. "What happened, Dad? As kids we admired you because you insisted we dealt with problems by talking them through and finding a solution together. What happened to that tolerance?"

Not even the robin breaks the silence that follows. Rebecca looks at Dorothy.

"Mum, is that how you feel too?"

Dorothy looks at Rebecca and then at George, tears appearing in the corner of her eyes. She says nothing.

After a few moments Rebecca says, "Right then. Well, I think it's time for me to go."

"Don't leave, Becky, not like this."

"Sorry, Mum, but there's no point in staying. Not now."

"Becky, I'm sure we can sort this out."

"Nothing to sort out. She's made her choice," though George sounds less sure than a moment ago.

Rebecca's voice is choked. "Then that's that. I came here to tell you how happy I am and I'm not going to let you spoil that. But if I can't come home with Chris then I won't come home at all."

Dorothy is distraught. "No, Becky, please don't say that."

"Sorry, Mum." She picks up her bag and leaves the table, pausing only for one parting shot.

"You say you're broadminded, Dad. You might want to

rethink that definition."

For a moment George and Dorothy sit in stunned silence. Then with a cry of "Rebecca, wait …" Dorothy leaps to her feet and runs after her daughter. She is too late. They hear the roar of her car's engine and the crunch of tyres on the gravel as Rebecca speeds off down the drive.

Dorothy slumps down on the grass and bursts into tears. George just sits at the table gazing into space.

SO MANY YEARS AGO. SO MUCH REGRET. SO MANY HOURS WISHING the past could be undone but to no avail. That evening Dorothy had rung Rebecca's London flat to find the line had been disconnected. She contacted Steven and Linda but neither of them knew where Rebecca was or had an address in America for her.

Dorothy was desperate. George was sunk in a personal hell. The next day they had rung her old employer but they had no forwarding information either. George, roused from his misery, realising the finality of what he had done, even tried ringing some of the major airlines to see if he could trace her that way, but none of them would give details of their passenger lists.

Rebecca had vanished into the blue.

Until now.

The door to George's room opened and there she was. Rebecca. Coming across the room, smiling. Summoning strength he didn't know he had, George half rose from the bed and held out his arms. Her arms went around him and suddenly they were both crying.

TUESDAY 9:20 PM

GARY SAT ALONE IN THE RESIDENTS' DINING ROOM, SURROUNDED by the debris of their pizza supper. He felt quite disturbed that the day wasn't working out as he had expected. It had all seemed so clear to him when George had first phoned that morning. It was time to put their plan into action. George wanted everyone round him one last time so Gary had to get all the family to the care home, including Rebecca, for a final family gathering, then George would be free to die. In Gary's mind it was all perfectly straightforward but it wasn't working out like that.

People. That was the problem. People always got in the way. First Steven and Linda initially not wanting to come, then the unnatural, at least to Gary, excitement over the arrival of Kate, the pressure for him to talk about himself, something he never did, and now, with the arrival of Rebecca, there would be tears. He just knew there would be. Gary didn't like tears. He didn't know what to do about them.

In Gary's mind they should all be sitting round George's bed now, all of them, including Dorothy, so George could have his family reunion. Instead Dorothy was still in her room and Steve had made it clear that he thought George and Rebecca should have some time on their own. What did they need that for? The whole point of today had been one last family gathering and that wasn't happening.

Gary was well out of his comfort zone.

TUESDAY 9:25 PM

AFTER THEIR FIRST IMPULSIVE HUG, REBECCA DREW BACK A little, wiped her eyes and looked down at her father. He looked so frail lying there, such a contrast to the strong, if angry, man she had last seen all those years ago.

"Oh, Dad ..." she began but George interrupted her.

"I'm so sorry, Becky, what a stupid fool I was."

"We both lost it, didn't we?"

"Yes, we certainly did. And now ... and now ..."

"Gary said ... well, he said you weren't too good."

"I'm 93 years old, Becky. Aches here, pains there, all a bit grim."

"But they're treating you for it, surely?"

"Controlling, rather than treating. It's not a problem, Becky. I've had a good run."

"And a good way still to run, I hope."

"I don't. Can't see the point of prolonging the agony. Time to move on, call it a day. But I couldn't go without seeing all the family again. Especially you, the chance to tell you how much I regret all those wasted years."

She looked round then dragged a chair over to the side of the bed, sat down and took his hand.

"No recriminations, Dad," she said, "I wasted them too. It won't help and I'm here now."

"I was afraid you wouldn't come."

Rebecca was silent for a moment then she decided that total honesty was the only way forward.

"I nearly didn't," she said, "when you first wrote I was in two minds about answering."

"But you did."

"Yes, but very non-committal, as I remember."

George grinned. "Non-committal? It was more like a polite note to the milkman asking him to leave two pints."

"Well, I didn't know what to say. It had been such a long time and the news about Mum really shocked me."

George's face fell. "It's awful, Becky, she doesn't know any of us anymore and I can't tell you how hard that is to bear."

"I can imagine. Will I be able to see her?"

"Yes, Gary's arranged it with the manager. They'll bring her along here soon."

"She's here? In this same home?"

"Oh yes. Gary fixed it. He's been wonderful, Becky."

"He's certainly been wonderful to me today. Talk about a red carpet. I wouldn't have thought it possible for me to be here so quickly. What on earth does he do that he can fix all that stuff?"

"No idea. He never talks about himself."

"Never?"

"No."

"But you must know something about him. I mean, he has a daughter. What's all that about? Is he married?"

George shook his head. "Not as far as I know. I've never met Kate's mother. She lives in the States I believe."

"Does she? Where? D'you know?"

"No idea."

"I'll have to ask Kate. Don't suppose I'll get much out of Gary."

"Are you still happy over there, Becky?"

Rebecca patted her father's hand. "Yes, Dad, very happy."

"And are you still with … with … Chris?"

"Yes, I am."

"Good."

"That's not what you said last time we met."

George was silent for a moment. Then he said, "No, it wasn't, was it? But if you're still together it must mean that it's a good relationship. One that works."

Rebecca felt tears starting to come again. "Yes, it does, Dad. Chris and I love each other very much."

"And that's the important thing, I realise that now. Forget what I said back then, Becky, we all need someone to love and someone who loves us. I've always had that and I am glad that you have too."

"Oh, Dad …" and suddenly Rebecca was crying again and burying her face in her father's neck. She felt George's hand patting her on the back as he had done all her childhood when she had been upset.

"There, there, Becky. It's okay."

After a few moments she sat back, sniffing. She opened her bag, found a handkerchief and blew her nose.

"It's been quite a day one way and another."

"You've seen Linda and Steven?"

"Yes, briefly. Gary says you want a full family reunion."

"One last time. All together. Yes."

"I hope it won't be the last time."

"It may well be," said George firmly.

Rebecca looked at him. "What are you going to do, Dad?"

"Do? Nothing. Just let nature take its course."

As Rebecca thought about the implications of this George added. "There's no point in being sad about it. I've reached the end of the road that's all. I'm falling to bits, I've lost Dorothy …"

"And she was always the most important thing in your life, wasn't she?"

"Yes. With all respect to you and others, it was always Dorothy first. I love her, you know, Becky, love her so much."

"I know, Dad, you never made any secret of that."

"I loved her the moment I met her – I've told you how I first met her, haven't I?"

In spite of everything Rebecca smiled. "Yes, Dad, you've told me. Several times."

"Well, I loved her then and I love her now. Even though she doesn't know it anymore."

"It must be very hard."

"It is, but in the last resort we're all alone, Becky. People can help, advise, offer comfort, but it's only you who makes the decisions that really matter."

"Dad, that's all over. Forget the past."

"I wasn't talking about that decision."

"Oh."

There was a pause then George said, "Think it's time you went and got the others, please."

"What about Mum? It's getting pretty late."

"It'll be okay. Gary will go and get her."

Rebecca hesitated, then said. "Actually, Dad, I rather think I'd like to see Mum for a few minutes on my own. Can I do that?"

George looked up at her. "Oh, I see. I hadn't thought of that." He paused. "She won't know you, you know."

"No, I appreciate that, but all the same ..."

George nodded. "Okay. I understand. You'd best speak to Gary. He'll fix it for you."

"Thanks, Dad."

"Off you go then. See you in a bit."

Rebecca bent and kissed him, then with a little wave went out of the room.

TUESDAY 10:14 PM

GARY'S PLAN FOR THE DAY WAS STILL VEERING OFF THE RAILS. HE had taken Rebecca to see Dorothy and later he had gone back to collect his mother so she could join them all in George's room. However, Angela, one of the night care assistants, was adamant that Dorothy was not going anywhere else tonight.

"By rights she should be in bed now. We let her stay up to meet her daughter who, I gather, has only just arrived from America, but that's it. Disruption to routine is very hard on people with dementia. I'll bed her down in a moment and you can see her again in the morning."

"But that's not the plan." Gary didn't understand what was going wrong. "She needs to come along to my dad's room with the rest of the family. He wants to see us all together."

"Then he can see you all together in the morning."

"But he won't be here in the morning. He's going to die, tonight."

"Really, Mr Redmond, that's a terrible thing to say."

"It's not terrible. He told me so himself. He wants to die. He's had enough. He's tired."

Angela turned away. "I don't want to hear any more about this. We can't just choose to die when it suits us."

"You know, Angela. I wouldn't be so sure of that." Gary and Angela turned to see Ken, George's favourite night care assistant, coming down the corridor. He went on. "I guess this is Mr George we're discussing here?"

"We are discussing *George,* yes," said Angela primly.

"Then I would say that he'll go when he wants to go. That man has a real powerful personality."

"Ken, can you just leave this to me please."

"No, I'm very sorry, Angela, I don't think I can. I've come to collect Dorothy and take her along to Mr George – just like Miss Belfort said I could."

"Pauline Belfort knows about this?"

"Indeed she does. And approves. I know this is not exactly normal but Mr George's family are here assembled and he wants to see them altogether. If he did happen to pass over tonight you wouldn't want to deny him the chance to say goodbye to his family, would you?"

"Well, no, of course not, but—"

"Then why not just leave it to me. I'll take Dorothy along now then, when the family have done, I'll bring her back here and you can see she is tucked up safe and sound. I'll take full responsibility."

"Well, I suppose, in that case …"

"Thank you, Angela. I'll see you later and perhaps you'd like to share my banana cassava cakes when you have a break?"

To Gary's amazement, Angela seemed to blush. "Oh … well … thank you, Ken. That would be very nice. I'll leave it to you then, shall I?" And nodding to Gary she disappeared down the corridor.

Gary gave a huge sigh of relief. "Thank you, Ken."

"No problem. Now let's get Dorothy along to your father's room."

TUESDAY 10:36 PM

THEY WERE ALL THERE, GROUPED AROUND THE BED LIKE PEOPLE in a Victorian painting. The room seemed more crowded now than it had done earlier in the day. George was propped up against his pillows, Dorothy was beside him in her wheelchair, a blanket round her shoulders. Linda was in the armchair, Kate and Rebecca sat on upright chairs next to Dorothy while Steven and Gary stood, slightly awkwardly, at the end of the bed.

George opened his mouth to speak but was caught by a fit of coughing. Linda leaned forward and handed him a glass of water. He drank and after a moment regained his breath.

"Sorry about that."

"Take your time, Dad."

George took a deep breath. "I was going to say 'thank you all for coming' but that sounds too much like the opening speech of a business meeting."

"Don't worry, Dad, we're all glad to be here." Steven looked round the room seeking agreement.

Various murmurs of "yes", "of course", "good to be here" dribbled round the group and vanished into silence.

"I wanted us all to be here one last time, the family as it once was back in the days when we were all together having fun. We haven't met as a family like this for many years now and it means a lot to me that you've all taken the trouble to come here today."

"Oh …" There was a small exclamation from Kate and they all turned to look at her.

"I guess I'm an intruder," she said, "I wasn't a part of your family back then."

"But you're part of our family now," said George, "so you're here on behalf of all those who can't come tonight, partners, grandchildren and so on."

"Thank you," she said in a small voice. "I'm honored."

"Right then," said George, "now I suppose you're all wondering what happens next. Probably thinking the old bugger's got some serious speech he wants to deliver and we'll have to pretend to listen, smile and hope it doesn't go on too long."

"You know us all so well," said Steven grinning, "so is that it? Can we all go home now?"

Gary was outraged. "No, you can't go. This is a serious moment."

A little ripple of laughter rang round the room.

"Don't worry, Gary," said Steven, "I'm not going anywhere. That was a joke."

"Oh! A joke? Okay."

Kate nudged her father's shoulder with her own. "Don't worry, Pops. Everything's cool. Grandpa knows just what he's doing."

"Grandpa does and, don't panic, this isn't going to be serious. Well, not yet anyway. Now I've said this before, and it's true, so forget all the polite denials, I am going to die very soon."

He held up a hand to forestall any protests. "No need to be polite, you know it and I know it. I'm 93, bits of me aren't working properly any more. I know it can't be long and I suspect it will be sooner rather than later." ,

There was a short silence then Rebecca said, "Of course we understand that, Dad, but understanding it and accepting it aren't quite the same thing."

Steven said. "We don't want to lose you, Dad, but we don't like seeing in you in pain either."

"Thank you, Steven. *Love me but let me go* as someone once said. I'm ready to go but I wanted this last together moment."

It was Kate who said what everyone was thinking. "You said this wouldn't be serious, Grandpa."

"And it won't be. Now we're all here together I want us to remember the good times, the family holidays, the parties in the garden, the jokes round the tea table."

"Oh, not the jokes," groaned Steven.

"Yes, the jokes. They may not always have been good jokes but they were fun. We not only laughed together as a family but we groaned together too."

"You can say that again," muttered Linda.

"So this is what we're going to do. We're each going to recount a special memory or if you can't do that, tell a joke. Then we'll say goodbye and at least we'll go away smiling."

There was dead silence in the room then Linda said. "You tell us you're about to die and then you want us to tell jokes?"

"Yes. A joke or some family memory. What's wrong with that?"

"Well, it just seems …"

"Nothing's wrong with that," cut in Rebecca, "it's a great idea, Dad, and I'll start the ball rolling."

She leaned across the bed and took George's hand.

"Do you remember the summer I won the talent contest on the pier at … oh, where was it?"

"I certainly do," said George. "Weymouth, was it? Sandown? Burnham-on-Sea? Can't remember. Too long ago, but it sure was one hell of a show. You brought the house down."

I'VE NEVER WRONGED AN ONION

REBECCA REMEMBERS THE SHOW SO WELL. THAT MORNING, walking along the promenade at … wherever it was … they had seen a sign announcing a talent contest on the pier at four o'clock. On the spur of the moment they decide to go.

So later that day the whole family stroll along to the pier and take their seats in the pavilion. The first half hour or so is fun, predictable but fun. Various people go up on the stage and sing or dance or tell jokes. It all works because the audience want it to work – they're there to enjoy themselves.

There is a brief interval, then the compere announces, "Now it's time for the kiddies to have a turn. Who'd like to come up here and entertain us?"

A few hands go up and the compere points to a young girl in the front row. "Come on up, my dear. Show us what you can do."

The little girl trips up onto the stage.

"What's your name, dear, and how old are you?"

"Jennifer, and I'm ten years old."

"Well, then, Jennifer, what are you going to do for us?"

"I'm going to read a poem about my dog called Spot."

"A poem? How lovely. Away you go then."

The little girl produces several sheets of paper from her pocket and starts reading in a low, monotonous tone. Each verse seems to be four lines long and the last line is always. "So I really love my dog, Spot."

After six of these verses the compere hastily intervenes. "That's lovely, Jennifer. Thank you so much Now let's have someone else shall we? How about you? The little boy in the third row."

Jennifer, looking slightly put out, leaves the stage to be replaced by a young boy who sings lustily, and occasionally tunefully, several nursery rhymes from *Little Boy Blue* through to *Sing A Song Of Sixpence*. This, like Jennifer's poem, is met with polite applause.

Various other children follow. Most do more nursery rhymes, one little girl attempts a ballet dance but her sandal buckles get entwined with each other and she falls over in tears. Another little boy, clearly encouraged by his mother, announces that his name is Robert but then gets completely tongue-tied and can't say anything else and finally retreats in some confusion.

The compere, game to the last, looks hopefully round the auditorium then, much to the amazement of her family, Rebecca stands up, pushes her way to the end of the row and heads purposefully for the stage.

She has an unmistakable air of confidence which the compere quickly latches onto.

"Hello, my dear. And what's your name?"

"Rebecca Redmond. And I'm eight years old."

"Well, then, Rebecca, what you are going to do for us?"

"I'm going to entertain you," says Rebecca, slightly scornfully, "that's what you wanted, isn't it?"

A ripple of laughter runs through the audience, even the compere smiles. "That will be lovely, Rebecca, the stage is yours."

He steps back and Rebecca turns to face the audience, her hands crossed across her tummy.

"What's she up to?" George whispers to Dorothy.

"No idea, but we're about to find out."

And they do find out. Rebecca coughs slightly, then bursts into song in a strong carrying voice.

> *I've never wronged an onion,*
> *I hope I never shall,*
> *I've never wronged an onion,*
> *I treat it as a pal.*
> *So tell me, tell me, tell me why,*
> *If I've never wronged an onion*
> *Why should it make me cry?*

The audience love it. As the song comes to an end there are cheers and whistles from all parts of the theatre but hardly pausing for breath, Rebecca goes straight on.

I had a friend and his name was Lord Jim,
He said that his wife threw tomatoes at him;
Now tomatoes are soft and they don't hurt the skin,
But these 'ere tomatoes were inside a tin.

There is no doubt that the audience prefer this to *Little Boy Blue*. The compere, looking slightly stunned, says, "That was lovely, Rebecca. Where did you learn those songs?"

"My mum sings them. She's always singing. All sorts of songs."

"Do you know any others?"

"Of course."

"More. More," yells the audience.

"Will you sing us another one?" asks the compere.

Rebecca looks completely composed. "If you like. I'll sing one of my mum's favourites." She waves out into the audience. "Are you listening, Mum?"

"I'm listening, my darling," whispers Dorothy.

Are the stars out tonight
I don't know if it's cloudy or bright
I only have eyes for you dear
The moon may be high
But I can't see a thing in the sky
I only have eyes for you
I don't know if we're in a garden
Or on a crowded avenue
You are here
And so am I
Maybe millions of people go by
But they all disappear from view
And I only have eyes for you.

George and Dorothy look at each other, not quite sure whether to laugh or cry. At the end of the show Rebecca walks away with first prize.

"I couldn't do that now," said Rebecca, "I'd be far too embarrassed."

"I don't know how you did it then," said Steven.

"It was Mum," said Rebecca, "she always said you can do anything you want, so long as you want it enough."

They all glance across at Dorothy, sitting there benignly gazing into space.

"And I was getting so fed up with dog poems and nursery rhymes, I just thought I could do better than that."

"You certainly did do better than that," said Linda.

"Precocious little madam," said Steven, but he was smiling.

"Yes, suppose I was," said Rebecca, "but it was fun and I won a box of chocolates."

"Which you didn't share ..."

"Why should I? You didn't sing anything."

"Well, I think it sounds real cool," said Kate.

"I don't remember it at all," said Gary.

"Well, you wouldn't, would you?" said Steven, "if Becky was eight you weren't even born."

"I think you came along later that year, Gary," said Linda, "I'm sure Mum was pregnant that summer."

"Well, even so ..." He was interrupted by George who suddenly had a violent coughing fit."

As Linda helped him to a drink of water, Kate quickly moved behind him and started massaging his shoulders again.

"There you go, Grandpa. Just relax. You'll be okay."

After a moment or two the coughing gradually eased and George flopped back against his pillows again.

"Sorry about that. It just catches me sometimes."

"That's okay," said Steven, "but if you're tired d'you think we should leave you in peace."

"No, no. We mustn't stop. This is just what I wanted."

They glance at one another, then Steven said. "Well, go on, Linda. Your turn."

"I can't think of anything. Or rather there's so many things."

"Well, just pick one. Any one."

"Oh, I don't know." She thinks for a moment. "Well, okay, then, this is a bit disgusting but … do you remember the time we came back from holiday to find we'd been invaded while we were away?"

ANTS IN YOUR PANTS

SHE IS EIGHT YEARS OLD, REBECCA IS SIX AND STEVEN ELEVEN AND it's one of the few times they ever see their parents completely shocked. They have been to Eastbourne for a week's holiday and they arrive home ready for a cup of tea before starting to unpack. Dorothy goes through to the kitchen to put the kettle on then they hear her scream.

"George, George. Come here."

They rush through to the kitchen to find the shelves, the work surfaces, the window ledge are all swarming with ants. They're everywhere, inside the cupboards, crawling over every surface. For a moment they are stunned, then George springs into action.

"Right. Steven go and get a bucket from the shed then fill it with hot water from the kettle. Linda, grab a broom – there's one under the stairs. Becky, go with her and get the dustpan and brush. Dorothy, have we got any old cloths, towels, anything."

They all leap into action. When the water arrives George takes the broom and begin sweeping ants off the surfaces and into the water. When he's got a good load he empties it out over the garden. He soon realises that hot water is not necessary, any water will do so Steven starts re-filling the bucket from the garden hose.

Dorothy comes back with some old dust sheets and they tear these into strips, soak them in water and use them to brush the ants out of the corners where the broom won't reach. It's not long before they find the cause of the problem. At the back of a cupboard are two jars of jam where the lids have come off and the smell has obviously attracted the ants. Those jars go straight into the dustbin.

Gradually they get the situation under control and then Steven is despatched to the shops to buy ant powder which they spread liberally round the back door as they assume that is where the ants made their entrance. Eventually they get their cup of tea but all that evening, and for several days afterwards, they continue to find ant stragglers all over the place.

Not an ideal end to their holiday.

"I DON'T REMEMBER THAT," SAID STEVEN.

"Neither do I," said George. "Ants in the kitchen? Are you sure?"

"Of course I'm sure," said Linda, "it makes me want to scratch just thinking about it again."

"I don't remember it either," said Rebecca, "but if you were eight at the time then I can only have been, what, six?"

"Well, it definitely happened," said Linda defensively. "It was horrible."

"It sure sounds gross, Aunt Linda," said Kate.

Steven suddenly realised that Linda was a bit upset that no one was sharing her memory so he tried to lighten the mood.

"Tell you what, Linda. Tell us one of your jokes. We always

liked your jokes." Steven turned to Kate. "Linda would come home from school with a joke she wanted to tell us but she could never get it right. She'd start telling the joke, forget how it went, so she'd switch to the end of a completely different joke so it didn't make any sense at all."

"I didn't always do that," protested Linda.

"Enough times to make it funny," said Steven.

"Did you always tell a lot of jokes?" asked Kate.

"All the time," said George firmly. "So come on, Linda. Make us laugh."

"Well, all right. I'll do some of the very short ones so I can't get the ending wrong."

"Want to bet?" said Steven but Linda ignored him.

"Okay. Here goes. I say, I say, I say. Why do cows wear bells?"

Steven, feeling slightly ashamed of himself, decided to play along. "I don't know. Why do cows wear bells?"

"Because their horns don't work. Da, da!"

George grinned, Rebecca and Kate smiled. Gary laughed. "Horns, I get it. That's funny."

"Okay, here's another one. Why did the bald man paint rabbits on his head?"

Rebecca laughed. "I know this one. Because from a distance they looked like hares."

Steven joined in. "What is the longest word in the English language?"

"*Smiles*. Because there's a mile between its first and last letters."

"What do you call a man with a seagull on his head?"

"Cliff."

"My turn," said George, "What's green, got eight legs, and would probably kill you if it fell out of a tree?"

There was silence for a moment. "That's a new one on me," said Steven.

Kate, trying to join in, said hopefully, "An octopus wearing armour."

They all laughed. "You've got the idea, Kate," said George, "but the right answer is a snooker table."

"Nice one, Dad."

Kate was puzzled. "What's snooker?"

"It's a billiards game, a bit like pool," said Steven.

"Oh, okay."

Gary was getting a little twitchy. "Look, can we get back to our memories. They're interesting."

"Okay, Gary," said Linda, "share one of your memories with us."

Silence.

After a moment Kate said, "Come on, Pops. Tell us something you remember from when you were a kid."

Another pause, then Gary said. "I can't remember anything I did."

Suddenly Steven felt a rush of compassion for his strange, much younger, brother.

"I know," he said, "how about your eighth birthday when you got your first bike."

"My first bike?"

"Yes, you remember. Mum and Dad organised a family party for you. We all came for the day. They gave you a bike. A Raleigh Chopper, if I remember rightly."

Gary's face lit up. "Oh, yes, of course. I remember that bike. It was very interesting."

"Interesting?" Kate looked puzzled. "Why 'interesting'?"

"New design. Interesting construction."

Steven laughed. "What Gary's trying to say, Kate, is that his reaction to being given a new bike was not a conventional one."

"No?"

"No. Most people given a new bike would get on it and ride it."

"Sure."

"Not Gary. His first response was to get a set of spanners and dismantle it completely."

"He certainly did," said George. "I wasn't amused. That bike had cost a lot of money and suddenly it's all in bits."

"But he put it back together again," said Linda, "I remember now."

"I wanted to see how it worked," said Gary. "What's wrong with that?"

"Nothing, son," said George, "it just surprised us at the time."

Kate smiled at her father. "It's cool, Pops. And so like you."

Gary frowned and then suddenly became excited. "I know, I know. I've remembered something."

"Come on then," said Rebecca, but Gary turned to George. "Do the mangle song."

For a moment George was puzzled. "The mangle song?"

"Yes, yes, the man and his braces, you know."

"What's a mangle" asked Kate.

For a moment they were all rather nonplussed then Steven stepped in. "It's a kind of very primitive tumble dryer only it doesn't tumble. It compresses the clothes between two rollers when you turn a handle."

"Oh, okay," said Kate, clearly none the wiser. "So what's the mangle song?"

"No idea," said Linda, but suddenly George nodded.

"I think I know what you mean, Gary. Is this what you were thinking of?"

He took a deep breath and then sang in a rather croaky voice.

Never let your braces dangle,
Poor old sport,
He got caught
Pulled right through the mangle.

"Oh, yuk," said Linda but Gary was laughing with glee.

"That's it, that's it. Pulled right through the mangle."

Steven laughed with him. "Hey, Gary, do you remember, we were singing that song on your birthday one time just as the postman arrived. He thought we were all mad."

"Yeah, and we all danced round him singing it. Great fun."

"Don't know where you get it from," said George but he was grinning.

Kate shook her head. "You guys are something else. What are braces? The things you put on your teeth?"

Rebecca smiled. "No, Kate, braces are what you'd call suspenders."

"Oh, okay."

Linda was watching George and saw a frown cross his face. "Are you all right, Dad?"

"Yes, don't worry. I'm fine. Enjoying this. Brings it all back."

Linda looked at him but he met her gaze defiantly. "I'm all right. Okay?"

"Okay, Dad." She turned to Steven. "Your turn, I think, big brother."

"Right. Well, let's think. Tricky, isn't it, just pulling these things out of the past." A brief pause. "Well, I don't know. This isn't really a shared family thing but it was very important to me."

"What was?"

"Being trusted to take the Christmas presents to Nan and Grandad Goring."

LIGHT AT THE END OF THE TUNNEL

IT IS DECEMBER 1967. HE IS FOURTEEN YEARS OLD AND SCHOOL has just broken up for the Christmas holidays. They've finished supper, Gary's asleep in his cot and his sisters have disappeared to do whatever it is sisters do, when his parents say they would like a word with him.

For a moment he's worried. What has he done that they've caught up with? But it's nothing like that.

"Steven, we'd like you to do something for us," says George.

"What sort of something?" he asks, rather suspiciously.

Dorothy laughs. "Guilty conscience, Steven?"

"No, but …"

"It's all right. Nothing's wrong, but how do you fancy making a train journey on your own?"

"A train journey?"

"Yes. We'd like you take the Christmas presents to my parents. We're not going to be able to get over there ourselves this year. Too much going on here."

"Oh, I see."

"And they can't come to us. My mother's not been well, as you know."

"Yes, I know."

"So we thought you could go," says George. "They'd love to see you."

"On my own?"

"Why not? You're fourteen now."

"How do I go?"

"It's quite simple," says George, "you get the train from here up to Waterloo. Then you catch another train to Salisbury and then get a bus. You can do that all right, can't you?"

Can he? Well, yes, he supposes he can. It will be an adventure.

And so it is. George gives him the money for his ticket and two days before Christmas Eve he makes his way to their local station and books straight through to Salisbury. At Waterloo he has half an hour to wait so he treats himself to a doughnut. He finds a window seat and as the train rattles through unfamiliar countryside he feels a great sense of pride. He realises how much his parents must trust him to let him make this journey on his own. He must be grown up.

Everything goes very smoothly. His grandparents are pleased to see him and very complimentary that he's made this journey by himself. He spends a happy day with them and then Grandad walks down to the bus stop with him and gives him a big hug.

"Well, done, Steven. Now you've got all those Christmas parcels safe, haven't you?"

"Yes, Grandad."

"Off you go then. Give our love to the rest of the family, eh."

"Yes, of course."

And so the return journey begins.

It's getting dark now and he's feeling a bit tired but the sense of adventure is still on him so when he arrives at Waterloo and finds he has three-quarters of an hour to wait for his next train, he has a sudden idea. Clutching the bag of presents, he walks out of the station and up onto the footpath on Hungerford Bridge across the Thames. He walks right across the bridge to the other side and stands there, looking out across London and all the sparkling lights.

When he turns to go back he sees lights in the windows of the Shell Building across the river and suddenly realises they're not random. Someone has switched on lights in certain offices so that it looks like an illuminated cross on the side of the building. He thinks that is amazing.

He returns across the footbridge, back to Waterloo and

catches his train home.

He has made it. This is a milestone in his life. His first grown-up adventure.

"I DON'T REMEMBER ANY OF THAT," SAID LINDA.

"Why would you?" said Steven.

"I remember it," said George. "I wasn't at all happy about it at first. I thought you were a bit young for a journey like that."

"Then why did you let me go?" asked Steven, then before George could answer he said, "it was Mum, wasn't it?"

"Of course, it was," said George, "and she was right, as usual. You were fine, and I bet it gave you a lot of confidence, didn't it?"

"It certainly did. I've never forgotten it."

"A lot of places do that thing with window lights at Christmas," said Linda.

"Maybe they do now, but it was the first time I'd seen it and it made a big impression."

There was silence for a moment then Kate said, "Why should you never marry a tennis player?"

They all turned to look at her. Gary's face was worried. "You're not getting married, are you?" he said.

Kate laughed. "'Course not. It's a joke. I've just remembered it."

Steven said, "I think I know this one but I can't remember it."

"Okay, Kate," said Linda, "Why should you never marry a tennis player?"

"Because love means nothing to them," said Kate and burst into peals of laughter and Gary looks at her with pride.

"There you go," said George, "a real chip off the old block."

"And I've got a memory too. Can I say it?"

"Of course you can," said Linda.

"It was my first visit to London. I was eight years old, the same age as you were, Pops, when you got that bike. One afternoon Ma took me down to the river Thames and there we met this man."

She turned and smiled at Gary who, rather embarrassed, smiled back.

"I didn't know who he was, not then. Ma sent me over to the wall, to count boats, she said, but I knew she wanted to talk to this man on her own. I did count boats, I was a very obedient child, but I also took a peek back at them from time to time. They looked good together. It made me feel very warm. And suddenly I kinda got this real crazy idea. What if this guy was my Pops, the Pops I'd never met. Wouldn't that be great?"

Gary came over and put his arms round Kate, pulling her close to him.

"And it was great." Kate's voice was slightly muffled but the emotion came through. "He was my Pops and he bought me an ice cream. I could see that he and Ma were real cool together and … and" – her voice broke slightly – "I think that was one of the best days of my life."

Gary said, "Mine too."

There was a pause and then George said, "That's beautiful, Kate, thank you for sharing that with us."

Steven lightly touched his brother on his shoulder. "You're a dark horse, Gary," he said, "but you've got a wonderful daughter."

Gary just nodded.

"Okay, my turn." With an effort George pulled himself a little more upright. "As Linda said, the problem isn't the memories, it's choosing which one to share."

"Well, then, don't just pick one, Dad," said Rebecca, "give us a few highlights."

"Okay. Good idea." He thought for a moment. "D'you remember that time your mum put Steven's PE kit into the washing machine with one of her old cardigans? The colour ran and she had to send him off to school with pink shorts and vest."

"I remember that," said Steven with feeling, "got laughed at something rotten that day."

"Then there was the hamster affair," said George. "Which one of you was it that had the hamster? I can't remember."

"I had a hamster," said Gary, "until Steve sat on it."

"You can't forget that damned hamster, can you?" said Steven.

"Well, whatever. The hamster I'm thinking of was very much alive. I'd just wallpapered the dining room and we moved all the bits and pieces back in. Your mother must have put the hamster's cage too close to the wall 'cos when I came down the next morning there were teeth marks all through my lovely new wallpaper."

Kate gave a giggle and Linda smiled. "I don't remember that. Bet you were cross."

"Just a bit, but your mother was completely unfazed. 'Don't fuss, George,' she said, 'just hang a picture over it or something'."

"Nothing ever really stressed her out, did it?" said Rebecca.

"Don't you believe it," said George, "she was a bit of a maverick, your mother. I remember the time when we were still living in Ringwood. You could only have been three or four, Steven. Linda was a baby and Becky wasn't born. New neighbours moved in next door and filled their front garden – they were only very small gardens – with these ghastly plastic gnomes."

"Oh, yuk."

"Yuk, indeed. Your mother hated them. She was very fond of her garden and had taken a lot of trouble to make it look nice and now here was this gnome invasion."

"You're not going to tell us she bought an air rifle and started taking pot shots at them from an upstairs window, are you?" said Steven.

George laughed. "Not quite. She was much subtler than that. She sneaked out in the middle of the night and smeared luncheon meat all over the gnomes. Then she laid a trail of it down the pavement to a house a few doors down where they had two Alsatians. The next day it didn't take those dogs long to track back along the luncheon meat trail and find the gnomes. By late afternoon they had all been removed and crunched and there's your mother looking wide-eyed and innocent while the neighbours fought it out amongst themselves."

There was a moment's silence as they contemplated Dorothy's devious nature. Dorothy, herself, just sat there smiling gently and gazing into space. Linda said, "You do realise, Dad, that all the memories you've just told us relate to Mum."

George nodded. "All my best memories relate to your Mum. I've told you how we first met, haven't I?"

"Many times, Dad."

"Well, then. Those are the memories I treasure." His voice grew firm. "And memories she no longer shares."

"It's lovely to have her with us," said Linda, "even if she can't take part."

"Just a moment." Rebecca stood up suddenly and they all looked at her. "Perhaps she can share something with us."

"Becky, darling, it's no good. I have to accept she's gone."

"Yes, but maybe not entirely. Let me try something. It worked, at least for a bit, when I went and sat with her earlier on, so let's try again."

REBECCA TOUCHES A CHORD

DOROTHY SITS IN HER ROOM GAZING OUT OF THE WINDOW AT the dark shapes of bushes in the garden. She is vaguely conscious of a change in her normal routine. Surely she should be in bed now but instead they have put her in this chair and wrapped a rug round her. She doesn't understand but it doesn't matter. She is warm, she is comfortable. Whatever would happen, would happen.

She sits there watching the clouds drifting across the night sky, crooning softly to herself from some memory buried deep inside her.

When I pretend I'm gay,
I never feel that way,
I'm only painting the clouds with sunshine.

She hears a footstep outside her door, then the handle is turned and the door opens.

For a moment, so fast it barely registered, she feels a feeling rush through her – something valuable, something remembered, but then it is gone again.

A voice, a vaguely familiar voice, says softly. "Mum, it's Becky. Do you remember?"

She looks up to see a woman coming towards her across the room. For another split second she thinks, "Yes, I do know you …" but then the moment passes. She smiles.

"Hallo, dear."

The woman moves a chair close to her, sits down and Dorothy sees she has tears in her eyes. She pats the woman's hand. "There, there, dear. Don't cry. I'm sure everything will be all right."

She doesn't like tears. They disturb her, so she turns away and looks out at the night sky again but she keeps hold of the woman's hand.

When I hold back a tear
To make a smile appear,
I'm only painting the clouds with sunshine.

"Mum? It's me. Becky. I've come home. I'm so sorry it's been so long."

Though things may not look bright,
They all turn out alright,
If I keep painting the clouds with sunshine.

She feels her hand gripped more tightly but she continues to stare out of the window. The woman goes on.

"I've seen Dad. We're friends again. I shouldn't have left it so long. I'm so sorry, Mum. I was angry and upset when I went away but I should have stayed in touch. And now you've gone away too. Only you can't come back, I know that. But I'm with you now, Mum. It's Becky come home at last."

Becky. Somewhere in the depths there is a brief flash of recognition. Becky? There is a sadness there somewhere but she doesn't want sadness. She withdraws her hand and lets it lie in her lap.

"Oh, Mum ... what can I say?"

Silence. Then Dorothy hears the woman swallow as though trying to control her feelings. It makes her uncomfortable. Why is this person here? Is there something she's meant to do?

"I know you don't know me, Mum, but if you can understand, somewhere down there where I can't reach, I want you to know I love you."

"Thank you, dear," she says. The unspoken words, "whoever you are," hang in air.

Silence again, then the woman says softly, "I wonder ..."

A brief pause then Dorothy hears gentle singing ...

Are the stars out tonight
I don't know if it's cloudy or bright
I only have eyes for you dear.

Ah, that was more like it. This she could understand. She opens her mouth and sings.

The moon may be high
But I can't see a thing in the sky
I only have eyes for you

Then suddenly they are both singing as two voices – if not two minds – come together.

I don't know if we're in a garden
Or on a crowded avenue
You are here
And so am I
Maybe millions of people go by
But they all disappear from view
And I only have eyes for you.

Then, moved by an impulse she doesn't understand, Dorothy throws her arms around this woman and holds her close.

BACK IN GEORGE'S ROOM REBECCA TOOK HOLD OF DOROTHY'S wheelchair and turned it through ninety degrees. Then she took her own chair and placed it in front of her mother. She glanced at the others. "She always like to sing, didn't she?"

"Oh, yes," said Steven with feeling.

Rebecca smiled then she sat down, took Dorothy's hands in hers, looked straight into her eyes and began to sing softly.

Every kiss, every hug
Seems to act just like a drug
You're getting to be a habit with me

The rest of the family looked on, as slowly Dorothy's face came awake and she joined in with the song.

Let me stay in your arms
I'm addicted to your charms
You're getting to be a habit with me

Rebecca stopped singing but Dorothy continued, her eyes sparkled and a smile drifted across her face.

Oh, I can't break away
I must have you everyday
As regularly as coffee or tea
You've got me in your clutches and I can't break free
You're getting to be a habit with me

As Dorothy sang, Rebecca very gently turned the wheel-chair sideways again, took George's hands and linked them to Dorothy's.

Oh, I can't break away
I must have you everyday
As regularly as coffee or tea
You've got me in your clutches and I can't break free
You're getting to be a habit with me

The song died away and there was dead silence in the room, broken suddenly by George starting to cry.

"Oh, Dottie, Dottie, I do miss you."

Rebecca put her arm round George's shoulders. "There's still something there, Dad. Not much, I know, but something."

Linda glanced across at Steven. "Don't think we can top that, can we?"

"No."

Dorothy was now sitting passively again but the smile remained. George let go her hands and turned to face the room.

"Well, that would seem to be that. Thank you all for indulging me. Now I think it's time to say Goodnight. I can't tell you how good it's been to have this time with you all. It's been exactly what I wanted."

The atmosphere in the room had changed. The echoes of laughter remained but an air of finality seemed to have crept in.

George glanced round at them all. "Thank you. You've all been wonderful but now I'd just like a few minutes on my own with Dottie."

Steven made the first move. "Okay, Dad." He bent over the bed and kissed his father on the cheek, the first kiss for many years. "Sleep tight."

Linda took both of George's hands in hers. "It's been fun for us too, Dad. See you in the morning." And she too kissed him before following Steven out of the room.

Rebecca glanced at Kate and gave a little wave of her hand. "Your turn."

"But don't you want to ...?"

"Yes, in a minute. Go on."

Kate moved round behind the bed again and laid her hands on George's shoulders.

"One more little massage, Grandpa, to help you sleep."

"Thank you, Kate."

Her hands moved rhythmically into his neck and shoulders.

"Thank you for everything, Grandpa George. Thank you for letting me be part of this family."

"The pleasure is all ours, Kate."

"That's such an English thing to say." As she was standing behind the bed only Rebecca and Gary could see the tears falling slowly and silently down her face. "You don't know what it means to me to have a real English family of my own."

George reached round behind him and captured one of her hands in his. "You're my grand-daughter, Kate. You'll always be part of this family."

"Oh." She withdrew her hands and Rebecca saw her fumble for her handkerchief. By the time she came round to the front of the bed the tears were dried though her eyes were still a little red.

"Goodnight, Grandpa." She bent over and kissed him then hurriedly left the room. After a moment's hesitation Gary followed her.

Left alone – apart from Dorothy – George and Rebecca regarded each other for a moment, then George said.

"Well, that's that." A pause. "I can't tell you how good it is to see you, Becky."

"I know."

"I'm so glad you got here in time."

There was another pause and then Rebecca said, "You're serious about dying soon, aren't you?"

"Oh, yes."

"I don't see how you can be so certain."

George smiled faintly. "Because it's time. But I couldn't go leaving loose ends unresolved."

"You mean me?"

"Mostly, but not just you. The Linda and Steven quarrel, Gary meeting his siblings again, making sure Kate knows she's part of this family. All that stuff. Result I think, but now there's nothing more I can do."

"I think you've done pretty well."

A tired smile. "Thank you. Now you run along. I want to talk to Dottie."

"Okay, Dad." She stood up but George hadn't finished.

"Just one thing before you go. Can you open that cupboard, that one there" He indicated the bedside table. "There's an envelope in there addressed to you. Take it away and open it later, not now."

"This one?"

"Yes, that's it."

"What is it?"

"Open it later, Okay."

"Okay, Dad." She bent and kissed his forehead then, turning, left the room.

TUESDAY 11:15 PM

IN THE CORRIDOR OUTSIDE HER FATHER'S ROOM REBECCA FOUND Gary hovering.

"Have you finished?" he asked.

Rebecca nodded. "All done."

"Then I'll just pop in. See if he needs anything."

"You do that, Gary. See you later."

As Gary went into George's room Rebecca hesitated, not sure what to do. She didn't feel ready to join the others yet. She needed some time to herself but she didn't know this building and didn't know where to go. In the end she took the obvious course, found a ladies' loo and locked herself in a cubicle.

She was very tired. The strain of the long day was starting to catch up with her but she was relieved that the reunion with her father had gone so well. Suddenly she realised she was still clutching the envelope he'd given her. She stared at it. A large white envelope with her name written on it. She tore it open and pulled out a card. The picture was of a sunlit village green, a very English, if nostalgic, atmosphere.

She opened the card and then froze. The inscription inside it read:

To Christina,

I am sorry we never met but I wanted to thank you for making my daughter Rebecca so happy.

With best wishes, George Redmond

She read it once. She read it again and then put her head in her hands and burst into tears.

TUESDAY 11:17 PM

AS HE CAME INTO THE ROOM GARY LOOKED AROUND AND NODDED to himself, his sense of order restored. He saw George slumped against his pillows. Next to him was Dorothy gazing into her own world but George had her hand gripped tight in his. Gary stood at the end of the bed looking down at them both.

"Well, we did it, Dad. All the family together as you wanted."

George nodded. "We did it, son. Or at least you did. Thank you. Thank you so much. It's been wonderful."

There was silence for a moment then Gary said, "I'm not quite sure what happens now, Dad, but I'm going to have to get Mum back to her room and into bed soon. It's only fair on her and I promised Ken."

"'Course. Just a couple more minutes."

Dorothy had been humming softly to herself and suddenly the words broke through.

"Somewhere the sun is shining,
So, honey, don't you cry.

George gripped her hand tighter. "Oh, Dottie," he said, "we've had quite a journey, haven't we? Torquay to here, but at least we took the pretty route."

We'll find a silver lining,
The clouds will soon roll by.

"But I think we've finally run out of petrol. Thank you for everything, my darling – seems inadequate but there's nothing else to say."

I hear a robin singing
Upon a treetop high.

Very gently George disengaged his hand.

"Time for bed, Dottie," he said and nodded to Gary. "Okay, son, over to you. Settle her down and then pop back for a moment, will you?"

"Sure, Dad."

As Gary took hold of the chair George grabbed Dorothy's hand, lifted it to his lips and kissed it.

"Goodbye, my darling," and he closed his eyes as Gary wheeled Dorothy from the room.

I hear a robin singing
Upon a treetop high.
To you and me he's singing,
The clouds will soon roll by.

TUESDAY 11:29 PM

AS HE PUSHED DOROTHY'S WHEELCHAIR ALONG THE CORRIDOR
Gary's mind was full of the day past. He had done it, done what
George had wanted, or most of it. It had looked a bit sticky at
times but it had finally all come together.

As he turned the corner towards Dorothy's room Ken
appeared.

"I'll take over now, Mr Redmond, I'll give Angela a call and
she'll get Dorothy to bed. Was everything okay?"

"Everything was fine, Ken, thank you."

"Mr George alright? Does he need anything?"

"No. I'll just pop back to see him for a minute."

"That's good then." There was a pause then Ken said. "You
need anything, Mr Redmond, you just let me know. Mr George,
he's a good man."

"Yes. Yes, he is. Thanks, Ken."

For a moment Ken held Gary's gaze. Then he turned away
and began pushing Dorothy's chair towards her room.

"See you later, Mr Redmond. You take care now."

TUESDAY 11:31 PM

SITTING, SOBBING IN THE TOILET CUBICLE, REBECCA WAS STARTLED to hear a gentle tap on the door. She froze then a voice said, "Aunt Becky? Is that you?"

She hastily wiped her eyes then opened the door to see Kate standing there looking very worried.

"I heard you crying. Are you alright?

"How did you know it was me?"

"Well, Nanna Dorothy is still in the room with Grandpa and Aunt Linda is in the dayroom with Uncle Steve so it had to be you. What's wrong? Can I help?"

Rebecca managed a weak smile. "No, I don't think you can, Kate. In fact, there isn't anything wrong at all. I'm just feeling a bit overwhelmed at the moment."

"I guess we're all a bit wrung out."

Rebecca moved across to the hand basins and rinsed her face. Behind her Kate said, "Can I ask you something, Aunt Becky?"

"Sure. But forget the 'aunt' it makes me feel old."

"It's been a very strange day."

"You can say that again, honey."

"I mean for me, meeting you all for the first time. It must have been a shock for you all, not knowing about me, I mean."

"The day's been nothing but shocks. An American niece is neither here nor there."

"Oh."

Rebecca suddenly realised how that must have sounded. "Oh, look, Kate, I didn't mean it like that. I'm delighted to meet you. It's just ... well ... as you said, it's been a very strange day."

"Pops said you live in Boston. Is that right?"

"It is, and you're in the States too, aren't you?"

"Ma and I live in Philly, well, that is at the moment I'm living in London, but Philly's my home."

"Just down the road from me then."

Kate giggled. "That's what I told Uncle Steven but he seemed to think it was a long way."

"He would. So would I have done once, but not now. Do you know the saying, *'Americans think 100 years is a long time, the English think 100 miles is a long way'.*"

Kate giggled again then she said abruptly. "What did you and Grandpa quarrel about?"

Rebecca looked at her for a moment. "How very American. No English person would be as direct as that."

"Have I upset you?"

"No, not at all." A pause. "Well, why shouldn't you know. When I left London for my first job in the States, 1993 it was, I finally told my parents I was gay."

Kate frowned. "Okay. So ... that's no big deal."

"It was to my father, at least back then. I also told them I probably wouldn't be coming back to England again. It all got out of hand and we both said things we later regretted."

"Wow. And that's it?"

"Yup."

"And you've not seen him since?"

"They didn't know where I was and I made no attempt to contact them. I still don't know how Gary found me."

Kate smiled. "That's Pops for you. He sorts things."

"Well, he certainly sorted today."

"Are you pleased he did?"

"Yes. Yes, I am."

"Is that why you were crying? 'Cos you and Grandpa are friends again?"

Rebecca looked at her for a moment then made up her mind.

"Only partly. He gave me this." And she held out the card to Kate.

Kate took it but paused. "Are you sure you want me to read this?"

"Yes, I'm sure."

"Okay then." Kate opened the card and read it. "Wow." She read it again and then lifted her head. "I'm guessing this Christina is your partner, right?"

"Right."

"But hey, aunt ... Sorry ... Becky. This is like huge."

"I know."

"Grandpa must have been desperate for you to have this."

"Yes."

"That's why he was getting so twitchy because you weren't here."

"I guess."

"What you going to do now?"

"Do? Well, take it home and give it to Chris. What else?"

"And Grandpa? Do you think you'll get another chance to visit him after today?"

"I don't know, Kate. But at least we've made our peace with each other."

"Sure." Kate paused, then she said. "I wonder ... would you mind if I went and found Pops. I kinda think he's a bit sad too."

"Of course." Impulsively Rebecca reached out and hugged Kate. "I think you've been marvellous, both of you, you and your 'Pops'. You and I must stay in touch. Okay?"

TUESDAY 11:43 PM

THE LITTLE FELT ELEPHANT WITH THE FADING COLOURED PATCHES on its flanks sat on the chest of drawers. The orange glow from the lamp in the care home car park could just be glimpsed round the edge of the curtain shining directly onto the elephant's tail which moved gently in the breeze from the half open window.

Gary sat beside George's bed. He held his father's hand.

"You can rest now, Dad."

"Dottie okay, is she?"

"She's fine. Ken's sorting her out."

"Good old Ken."

"How you feeling?"

"Tired, but peaceful."

There was a long pause, then George said, "Right then. Well, that's it, son. Thanks for giving me such a happy evening."

Gary said nothing but he felt George's hand tighten on his.

TUESDAY 11:57 PM

GARY SLOWLY MADE HIS WAY ALONG THE CORRIDOR, NOT SURE what to do next. He wasn't ready to face the others so he turned and made his way out of the building to the car park.

Without much surprise he saw Kate sitting on the wall and moved across to join her.

Her eyes were serious as she said. "I thought you might come out here so I waited for you. Guessed you could do with some company."

"Thanks."

"It's been an amazing day."

"Yes."

"How's Grandpa?"

"He's peaceful."

Kate said nothing for a moment and then said. "How peaceful?"

Gary turned and looked at her. "Very peaceful, Kate."

TUESDAY 23:59 PM

IN THE DAY ROOM STEVEN LAY BACK IN AN ARMCHAIR, HIS EYES closed. He wasn't asleep. Images of his father and mother flitted through his mind. He felt exhausted as though he had run a gruelling race and yet he also felt more of a sense of peace than he had felt for a very long time.

Linda sat in the passenger seat of her car in the car park. She too felt exhausted and knew she needed some time alone. She was also thinking of family but mostly her own husband and children. She had been very moved by the memories that today had brought back but she felt very strongly that it was important to always move forward.

Rebecca had left the care home and was walking along the dark lane. She needed space and the night air was very refreshing. She felt drained and knew she needed to walk and think. The card for Christina was safe in her bag and, after the initial shock, it gave her great joy. The final bridge mended.

Gary and Kate sat on their car park wall, not talking, both lost in their own thoughts. Kate was nestled close to her father and Gary's arm was round her shoulders.

Dorothy, now safely tucked up in bed, was still awake. There was a smile on her face though it wasn't a conscious smile. She just knew, somewhere deep inside herself, that she was happy. For a few moments that evening she had had pin-point flashes of familiar things. The sound of the sea, the smell of leather seats in a coach, chattering voices all round her and the echoes of laughter. She couldn't put pictures to any of them but they were comforting. She hummed gently to herself.

Are the stars out tonight
I don't know if it's cloudy or bright
I only have eyes for you dear

She gave a contented sigh and went to sleep.

The church clock struck midnight – the hour of passing.

In George's room the little felt elephant gazed passively down at the man lying very still in the bed. The man's eyes were closed but he was smiling.

Read on for an exclusive extract from:

'Some of the best stories are quests ...
This is a book to make everyone think twice
about easy assumptions'
SIMON BRETT

Dreams
of Eleven

MICHAEL BARTLETT

When Richard Kirkwood announces he's looking for Julie, a
girl he last saw 40 years ago, everyone suspects he's been
carrying a torch for his childhood sweetheart all these years.

But this search is so much more.

DREAMS OF ELEVEN

RICHARD

IT'S A DARK, DRIZZLY EVENING IN EARLY OCTOBER 2006. I'M driving home to Weybridge from Gatwick after ten long, tedious, tricky days in Stockholm. I'm very tired but the problem is solved. I've informed the office that the risk of legal action has gone away. I've negotiated a slight over-run in the duration of the contract but the project can go ahead. I've found a Kit-Kat in the glove compartment and there's some decent folk music on Radio 2. All is well.

It's around half past eight and I'm approaching the Guildford exit on the M25 when my phone gives two beeps. A text. I assume it's Lauren saying she's been delayed at the office yet again so I wait until I'm off the motorway and can find a safe place to pull over. It's not Lauren. It's Francesca Thompson and the message reads:

> An issue has arisen with your contractor. Their company
> is under investigation by police. Situation sensitive. Do
> not come into office. You're on garden leave till further
> notice. Will phone tomorrow. FT

I gaze at the screen in disbelief. I'd heard vague rumours a few weeks ago about possible accounting irregularities with this contracting firm but I'd dismissed them as idle gossip. But now this. And why me? Do they think I'm involved in some kind of fraud?

The wording of the text is final. Non-negotiable. Absolute. I sit in a layby on the A3 trying to come to terms with the fact that I've been suspended for something I know nothing about. With a single text I am taken out of the loop, all my clients have become someone else's problem. From a full diary I'm suddenly faced with empty days – and I don't know what to do with empty days. If I'm not working I don't have any purpose. Suddenly I find I'm very angry. I know being suspended isn't the same as being judged, but that's the way it feels.

I have no doubt the timing of this text is not accidental. It has been sent after the office has closed so I can't make an instant response. My first instinct is to call Hunky on his mobile and demand an explanation but I hesitate. I push personal anger aside and let my professional self take over. In any crisis, the instant reaction is almost certainly the wrong one, and in any case the message does not even come from Hunky Dory himself, but from his PA, Francesca Thompson.

That's not so surprising though. Vincent Dory, 'Hunky' behind his back, is the Managing Director of my division of *Swamplett, Benson and Dring* and a moral coward. Francesca is his Swiss Guard forming a cordon around his private Vatican. She isn't my favourite person, but then she isn't anyone's favourite person including – I've often suspected – Mr Thompson.

Hunky's not relevant anyway. It's Francesca's views that really matter in our office. If she thinks I've been involved in fraud then she'll show me the kind of sympathy a Rottweiler offers a one-legged burglar.

Anger is now struggling for first place with panic but there is nothing I can do for the moment so I drive on home.

Lauren is in the living room when I get there, sitting on the sofa with papers spread in a wide semi-circle around her.

"Hi," she says, then glances at the clock. "Hey, is that the time? You're late, aren't you?"

"Contraflow on the M23," I say, "but it won't be a problem anymore."

She glances up, amused. "They've put you in charge of contra flows now, have they?"

"No. I'm no longer in charge of anything." And I tell her about the text message.

She's silent for a moment. "What kinda fraud we talking about?"

"I don't know. It was just a handful of rumours. Something to do with money laundering, I think. Frankly, I didn't pay much attention. I've been working with those guys for years and I find it hard to believe that they were using our contracts as a front."

"Not relevant." Lauren is an American and a lawyer which means she has very few illusions. "You'd probably be the last to know if they were running a scam."

She pauses for a moment in thought. "This garden leave thing – almost certainly a formality. You're the main point of contact for these guys. You need to be isolated so the investigation can go ahead."

"I hope you're right.. Or maybe they think I really am involved."

"But you're not, as we know, so we can kick that into touch."

For the first time I feel a little glimmer of happiness. Lauren's unquestioning assumption that I'm innocent does me the world of good. But her next words dispel that feeling.

"So, they can't prove you're actively involved in any fraud, because you're not, but if it all goes belly up it might not be possible to prove you weren't. Not proven, as your Scottish neighbours would say."

"Not proven?"

"Yeah, you wouldn't face any charges but there'd still be an element of doubt. That can be very damaging."

I hadn't thought of that, and I find the prospect terrifying. "If that were the case then I might not be able to go back to work."

"I guess that's a possibility."

I feel the panic beginning to rise. "But … but that would be appalling."

Lauren looks slightly surprised. "Well, not ideal, sure, but not catastrophic. They'd probably do some kind of early retirement deal. You should be fine financially."

She doesn't understand. How could she? It's not the money. It's the empty space. Time to brood. Time for unwanted memories to come flooding back. They must be kept at bay, but she has no idea about that. I've never told her.

"I can't let that happen. There mustn't be any doubt. I've not been involved in any kind of fraud and that must be made absolutely clear."

Lauren is clearly a little taken aback by my vehemence. "Well, let's hope it's all wrapped up pretty quickly. Seriously though, you might want to think about getting a lawyer."

"You offering?"

"Not likely. Vested interest."

I think about the suggestion. "Don't think I'll go the lawyer route yet. Bit heavy handed. Let's see how it plays out first."

"Fair enough, but if you change your mind, why not give

Max a call? If you can't have me then he's the next best thing."
She grins. "So, what support d'you reckon you'll get from the
company?"

"The company in general, no idea, but I wouldn't expect
any support at all from Hunky and Francesca."

"I've never trusted Hunky or that bitch who works for
him." Lauren, like many Americans, believes in calling a spade
a bloody shovel. "So, what's your next step?"

"I don't know, I really don't know. I'll speak to Francesca
tomorrow and see where we go from there."

"Sure. Guess that's all you can do."

I nod and she gestures to her papers. Lauren's very good at
getting her priorities right. "Well in that case …"

"You carry on. I'm going to bed."

I lie on the bed but I can't sleep. I'm not so fond of the job
that I'd miss the long hours, the stress, the delicate negotia-
tions, but that job is who I am. It gives me a structure, it gives
me respect, it gives me a purpose. Without it I am nothing,
and left to my own devices all the old insecurities will come
back and drown me.

But I have to face the fact that for a while at least there is
no choice. How the hell am I going to fill the hours and keep
the demons at bay?

I lie there sleepless in the dark. I am very frightened.

ABOUT THE AUTHOR

Michael Bartlett has been a regular writer for hit programmes for radio and television, and he has also written numerous original plays which have been staged for radio, TV and theatre across the UK. He lives with his wife in Norfolk.

He is the author of numerous short story collections. *Mr Redmond's Mending Day* is his third novel, joining *Dreams of Eleven (2022)* and espionage thriller *Hunting the Hornets (2023)*.